I
THOUGHT
OF
You

JEWEL E. ANN

I THOUGHT OF YOU

JEWEL E. ANN

Cover Design: Sarah Hansen

Photo: © Regina Wamba

Formatting: Jenn Beach

For Logan, Carter, and Asher
Count every breath because every breath counts.

"There are only two ways to live your life. One is as though nothing is a miracle. The other is as though everything is a miracle."
—Albert Einstein

CHAPTER

one

If I give you today, there will be no tomorrow.

Price

TWO MONTHS AGO, I slid a handwritten note onto the nightstand next to a white tissue box and a gold-framed photo of a blue-eyed Himalayan cat.

I can't do it. Please forgive me.

Can't or won't?

"Can't" made me weak. "Won't" made me selfish.

Either way, it was with an insufferable and unavoidable pain that I'd come to that conclusion.

Conclusion or decision?

Hell, I didn't know. It didn't matter.

Nothing could prepare a person for that kind of moment. But they'd left me with no choice. Well, that wasn't true. There was always a choice. Was mine an

1

unforgivable one? That was hard to say. After all, they were my people. I would have died for them, but not like that.

———

MY NEW PLACE doesn't have a picture of a Himalayan cat on the nightstand, my favorite black weathered recliner from college, or a warm body waiting for me in bed.

It's a fully furnished two-bedroom home in Austin, Texas. It's all very Pottery Barn. There's a tufted crushed velvet sofa in twilight blue, mid-century wood tables with fake flowers in vases, and marble bookends flanking a collection of everything from Stephen King to Margaret Atwood.

Wood floors.

Modern rugs.

And a few contemporary pieces of framed art—red poppies and birch trees on cobalt canvas.

In the primary bedroom, above the bed, there's a photo of a young boy on a bicycle with a yellow lab chasing him down a sidewalk. The boy looks like a younger version of myself.

Maybe it's that I had a yellow lab.

Maybe it's because my parents made me ride my bike everywhere while my friends were in their rooms gaming.

Maybe it's his twiggy arms and legs and wavy brown hair in a mess. Since then, I've added muscle and discovered that a little hair gel goes a long way to taming thick, wavy hair.

Whatever it is about that boy in the photo, it's comforting.

Before five in the evening, I add a blue Honda CRX to the driveway. It has a dent in the rear bumper, which complements my new life and motto: Perfection is over-rated. My whole life has been overrated. For a decade, I've been the happiest, miserable overachiever. It's a complicated oxymoron that makes sense if one takes a step back to see the whole picture.

However, I'm six weeks into remedying that situation —well on my way to underachieving the hell out of my life.

Now, there's only one thing left to do. Find *her*.

————

Scottie Rucker looks exactly as I remember— wayward, cinnamon-brown hair just past her shoulders. Bangs brush her eyes, always a quarter inch too long. When she laughs, her head shakes, and her chin lifts to flip those unruly bangs away from her gleaming eyes of gold and brown.

Always hopeful.

Always pleasant.

I don't have a single memory of her that's less than perfect. Even our breakup felt like fate because she said all the right words. The world makes sense with Scottie in it. And right now, I need things to make sense.

A whoosh of cool January air whistles when a customer exits Drummond's General Store, leaving me and a handful of other customers milling around the aisles of industrial shelving surrounded by white shiplap exterior walls with sliding ladders. This place bleeds nostalgia.

There's a vintage soda fountain with a draft arm, an ice cream cabinet, and rows of syrups. Bulk goodies—everything from fireballs and taffy to Tootsie Rolls and Bit-O-Honeys—line the far end of the bar with sparkly red swivel stools. A stand with fresh floral bouquets anchors one end of the register, while a display for local artisan-made goods anchors the other.

"Let me know if you need help finding anything." Scottie's melodic voice floats through the air.

Twelve years ago, I met her by accident at a modern-day apothecary a few blocks from Independence Hall in Philadelphia the summer between my junior and senior years of college. My dad conned me into working at his law firm for the summer in hopes I'd consider changing my major. But I've always been a numbers guy: mathematics and economics.

And Scottie's always been the girl who wears healing stones instead of diamonds and thrives on thirty minutes of meditation in the morning instead of eight ounces of coffee.

A torrential downpour around two in the afternoon on a Thursday in June sent me dashing into the corner apothecary. To avoid being an asshole using her place of business for cover, I emptied my wallet on miscellaneous shit I'd never heard of, including a Tiger's eye bracelet that was supposed to help me achieve wealth and vitality while protecting me against negative energy.

Perhaps it did, at least for that summer. I still have that bracelet.

Halfway between the chips and canned goods, I glance at her, and I feel like time is transporting me to that day in Philly.

A pleasant smile touches her lips as she drops her gaze to the abandoned receipt on the counter, only to do a quick double take.

I hold her gaze, letting this moment sink in. A slow-growing smile steals her glossed lips. Recognition takes on a whole new meaning. I feel alive.

She slides around the counter, her Birkenstock clogs scuffing along the black and white lattice vinyl tile. "Are you real?"

With a tiny laugh, I nod.

"Price Milloy," she says my name with a content sigh.

"Scottie Rucker."

"What are you doing—"

I interject by holding a finger to my lips. "Shh. Stop interrupting the universe."

Her eyes widen. "Did you steal my line?"

"I'm just quoting the most profound person I've ever known."

She snorts. "So much gibberish." Throwing her arms around my neck, she whispers, "My god, it's so good to see you."

It's like she knows exactly what I need.

Twelve years get erased in a single breath.

With my face buried in her hair, I inhale. She never wore perfume from a department store, always an essential oil concoction she made—vetiver and amber. On occasion, she wore patchouli.

She steps back, beaming with a face-splitting grin. "What brings you to Austin?"

"I live here." I lie (sort of), knowing it's the first of many to come. Technically, I am living here while I see her. She's why I'm here. It's not as creepy as it sounds. On the surface, it's mind-bendingly complicated. Yet, at its core, it's as simple as I'm here for her.

More on that later.

"No kidding? Wow! Have you lived here long?"

Less than forty-eight hours.

"Hmm ... I'm trying to think how long it's been." I scratch my chin. "Six? Seven months? What about you?"

"I've been here ten years. I needed a change and decided to try Austin. No job. No place to live. I just packed a few bags and headed south." A slow grin creeps up her face while she shakes her head. "I can't believe we're running into each other. It's been so long. Are you married? Kids? I want to catch up."

Another gust of wind announces an older couple entering the store. Scottie shoots them a grin before turning back to me.

"Catching up sounds amazing. Can I take you to dinner tonight?"

"Oh! Tonight? That's soon."

I shrug. "Carpe diem."

Her soft lips rub together for a beat. "Why not?"

"Wonderful. Give me your address. I'll pick you up around six?"

"Eight." She fiddles with her hair. Yet another thing that's not changed about her. Always fiddling.

"The store closes at eight. Until I get someone else hired, it's just me. If that's too late—"

"Eight it is. Write down your address."

"It's here."

"Here?"

She jabs her thumb over her shoulder. "I live in an Airstream behind the store."

Things make sense now. The only address I found for her was this store, which I assumed had an apartment above it.

"Then I'll see you at eight."

"Let me give you my number in case something comes up and you need to cancel."

Nothing will come up. I'm here for her.

The rented house.

The vehicle.

It's all for her.

I don't have a phone, at least not one I plan on using anytime soon. It's just for emergencies.

She jots down her number on the last customer's abandoned receipt.

"Perfect. Then I'll see you in," I peek at my watch, "five hours and twenty-seven minutes."

"Price Milloy." She shakes her head. "I'll be pinching myself all afternoon."

I grab a small bunch of bananas from a basket and set them on the counter because not buying something feels weird.

She weighs them and hands me the change. "Five hours and twenty-five minutes now." I can't remember the last time someone looked at me with such wonder and sheer happiness in their eyes. In truth, it hasn't been that long, but life has messed with my recollection of those moments.

I steal a few extra seconds to return what I hope feels to her like the same expression.

Coming here was the right decision.

CHAPTER

two

Remember me? Yeah, me neither.

THIS IS what it feels like to relearn something basic like walking and talking. Even after six weeks of practice, I stare at the black TV screen. The batteries in the remote control are dead, and I have no intention of replacing them.

No internet.

No computer.

No social media.

No email.

I've never sat for this long with nothing to do and no company besides my thoughts. How does one exist with only one's thoughts? I'll get a library card tomorrow and purchase some hobby things—Legos and ...

I've got nothing. If I had the internet, I would search for enjoyable hobbies.

It's misting outside, but I throw on my rain jacket and take a walk for fresh air and exercise before I reward myself with a nap, or what I'm calling meditation, until I learn how to meditate.

I'm tired.

The pain fluctuates between a five and a six. I've been at a ten.

By seven thirty, I'm parked across the street from Drummond's General like a stalker. As soon as eight o'clock rolls around and the store's lights dim, I meander to the back alley, where there's a vintage Airstream trailer and an old, rusty red Ford pickup truck.

I knock on the trailer door.

"Come in!"

The door sticks when I press the handle, so I give it a jerk, and just as it opens, Scottie applies lip balm. "Hey. Welcome to my humble abode." She beams like always.

I close the door behind me to keep the warm air inside. The Airstream is a mix of hickory and cedar with copper-plated hardware. A narrow galley kitchen separates the bedroom from the bathroom. But those details feel like an afterthought once I get a whiff of the mint.

Mint candles?

Mint air freshener?

I'm not sure, but her apartment in Philly always smelled like a candy cane. To this day, I have a weakness for all things peppermint.

"The simplicity with which you live your life is still one of your most endearing qualities," I say while surveying the cozy space—a minimalist's dream.

Scottie threads her arms into her white cardigan and flips her bangs away from her eyes. "As I recall, you didn't use to find my simplicity so endearing. I think you called my taste in things 'cheap.'" She shoots me a wry grin while sliding her purse over her shoulder and slipping her feet into the same Birkenstock clogs she had on earlier.

"I don't remember that." I frown. "But if I said that, I was an asshole, and I'm sorry. The world would be a better place if more people lived—"

"Cheaply?" She lifts an eyebrow—a real eyebrow, not one of those fake stenciled ones that looks good from across the street but gets creepier the closer you get.

"Frugally. Consciously." I clarify.

"Bravo, Price. Your vocabulary has improved. I hope your taste in food has, too. I haven't chosen a steakhouse for dinner. Sorry. There's a new plant-based restaurant a few blocks from here. We can walk." She locks the door and leads me around to the street.

"It might surprise you, but I love plants. The healthier, the better."

She laughs, making a quick sidelong glance while we stroll up the quiet street sandwiched between a mix of old homes and small businesses adorned with hanging planters and string lights. "Earlier, when we hugged, I sensed something was different about you, but I never dreamed it was a red meat withdrawal. Do tell. How long have you been without meat?"

"Not long enough."

Sixty days ago, give or take, my last animal sacrifice consisted of poached salmon with yogurt dill sauce, asparagus on the side, and lemon-herb rice. It paired nicely with the three-hundred-dollar bottle of Chardonnay.

"You didn't answer me earlier. Are you married? Do you have kids?" She prods.

I feel her gaze on me as I keep mine pointed down the street at the couple approaching us with their little dog in a red harness. "That was the dream."

"Was?"

"When I graduated from college, I thought I'd get a job and work my way up in an investment firm. Marriage. Kids. A mortgage for a home just out of my price range. A car with enough room to accommodate two-point-five kids and a dog. A real dog, you know? A lab or a German Shepherd. Not a designer dog. Maybe a rescue dog with a missing eye or something that not only gave it the character of a survivor but one that would make it look like all of my donations to the animal shelter weren't just meaningless contributions. We all know those who want to look generous and caring but refuse anything but a purebred with bloodlines of a Westminster Kennel Club winner."

Scottie playfully nudges me and chuckles. "So what happened?"

"Despite my efforts to conquer the world and claim the American dream, I instead worked myself to death. Well, nearly to death. So I stopped."

"What do you mean stopped?"

As we pass them, I politely smile at the couple with the dog. "I stopped working. Stopped chasing."

"You're jobless?" She laughs like it's ridiculous.

"I am."

She hums for a few seconds, her head bowed and her hands in her pockets. "What do you do all day?"

"I contemplate life, but I'm thinking of finding a

hobby. Do you think my hands are too big for knitting?" I hold out my hands in front of me, fingers spread wide. "Curling has always intrigued me. If it's good enough for the Olympics, surely it's a challenging hobby."

"Ha! I'd pay money to see you in a curling club." She nods to the right.

I open the door to the bustling restaurant, catching an immediate aroma of herbs and something sweet like a fruit pie.

She steps inside. "Table for two?"

"I can seat you at the bar."

Scottie eyes me.

"I'm good with that," I say over the woman on the corner stage with a guitar singing "Stay."

We're seated at the bar at a ninety-degree angle to each other. The shaven-headed waiter hands us menus and begins his spiel about tonight's specials.

"I'll have the hot bourbon apple cider and the falafel wrap," Scottie says.

I quickly scan the menu. "I'll have the warm veggie salad, and water is great."

As I hand him the menu, Scottie gives me another wide-eyed look. "If you're trying to impress me, don't. I plan on getting dessert."

Inspecting the dimly lit restaurant with candles on the tables and walls of hanging plants, I grin. "I promise I'm not trying to impress you."

"Did you have bypass surgery? A near-death experience?"

My gaze returns to her. She's never looked more beautiful. "No bypass. No near-death experience. It's time I take my life and my health more seriously."

The bartender delivers my water and her spiked cider.

Something flits across her face, making her smile falter for a second. She just as quickly recovers. "Kudos on taking care of your health, but never take life too seriously." She winks.

"True." I laugh. "Tell me about your life. You own a general store. That Airstream is in great condition. And you haven't aged a bit. Well done, you."

Scottie smirks after sipping her drink. "I'm an overworked, underpaid employee at the general store I don't own. And speaking of not owning things, the same couple who own the store also own that vintage Airstream. However, that rusty truck is all mine."

"But you're happy." I cross my arms on the bar.

She doesn't have to answer. I already know she's happy. It's why I'm here. People like Scottie don't need to search for happiness. They are the happiness that everyone around them desperately wants to experience.

"I am." She cups her mug with both hands, eyeing the rising steam for a second. "I've been here for ten years and love it here. I have a satisfying job, as simple as it is. Some people think Austin is pretentious. But I adore the kind of people who shop at a general store—kind people who appreciate simple things and a simple life. They don't haggle over prices and appreciate local goods and the people who make them."

This woman doesn't disappoint.

"That's great, Scottie. Really. I'm not surprised you've stayed true to what matters in life."

She eyes me as if she's weighing my sincerity. "Thanks."

"Is it a fair assumption that you're not married? No kids? And yes, I'm assuming because your residence is rather small."

She nods several times. "Fair assumption. I've never been married. No kids. I'm waiting for the universe to open that door. But I do have a date next weekend, so there's hope for me. However, I'm a little nervous." Her nose crinkles.

"Why is that?"

"He's the grandson of a customer who shops at the store nearly every day. Herb is my favorite customer."

My eyes widen. "A matchmaking grandfather. That's pretty special."

"And scary." She sips her drink and rubs her lips together before canting her head. "What?"

I grin. "Nothing. I just can't believe I'm having dinner with you."

"I know. It's such a small world."

No, it's not. It's a massive world with nearly eight billion people, and it took a while to find her.

"Why is your date scary? Have you at least talked on the phone?"

"No."

"Just texts?"

"No."

"What?" I laugh.

"Herb, the grandpa, set it all up. One day, he asked if I'd consider going on a date with his grandson, and the next day, he gave me a date and time to meet said grandson for dinner at a sushi restaurant thirty minutes from the store."

"That's it?"

"I know he's a 'shy' welder who loves kayaking and hiking."

The waiter delivers our food and refills my water glass.

"And you said yes?" I retrieve my fork from the rolled napkin.

She bites into her wrap and chews for a few seconds. "Herb is the nicest guy. So I figured it's worth one date if his grandson is anything like him."

"Shy sounds like code for you'd better be ready to carry the conversation for the entire night."

Scottie wipes her mouth and nods. "Yes. I thought about that. If I'm not getting a good vibe, I'll bore him to death with the minute details of my hobbies. If I like him, I'll work my magic and get him to tell me his deepest secrets."

"Magic? Is that like a spell?"

"You were under my spell, Price Milloy. Don't act like you don't remember." Mischief shines in her eyes.

"That was a long time ago. I don't think you remember me as well as you claim to." Am I fishing for just the opposite? Absolutely. I remember everything about Scottie Rucker. But she walked away from me too easily to imagine I made much of an impression on her.

"You weren't the guy who sat around contemplating life and eating salads. *That* I remember with complete clarity. You had a plan, and it was pretty darn close to world domination. You woke up at five to exercise. Showered by six. And you made it to your dad's office before anyone else."

"Ah, yes. I was an exhausting overachiever. A real ass."

She remembers. Damn! My whole day has been made.

"Price." She laughs. "Stop. You weren't an ass. I envied your drive and work ethic. Your passion for setting goals and achieving them. I felt goalless." Her chin drops, and the lighting isn't great, but I think she's blushing. "You were the one who got away."

Scottie remembering absolutely anything about me is enough. I don't need to be the one who got away. But I'll take it. I'll take anything she'll give me. I'll swallow each morsel like a pill that will let me live forever. I'll wear her words as a magic cloak of immortality. Unfortunately, I have nothing to give her in return.

"As I recall, you gave me the boot. You punted. That's not the same as *getting away*. If a certain someone let another someone get away, it was I who let you get away … or push me away."

She lifts her gaze. "You didn't fight me on it."

"I did what you asked me to do."

Her head tips backward in a hearty laugh. "Who does that?"

"You told me not to take myself too seriously, to slow down and accept a few things in life that were less than perfect. And you told me I'd die before I reached thirty if I didn't get more sleep and drink less coffee. Sometimes, I send my mom cards with handwritten notes 'just because,' per your sage advice. And you told me that letting go shows more love than holding on."

Scottie's lips part. "I-I can't believe you remember all of that."

I shrug, glancing out the window just over her shoulder. "My point is … I took my cues from you. Maybe I was the overachiever getting good grades, but you were the more emotionally intelligent one in our relationship. So I listened to you. I trusted you. And I wanted to love you how you deserved to be loved, so I let you go, too." When I return my gaze to her, she blots the corner of her eye.

"Jesus, Price, that's not fair. I knew nothing. I was a nineteen-year-old girl with too many feelings about you and life. So I wrapped them in false confidence and tried to Yoda you."

"Yoda me?" I chuckle.

"I feigned wisdom and maturity so you didn't get stuck with a girl who had no idea what she wanted to do with her life."

I wait for her to look at me because I'm not sure I've ever seen her this vulnerable. "Yes, you did," I say. "You knew you wanted to *live* it. And you knew I wanted to conquer it. I would have stolen the essence of what made you so extraordinary. And you would have ..." I find the hint of a sad smile. I can only imagine what she would have done for me, but I don't want to say it.

"We would have ended badly," she says, resting her hand on my knee. "Your dreams were too big, and mine were too small."

I shake my head. "Mine weren't dreams. They were goals. I'm not sure I've ever really dreamed—not consciously."

"Well," she removes her hand from my leg and pops a tomato into her mouth, chewing it around her smile, "it's never too late."

My lips part to refute that, but I press them together and opt for a slow nod. What would happen if I let myself dream? What would my dream be? I can't imagine. Not now.

After eating and enjoying the live music, I set my napkin on my plate. "Thank you for having dinner with me."

She curls her hair behind her ear, staring at the half-eaten cake on her plate. "Give me your phone. I'll share my contact information. We need to do this again."

"I uh ... don't have a phone."

She laughs, but it quickly dies. "Are you serious?"

"Serious. But I know where to find you. And I can give you my address. If you're ever in my neighborhood, we could take a walk or sit on the sofa together."

She pulls her phone from her purse, giving me an incredulous expression. "Sit together?" After bringing up a new contact and adding my name, she hands me her phone. "Sure." She chuckles. "I'd love that."

CHAPTER
three

If you wait long enough, you'll forget what you're waiting for.

Scottie

I DON'T HAVE Price's phone number, just like I don't have Herb's grandson's number. If Herb comes in tomorrow morning, I'll ask him to cancel my date with his grandson. When I said yes, I never imagined Price Milloy sliding back into my life. I never imagined he'd ask me to dinner and say things that made my heart skip a few beats.

He's just as handsome as I remember. Men age well, not that thirty-four is old. However, most people put on a little weight as they age, but Price's cheeks are a little more hollow, and his pants hang looser than I remember. He's always had wavy brown hair, but it's a little longer, and his velvet brown eyes don't hold as much glimmer. His aura makes me uneasy.

"Let me know if I can help you with anything," I say to the gentleman entering the store in a red baseball hat and a black zip-up hoodie. My gaze follows the clinking sound of the dog with jingly tags behind him—an adorable white Fox Terrier with a black patch on its back, a tan mask, and button ears.

The man scratches his scruffy jaw and nods, offering me the quickest of glances before heading toward the back of the store with the dog right behind him.

Every time the door has chimed today, I've secretly hoped for Price. I glance at my watch. The store closes in ten minutes. The guy didn't grab a cart or basket, so he shouldn't be here long. While I wipe down the counter and finish sweeping the floor in front of the bulk bins, the man in the red hat strolls down each aisle with his hands in his jacket pockets, occasionally stealing a glance in my direction with his blue eyes that are almost too blue to trust and full lips pressed into a hard line.

Why does he keep looking at me?

And why does it look like there's something in his pocket? A gun. It has to be a gun, but it's not in a holster.

My spine stiffens, and my heart beats so fast it pulses in my ears. This makes no sense. Someone doesn't rob a store with their dog. Do they?

There are cameras, but no one is monitoring them; no one would save me.

"Um ..." I clear my throat. "We're closing soon. Are you sure there's nothing I can help you find?" My voice trembles as I make my way behind the counter again— the broom clanks when my shaky hand leans it against the door to the back room.

Keeping his head bowed, he steps up to the counter,

grabs random items within arm's length of the register, and tosses them in front of me.

"Are you paying with a credit card? We only accept credit cards. There is no cash in the store."

Nothing for you to rob.

He slowly lifts his head, giving me my first good look at him. Beneath the dark blond scruff on his face, he has a strong jaw, high cheekbones, full lips, and distrusting cobalt eyes. A half-inch scar slants toward his temple just above his left eyebrow. It's flat and a shade lighter than the rest of his skin, like it's been there for years.

I mentally note it, along with his curled, dirty blond hair peeking out in all directions from his hat. If I live to talk to the cops, I'll tell them he's over six foot, maybe six-two or six-three. Athletic build with broad shoulders. Robust hands with thick knuckles. He'd easily be able to strangle me with just one of them.

"You take cash," he says matter-of-factly.

Chills claim my skin like a pond's surface, surrendering to winter. And I feel just as frozen in place. Still, who brings their dog to a robbery? Or is this a homicide in the making?

He's calling my bluff. He and his dog have sniffed out my lie. I want to scream, but I'm too terrified to scream. I've had this nightmare, the one where the fear is so great that it has me in a choke hold, so when I open my mouth to cry for help, nothing comes out.

"Please don't hurt me," I whisper before pressing my trembling lips together.

I would give anything for someone to walk through the door. There have been so many nights when someone has rushed into the store, grateful they caught me before I locked the door because they needed something.

Not tonight.

He narrows his eyes briefly before his pinched brows release and spring up his forehead. He holds up his hands as if I'm the one who might harm him. "Scottie, I'm not going to hurt you."

I yank open the drawer below the register and pull out a pair of scissors before taking several steps backward. "How do you know my name?"

"I'm Koen."

I shake my head. I didn't ask his name.

"Herb Sikes's grandson."

I hear him, but it still takes a few seconds for everything to register. "W-what are you doing here?" I lower the scissors but keep a firm grip on them.

Killers have families and grandfathers who probably adore them because they don't know they're killers. Herb said Koen's the silent type.

Just like a killer.

Most killers have above-average IQs. And cute dogs. Unsuspecting little accomplices.

"I was just checking you out." He cringes, pinching the bridge of his nose. "God, that sounded all wrong. I meant I wanted to see if you were ..." He shakes his head. "I don't know how to say this." Koen pulls off his hat and scratches his head, ruffling his thick, mussed hair.

"You were afraid he fixed you up with a dog," I say, letting the tension fall off my shoulders while I return the scissors to the drawer and blow out a slow breath.

"I like dogs," he nods to his dog, "so that would have

been an acceptable arrangement." A shy grin steals his lips. "Sorry, bad joke." He glances around the store.

He's nervous. I can't believe I feared for my life just seconds earlier.

Do I tell him I was hoping to cancel our date?

"My grandfather is a kind man. He once tried to fix me up with a woman who was six months pregnant and going through a divorce." He wrinkles his nose.

It's kind of cute.

"I'm not pregnant, and I've never been married."

But my first love is back in my life, and that has me confused. I should tell him and cancel our date. I'm not good at seeing more than one guy at a time, not that I've tried.

"I'll come back another day when I have cash." He smirks with a James Marsden smile, the kind that involves his eyes, forcing them to squint a fraction.

And just like that, I no longer wish to cancel our date.

"How did you know I was lying?"

"My grandfather doesn't have credit cards anymore."

I frown. "I'm sorry. I'm not usually a liar."

"I'm sorry I scared you."

"You didn't—"

He lifts one eyebrow.

I blush and shake my head. "You nearly scared the crap out of me. I saw my life flash before my eyes."

"God! I'm an idiot. I shouldn't have come." He returns his hat to his head. "If you don't want to go out next weekend, I won't blame you."

"I hate first dates," I say.

He glances up at me, and his anguish multiplies.

"I have to find the right outfit. My hair never cooperates. The restaurant is usually overpriced, and I hardly taste the food because I'm too focused on making sure it doesn't stick between my teeth." I shrug. "There are many reasons why I'm thirty-one and still single, but hating first dates is at the top of that list. So ..." I turn and retrieve two soda glasses. "Do you have a curfew?" I glance over my shoulder.

His expression softens. "No."

"Great." I snag my keys and hold one out to him. "Lock the door, flip the switch on the *Open* sign, and sit on a bar stool."

He hesitates for a few seconds before taking the key. I turn toward the fountain machine and mix up a cherry-lime Rickey and a brown cow.

"Chips, pretzels, or popcorn?" I ask with a grin, sliding the drinks in front of him.

Koen gives me that winning smile again. "We're really doing this?" He unzips his jacket.

"I think we should."

"Then popcorn, of course."

I laugh. "Of course." Stealing a bag, I peel it open and set it on the counter between the two sodas before hopping onto the sparkly red swivel stool beside him.

"You haven't introduced me to your sidekick." I nod to his dog.

He follows my gaze. "This is Scrot."

"Scrot?"

"Yes. Rhymes with boat."

"Nice to meet you, Scrot."

He slides into a down position below Koen.

When I glance up, Koen chooses the brown cow,

sipping from the stainless steel straw. "Is this a first date?" he asks.

I toss a few popcorn kernels into my mouth and grin while chewing. "Heck no. This is a chance encounter, not a first date."

He grabs a handful of popcorn. "So, how long have you worked here?"

"Nope." I sip my soda. "That's a first-date question."

He chuckles. "Okay. Uh ... my boss is sleeping with his daughter's best friend."

I cup a hand over my mouth and giggle. "You're *so* good at chance encounters. How old is his daughter's friend? Please say she's of legal age."

"She's twenty-three. He's fifty."

"Yikes. Does his daughter know?" I stir my drink with the straw until it fizzes.

"No."

"Could you date someone twenty-seven years younger than you?"

Koen smirks. "That would make her six. So I have to say no."

"You know what I mean." I laugh.

He eyes me while sipping his drink. "I don't know. I can't imagine having much in common with someone that young."

I narrow an eye at him. "Do you think your boss is sleeping with her because they have a lot in common?"

"Fair point."

The momentum dies, and the popcorn bag's rustling and the refrigerators' hum are the only sounds in this space.

"Sorry. This is stupid," I mumble with a sigh. "I thought we could skip the first-date awkwardness, but this is even more awkward." I fiddle with my hair. "We're strangers."

Koen draws in a long breath, gaze surveying the store. Now that I'm not afraid of him, I sense his gentleness and patience in how he seems to give my words thought before responding. Herb does that, too, but I've always assumed it's his age, a man in no hurry to do or say anything.

"We could kiss." When his eyes shift, gaze landing squarely on my face, he grins, quickly rubbing the pads of his fingers over his lips to hide it.

I take a second to respond, a slight delay to ensure I heard him correctly. "Strangers kissing?"

He offers a one-shoulder shrug. "I would never suggest it if this were a first date."

"You think chance encounters involve kissing?" My cheeks ignite.

"There's a *chance*. Wouldn't you say?" Shy, my ass. He's bleeding with confidence.

My nose wrinkles. "I don't think I kiss strangers. It's too intimate."

Koen eyes me like he's giving it some thought, perhaps formulating a counterclaim. Then he leans toward a display on the counter and nabs a deck of Drummond's playing cards next to a Drummond's fountain drink jigsaw puzzle. He retrieves a five-dollar bill from his pocket. "For the cards." He pulls the tab, opening the new box of cards and shuffling the deck. "Golf?"

By this point, my grin is not only unavoidable, it's so obnoxious my face hurts.

"Golf."

He deals the cards, and we each flip two over. I quickly win the first game, but he wins the following three.

"Do you live nearby?" he asks, shuffling the cards.

My gaze shifts from his capable hands (he's obviously shuffled many cards) to his pleasant grin. "Pretty darn close."

"In this neighborhood?" He deals six cards each.

"Closer." I smirk, lining up my cards into rows of three.

Koen lifts an eyebrow. "Do you live in the store?"

"Not quite." I jerk my head toward the back door while sliding off the stool.

He follows me.

"Voila," I say, opening the door to the chilly night under a clear sky.

"That's your Airstream?"

"Yes. Sort of." I don't elaborate on the semantics.

"And we're playing cards in the store?"

I laugh. "Less than an hour ago, I thought you were going to rob me."

Koen inspects me with a curious gaze for a few seconds. "Listen, I should go, but I've enjoyed our chance encounter." He saunters back toward the counter and slips on his jacket.

I gather the cards, take the glasses to the back room, and load them into the dishwasher. When I return, Koen's waiting by the door with his hands in the pockets of his hoodie and Scrot at his side.

"I'd still like to take you to dinner next weekend if you're interested."

I slide my phone from my pocket. It's been twelve years since I've felt this kind of instant chemistry. Twelve years of dormant butterflies in my tummy waiting to be resurrected. "I'd like that too."

We exchange numbers, and I unlock the door.

He bites his lips together as if he's fighting a grin.

"What?" I ask.

He shakes his head. "I'm just thinking."

"Do I want to know what you're thinking?"

"I'm thinking, 'Well done, Grandpa. Well done.'"

I blush. Oh yeah, those butterflies are very much alive. "Thanks for not robbing me tonight."

Koen adjusts his hat and zips his hoodie to the top before shooting me a mischievous grin. "You're welcome."

He's sexy and playful. I don't want him to leave, but he's opening the door. I try to be cool. We just met. I should say goodnight.

"Goodnight," he says for the both of us since I'm too busy thinking of doing something impulsive, even for me.

Five seconds later, I step outside. "Hey?"

He turns, already halfway to his truck.

"I've thought about it and … maybe we could kiss." I can barely breathe. Bravery is exhausting.

"You're right, it's too soon. But if it makes you feel better, I've already kissed you a dozen different ways in my mind."

Dead.

A woman with more dignity would turn around, go inside, and wait for the next date. Regroup and play hard to get.

I'm not that woman.

Instead, I gawk at his sexy ass in those jeans. I smile

when he helps Scrot into the truck. And I watch him pull out of the parking lot.

Then, I play it cool.

Kidding.

I lock the front door and squeal while jumping up and down.

Then, I play it cool.

CHAPTER
four

The difference between a good idea and a bad idea is about ten seconds.

Price

THE DAY I MET SCOTTIE, I spent my whole week's paycheck on oils, healing stones, and incense because I felt bad for dragging my wet self into the store, dripping water everywhere. She asked me if I was into natural healing.

I nodded, gazing at the counter while handing her nearly all the cash in my wallet.

"Liar," she said with a laugh.

Narrowing my eyes, I glanced up. She didn't know me. I couldn't imagine why she was so quick to judge. Did I look like an unnatural person?

"If you're not lying, then you're obviously into kink." She smirked.

"Excuse me?" I pocketed the two dollars and thirty-

seven cents in change. The scent of essential oils hung heavily in the air, the herbaceous ones dominating the rest.

She held up a hexagonal pointed stone before wrapping it in tissue paper. "This is a butt plug, or sometimes it's used for rectal cancer healing. And these two oils are used during cancer treatment, *or* they are very common aphrodisiacs—especially when used together. So just be careful."

My hair dripped rainwater down my face, but it could have been sweat, too. And the rain continued to pelt the windows as I glanced over my shoulder and prayed for a reprieve.

"There is a third option." She added the incense to the bag, tucked the receipt next to the healing butt plug, and slid it in my direction. "Perhaps you don't practice natural healing or have kinks. Maybe you feel bad for tracking water all over my floor instead of paying attention to the forecast and packing an umbrella."

She pulled her cinnamon brown hair over her shoulder, slowly braiding it while wearing a beaming grin. I knew when girls were flirting with me, and Scottie Rucker was better than anyone—a flashing neon sign.

"It's my parents' anniversary." I winked. "No cancer. All kink. My sister always out-gifts me. But not today."

Scottie cupped her hand over her mouth and snorted. "Oh my god. You win."

"But I do feel terrible about the wet floor." I strolled toward the door just as the rain let up.

"Then come by on a sunny day around noon with a cherry hibiscus tea from Bea's Teas down the street. And for the love of god, don't let anyone stick that blue sodalite stone up their ass."

I turned at the door.

She shot a sharp arrow into my chest with one smile. "I'm Scottie."

"Price," I said while opening the door and heading home with my bag full of sexual healing.

———

I ARRANGE green glass bottles of water on the counter.

Wash veggies.

Pour dirt into my pans for sprouts.

Hang grow lights.

And nap.

When I wake, I open my fancy black box and dump the first bag of Legos onto the kitchen table. It's Harry Potter Hogwarts Castle.

Two hours later, I suddenly need something from the local general store. Of course, I hope Scottie will be excited to see me. And she delivers.

"Hey! I was just thinking about you," she says, unpacking a box of oranges. Her bangs are clipped back with a white barrette that matches her white, off-the-shoulder sweater, and the rest of her hair is braided into short pigtails. She bleeds youth.

"Yeah?" I pluck a basket from the stack and hook it over my arm. "What were you thinking?"

"I was thinking you need a job."

I stand beside her and inspect an apple. "Been there. Done that. What else do you have?"

She deposits two avocados into my basket. "You need to put on some weight."

"You're uncharacteristically bossy today. Or is this the newer, more mature version of Scottie Rucker?"

She arranges the oranges in a basket. "Haha. I'm serious. Is everything okay with you?"

I focus on finding two more suitable apples. "Indeed. I started sprouting today. You should stop by in a few days to see their progress."

"Who are you?" She laughs.

"Why do I need a job?" After I steal a green grape and pop it into my mouth (it's sour), I mosey a few feet from her to the bins of nuts and seeds.

"A job gives you purpose."

"Purpose? I just started a new Lego set. It's over six thousand pieces. It's not going to put itself together. I still haven't ruled out knitting. But let's be honest, curling is where it's at."

Her giggles fill the store. Do the other customers know how lucky they are to shop here and be in the presence of such raw joy?

"I think part of your purpose should be a part-time position at a lovely little general store."

Shooting my gaze to hers, I wait for her to elaborate.

She doesn't.

"I'm not qualified."

"Price, you're overqualified times infinity. That's what makes this so perfect."

"Sorry. You'll need to elaborate on your definition of perfect." I smile at a gray-haired lady who squeezes past me to reach for a brown bag.

"I bet you've never stocked shelves, made soda and ice

cream concoctions, operated a cash register, or mopped a floor at eight o'clock at night."

"Hmm. I need to bone up on my vocabulary. I don't recall Merriam-Webster listing any of those chores under the word 'perfect.'"

"It's the simplicity. It's doing something basic but necessary. It's not about the paycheck. It's contributing to society. It's the conscious or subconscious acknowledgment that no job is beneath you. We are all equal."

I set my basket on the counter, eyeing her with a healthy dose of skepticism she earned with her We Are All Equal speech.

Scottie sighs, barely hiding her grin. "I can't find anyone who wants to work here, probably because the owners can't afford to pay anyone but me. As much as I love this job, and I do love it, I need a little time off now and again. It would just be for a few hours, maybe two or three nights a week."

I have a long list of reasons why I can't work. A list I can't share because it's complicated.

"Easy work?"

She nods. "You can hardly call it work. In fact, if mopping is too much, I'll pop in and mop before I go to bed."

"I'm sure I can mop. Does it come with instructions?"

Her face breaks into a full grin. "The funniest part about this is that I do not doubt that you've *never* used a mop."

"You know, they make robots that clean hard surface floors."

She weighs my apples. "You know, if my boss could

afford a robot, I wouldn't be begging you to take this part-time job."

"Have you done that yet?"

Glancing up from the register, Scottie narrows her eyes. "Done what?"

"Begged me?"

Her smile fades. "I thought about it. But that was a long time ago."

It's like a sky full of clouds covering my sunshine. Who is this woman before me, radiating less warmth and more of an air of melancholy?

"Scottie—"

"Can you be here tomorrow at five for training?" She recovers so quickly that I question if the sad expression is hers or just a reflection of mine.

"I can."

She inflates with a big smile on her next breath. "Really? You're going to do this?"

I hand her cash. "How else can I contribute to society while simultaneously standing up for human equality?"

I swear she looks ready to burst with excitement, but she swallows hard and clears her throat. "Thank you, Price. I'm happy for both of us."

I hug my bag of groceries. "Me too. It's such a win-win."

Her mask slips, and she acknowledges my sarcasm with a tiny eye-roll. It feeds my smile. Who am I kidding? It feeds my fucking soul.

"Later."

"See you tomorrow," she singsongs.

As soon as I exit the store, I blow out a long breath. This is a terrible idea. Evenings and mornings are not my best times, but she didn't ask for a one-to-three shift. Maybe I can renegotiate my schedule with her tomorrow.

When I arrive home, my Legos await me. They're unfinished, just like my life.

"Goddamn." I wince, rubbing my lower back. I'm so tired today. The good days outnumber the bad ones, but the bad ones pack a punch.

Feel everything.

I shower, switching the water to straight cold for five minutes at the end. Shivering, I swipe the towel over my hair a few times before blotting my body and hobbling to the bed. Tugging on the neatly tucked sheets, I wrap them around my body, teeth chattering, heart pounding. I question if I've ever been in control of my life or if I've simply stacked the odds in my favor.

This is what it feels like to let go of control. Letting go of fear isn't as easy.

Closing my eyes, I blow out a slow breath. "There's nothing to fear."

Feel everything.

CHAPTER
five

Timing is nothing, if not everything.

Scottie

"HELLO?" Koen answers on the third ring. He sounds distracted—short and a little out of breath.

"Hey. It's Scottie. If this is a bad time—"

"Uh, no. Just a sec."

There are muffled voices in the distance and scratching noises like his phone's speaker is rubbing against something. Then there's a click, and it's quiet.

"Sorry. What's up?"

Shit.

Nothing is up.

"Really, if this is a bad time. I can call you later." I pick at a loose thread on the frayed cuff of my denim button-down.

"Nope. The time is fine."

My nose wrinkles while I silently berate myself. I

should have texted.

"Scottie?"

"Yeah, uh ..."

"Hi," he says in his confident tone. "Did you call just to say hi?"

My body relaxes as I slowly spin in circles on the swivel stool behind the counter.

"Or are you calling to cancel our date? That would suck, but I would understand. I was pretty creepy the other night."

I chuckle. "No. I'm not calling to cancel. I'm bored. It's a slow day in the store, and I thought maybe you were taking a lunch break. But you sounded busy when you answered. So yeah, I called to say hi." I can't stop smiling; I can't tame those butterflies. "Hi," I whisper, stopping the stool as a customer enters the store. "Hi," I say to the customer. "Let me know if I can help you."

"Sounds like someone came into your store."

"Yes. I'll let you get back to work. I'll try to control my bored impulses in the future."

"Hey, man! Are you coming?" A deep voice drifts from his side of the call, along with several thumps.

"Well, good chat," I say with a tiny laugh.

"Just some assholes banging on my truck window. They're lost without me."

"Are you their boss?"

"Nope. Just the only one who knows what to do."

"Ah, gotcha. Well, I'll see you in eight days."

"Eight of the longest days of my life."

I press a hand to my mouth to hold my squeal.

A dog barks.

With a deep breath, I regain my composure. Barely.

"Do you take Scrot to work with you?"

"Of course. At least when I can."

I don't know why this makes me happy, but it does. "I love that. Well, see ya."

He hums. It's deep and sexy. Is he slowly killing me on purpose? "Bye, Scottie."

I end the call and pull my shirt away from my skin to keep from overheating as the young woman who just came into the store reads the label of a bag of soup mix. Then, another customer comes through the door, and the rest of my afternoon turns into a steady flow of customers.

A few minutes before five, Price steps into the store. There's something different about him, more than just the long span of years we've been apart. I can't put my finger on it. When I'm with him, I have this urge to hug him and never let go. He's a man who needs an eternal hug. That wasn't the Price I met in Philadelphia. And I never thought I would see him again. There are so many things I want to say, but I don't know if I'll ever be able to tell them.

"Hi. Are you feeling okay?" I stare at him while stacking clean glasses on the shelf above the soda fountain.

He draws in a long breath and holds it while smiling. "Just nervous about my new job."

"I believe everything you've done in life until this point has prepared you for this. All that hard work is about to pay off."

Price's raised eyebrows don't seem convinced, but he manages a smile while averting his gaze to the display of crystal necklaces and bracelets.

I stack the last glass and retrieve a bracelet from the rack. "I make these."

Price eyes me with surprise, or maybe it's wonder in his eyes.

"This one," I slide the bracelet onto his wrist, "has selenite, which has cleansing properties, strengthens immunity, and helps protect you from losing control."

Price stiffens, gaze shifting to mine as I tighten the strings on the bracelet.

"Rose quartz for self-love, fluorite to replace negative energy with positive energy, and citrine for courage."

He swallows hard. "I fear you think I need a lot of help."

Holding his gaze for several silent seconds, I smile. "It is *I* who needs help. So let's get you trained."

Price pulls cash from his front pocket.

"Nope. It's a gift. Wear it every day. That's all the thanks I need. And when people ask you where you got it, send them my way."

He stares at the bracelet with a heartbreakingly somber expression, whispering, "Thank you."

Over the next two hours, I teach him how to make the sodas, malts, and sundaes and form a perfectly round scoop of ice cream to fit atop the sugar cones. Then I offer a tutorial on the cash register and finish his training by mopping the floor. I feel his gaze when I'm focused on showing him something. It's like the night Koen came into the store, repeatedly inspecting me when he didn't think I was looking.

"I won't make you close up yet. I'll be sure I'm here by eight to do that." I return the mop to the back room.

"You don't trust me with a key? Or you have to ask

your boss?" he asks, resting his shoulder against the doorframe while I wheel the mop bucket into the corner by the broom.

Wiping my hands on my jeans, I glance up at him. "Neither. I just don't want to overwhelm you."

"The soda fountain overwhelmed me."

I smirk. "As I recall, you mixed drinks like a seasoned bartender, trying to get a nineteen-year-old girl drunk. I don't believe sodas overwhelm you. There's a cheat sheet."

When I reach the doorway, he doesn't move but fiddles with his bracelet.

"You conquered the world, didn't you?"

The corners of his mouth twitch. "Why do you think that?"

"Because you look like a man who conquered the world."

He grunts. "I look like shit."

"You look like someone who trained for months to run a marathon, then collapsed at the finish line."

He seems to give it some thought before nodding several times.

"Well, I didn't conquer the world. In fact, I don't own this store or that trailer because I don't need much."

"To be happy?"

"To live."

A tiny crease forms along the bridge of his nose. "It's almost too simple," he whispers as if his words aren't meant for me.

"Price, I just wanna be here. I want to breathe the air, eat the food, converse with people, gaze at mountains, and dive into oceans. Make love. Watch movies that make me laugh until I nearly wet myself. Read books that tear out my heart. I want to *live*. Happiness is an emotion, a state of mind. But humans are not static. We're constantly evolving, and our emotions shift without warning. The question is: What do you need to feel like you're living?"

His lips part for a second. "I need not to—"

The door chimes.

"What do you need?"

He shakes his head as if the thought has gone. "I should head home. Or do you want me to help this last customer?"

"No. I'm the one who forgot to lock the door and shut off the *Open* sign. Can you work from five to eight this Friday? I'll be here by eight to close."

"Friday." He nods and turns. "Goodnight."

"Goodnight." I follow him out of the back room. Just as he exits through the front door, I catch a glimpse of my last customer of the night—and his adorable Fox Terrier.

"Sorry, sir. We're closed. I can't have you lingering too long." I turn off the *Open* sign and immediately feel those darn butterflies.

Koen grins, snagging a bottle of our local ginger beer. "Sorry, I'm just really nervous about our date. How are you feeling about it?" He sets the bottle on the counter with some cash and adjusts his baseball cap. He makes that navy flannel shirt look better than I ever knew flannel could look. Plaid is officially sexy.

And I don't believe he's nervous about anything for one second.

I squat beside him to pet Scrot behind his ears. "Terrified. You will ask me if working in a general store is my life's aspiration. And I will tell you that I also make crystal jewelry and essential oil perfumes. No 401K. No health insurance. I might even reveal that the people who own this general store also own the Airstream where I sleep. But in the next breath, I'll confess that I wouldn't change anything about my life. And you'll either find it endearing or pathetic. But either way, you'll stay through dinner, and I'll ask you about your job. Since you're a welder, I'll run out of follow-up questions because I know nothing about welding. So ... yeah. I'm nervous about our date." I stand, giving him a toothy grin before making my way around the counter to get his change for the ginger beer while he twists off the top.

"Damn." He takes a swig. "This is going to be a weird date. I've never thought to ask someone about their life's aspirations. You're the kind of woman who enjoys deep conversations, and I'm the guy who has a million things running through my head at once but can rarely articulate any of them in a way that makes sense. So I usually default to talking about sports or my favorite places to travel."

I slide his change to him. "I like tennis. I used to be pretty good at it, and I love watching it. I like college football more than professional. Golf bores me in every way imaginable."

Koen taps his knuckles on the counter several times while twisting his lips. "I need to walk Scrot. And I owe him a game of fetch. It was a busy afternoon."

"Because your date for next weekend disrupted you."

He chuckles before chugging the rest of his ginger beer. "Not even a little."

I toss his bottle in the recycling bin and turn off the register. "Why are we not going out this weekend?" I ask.

"Because I'll be out of town."

I nod. "I see. How do you play fetch in the dark?"

"A glow-in-the-dark Frisbee."

"Oh! That reminds me. I like Frisbee golf." I grin. "So not all golf bores me. And I like the card game we played."

"Would you like to walk with us to the park and play fetch too?"

I pull on my sweater. "I'd love to. I need to switch my shoes." I squeeze past him to lock the front door. "We'll go out back."

"Mmm, you smell good."

I pause for a breath before glancing over my shoulder at him just inches from me. Every time he hums, I feel it more than I hear it. And it makes me a little weak in the knees.

"Jesus, that sounded creepy." He takes a step back and covers his grin with his fist.

"Are you going to suck my blood?"

"Do you want me to suck your blood?" He smirks.

"Herb said you're shy."

"Did he? That's interesting."

I pull up my sleeve and lift my arm, scooting my bracelets away from my wrist while holding it close to his face. "It's my newest blend: clary sage and vanilla with bergamot, ylang-ylang, and jasmine notes."

He turns his hat backward and leans forward, taking a slow inhale. "What's it called?"

"Oh ..." I nervously laugh and slide my sleeve back down my arm while making my way to the back door. "It's called Foreplay."

"Is it now? That's a great name. Who doesn't love—"

"Don't." I giggle, stepping out back and waiting for him to follow me so I can set the alarm and lock the door. I can't look at him. "There's no need to reply. I named it for the women who buy it, not the men who ... you know." When it's set and locked, I turn toward him.

His lips press together for a beat. "So, what are your life's aspirations?"

I like him so much. This slow burn is starting to feel like an inferno.

"Well," I brush past him toward my trailer, "after we play fetch, I want to learn everything I can about welding so we don't have to talk about me and my erotic concoctions on our date. But other than that, I'm pretty open to whatever life wants to send my way. I'm a proud underachiever." I open my trailer door.

"If you need help with your welding research, call me. I can help you bone up on that before your big date."

Koen's quick wit and unyielding confidence are just two more things to add to the rapidly growing list of traits that make him irresistible. Just like my new perfume, it's a perfect combination.

It's foreplay.

"Come in," I motion with my head.

"Scrotum and I will wait—" He stops.

He should have kept going. I might not have noticed his error. Was it an error?

I slip out of my Birkenstocks, keeping my eyes on him while he stands unblinking with half his body inside and half outside.

"Did you say—"

He bites his lower lip and nods. "Yeah," he says slowly. "I found him on a camping trip in Wyoming. He was taunting a mountain lion. I'd never seen anything like it. Eventually, the lion ran off. My brother whistled and said, 'That dog's got big balls.' When we found no identification or a chip on him, I brought him home. And my brother said I should call him Ballsy." Koen bobs his head a few times. "And perhaps he was right. But I thought Scrotum would be a better name because ... well, a scrotum has balls."

I snort, cupping my mouth.

"I quickly discovered women don't find the name quite so cool, so I call him Scrot for short."

I have no words, so I duck my head to hide my grin while I shove my feet into my sneakers. "Well, he's the most adorable Scrotum I've ever seen."

"Is that saying a lot?"

While I finish tying my shoes, I glance up. "Are you asking if I've seen a lot of scrotums?"

Koen scratches the back of his neck and chuckles. "I might be."

"I've seen a handful." I roll my lips between my teeth while I step closer, and he backs out my door. Koen carries a rugged scent, one of those just-for-men soaps that go for a cedarwood but end up smelling like a mix of leather and campfire. He wears it well.

After I close the door behind me, he cups my wrist and lifts my arm.

"What?" I ask.

"Just seeing how big your hand is." He releases it. "So you've seen like ... two scrotums."

I like him *so* much I can't stop smiling.

CHAPTER
six

It's easy to love a good man. It's hard to love two good men.

SCROT CHASES the Frisbee for over twenty minutes. I try to outrun him a few times, but I fail. Koen's grin swells a little more each time I return empty-handed and out of breath.

"One more chance," I say, bent at the waist, catching my breath.

"You're really going to race him again?"

I nod since I can't talk.

Koen chuckles. "Okay." He fakes a throw, so Scrot heads off in one direction, and then he flings the Frisbee in a different direction to give me a head start.

"I threw it too far. Let it go!" he yells.

I have the edge. Why would I let it go? With a big jump, I nab it out of the air.

Victorious!

Except, the ground disappears and it's replaced with water.

Icy water.

Air fills my lungs when I surface, but they won't release it again.

"Shit! Scottie, I've got you." Koen holds out his hand, and I take it while Scrot barks. He pulls me out of the pond, which appeared out of nowhere.

"C-cold." I shiver, and everything smells fishy. I don't know if I'm tasting or smelling it.

"Crap. I'm so sorry." He removes his hoodie and his shirt.

"What are y-you d-doing?"

He removes his jeans. "We need to get you out of these wet clothes. It's only forty degrees tonight."

"I'm f-fine." I hug my shaky fists to my chest.

"You don't sound fine. Here." He peels off my sweater.

"My shirt—" I try to keep it from going over my head with my sweater.

"It's wet, too." Koen overpowers my weak resistance. "Can you put your arms through?" He works his shirt over my head and helps guide my arms through the holes.

"Ko-en ..." I fail at protesting as he peels my jeans down my legs, sliding off my sneakers and depositing the wet denim beside me.

"Can you hold the waist to keep them up?" He guides my hands to the waist of his jeans once he has them up my legs.

I nod quickly. "You're naked."

He guides my feet back into my sneakers. "I've got on underwear. And I'm not wet." He holds my clothes in one hand while wrapping his other arm around my shoulders as we walk back to my trailer.

Me in oversized clothes.

Him in black briefs and brown leather boots.

We garner more than a few looks over the mile walk. It's night, but it's hard to miss a man in his undies. Lord knows I can't stop taking a peek.

Abs. Sculpted quads and calves. Tight glutes.

Then Scrot does his part to make the night a little worse. He stops to take a dump.

"Are you fucking kidding me?" Koen grumbles.

I snort despite my chattering teeth.

"The uh ..." He wrinkles his nose. "Poop bag is in the pocket of my jeans."

"Oh. I'll hold the waist; you grab the bag."

He tries to fish the bag out of the pocket like he's on the verge of winning a game of Pick-up Sticks. "I'm trying really hard not to enjoy this."

"Just get it." I roll my eyes.

"I don't want to touch you the wrong way accidentally. As a rule, I never fondle someone when their lips are blue."

I giggle. "Just get it."

Koen scoops poop, and we continue on our way.

"I'm sorry," I say when we reach my trailer.

"Why are you apologizing?"

"Because you told me to stop, but I didn't. And you," I giggle, "walked all the way back in your boots and underwear." When we step into the trailer, I pull off my wet shoes.

"No big deal. It's not my first time."

With my teeth still chattering, I glance up at him. "It's not?"

"Okay. It is. I just didn't want to make you feel bad."

"I'm going to step into the shower. I'll toss your clothes out to you, and you can go. If you never want to see me again, I understand."

A tiny grin pulls at his lips while Scrot sits at his feet. "I want to see you again right now, but I'm trying to be a gentleman."

"Did Herb fix me up with a pervert?" I cock my head to the side and buy time to take a quick scan of his nearly naked body. He's wrapped in lean muscles. Hairy, but not too hairy. I'm the perv.

When he doesn't answer with more than a conspiratorial grin, I quickly open the door to the bathroom and slide inside to remove his clothes. "Here you go. Again, I'm so sorry," I call, cracking the door just enough to toss his clothes and jacket onto the floor. "Goodnight."

Once I stop shivering and wash the pond water from my hair, I wrap up in my robe and open the bathroom door. "Oh. You're still here."

Koen smiles, glancing up from my kitchen table and my thousand-piece puzzle of the colorful buildings along Cinque Terre, Italy. "Just making sure you're okay. Thawed out."

"Are you working on my puzzle?" I ask, even though I know the answer because he's finished adding the blue pieces of the water.

"Sorry." He sits back, folding his hands in his lap.

I grin, combing my fingers through my hair. "You like puzzles?"

"No." He bobs his head. "Well, that's a hard question.

I've never purchased a puzzle, and I don't sit around thinking about puzzles. And when I'm gifted a puzzle," he squints, "which is oddly quite often, I never open the box. However, if my mom or grandpa opens the box and spreads out the pieces, or if I'm at one of their houses and they have a partially constructed puzzle on the dining room table, I become obsessed with putting them together. Last year, on New Year's Eve, my mom went to bed at midnight, and I said I would find *one* particular piece before heading home. She woke up at three in the morning to use the bathroom, and I was still there."

My eyes widen, as does my grin.

Koen is not that sorry that he worked on my puzzle without permission because, in the time it took him to tell me that story, he found three more pieces.

He hums. "I guess I don't like unfinished projects. Or clutter. Or loose ends."

My gaze shifts to the dirty dishes by my sink and my unmade queen bed littered with clothes and bins of essential oils and stones. There's no way he hasn't noticed my clutter and unfinished projects. And yet, he's still here.

Price Milloy thrived on order. I bet he'd say I was a terrible influence on him. Why am I attracted to the tidy ones?

"Want some pistachios?" I pluck the open bag from the counter and scatter some on the table next to the puzzle pieces.

Koen's brows jump up his forehead while he stares at the shelled nuts. "Thanks," he murmurs, plucking one from the table before gently sliding the rest away from the puzzle pieces.

He's a puzzle, a bunch of pieces that seemingly don't fit until you stare at them long enough. He has calloused hands and fingernails that look clipped at best. He wears a baseball hat to hide his unkempt hair. Those dirty brown boots are probably the same ones he wears to work every day. His flannel shirt is missing two buttons, and his jeans have a small hole in the knee that's not there on purpose.

But he's not a fan of unfinished projects, clutter, loose ends, or pistachios scattered on the table.

"Is your dad alive? Or are your parents divorced?" I ask.

He makes a quick glance up at me before returning his attention to the puzzle. "Divorced."

"Is Herb your dad's father or your mother's?"

"Dad's." He finds another piece that fits.

My lips part to vomit my next question, but I swallow it.

"I'm going to get dressed."

"Do you want me to leave?"

"Uh ..."

"That was a stupid question." He stands. "You're too nice to ask me to leave." He whistles for Scrot to head to the door.

"I haven't had dinner. So I'm going to get dressed and eat something besides pistachios."

Koen nods before adjusting his hat. "I get up at five, so I should head home."

"Well—" I start my goodbye.

"But I don't want to go." He bites his bottom lip, which wrinkles his nose. This is the first time he's shown anything short of absolute confidence.

We hold each other's gaze for a long moment. I don't know what this is, but it's something.

My lips twist. "It's the puzzle, isn't it?"

"It's you."

I fight my grin.

"My Frisbee skills? My fancy home? The dirty dishes in the sink? Or the catastrophe on my bed?"

"I hadn't noticed—"

"Liar." I laugh.

His smile gives him away. "Why don't you get dressed while I get you something to eat? We can work on the puzzle for a little longer."

"Are you going to wash my dirty dishes while I get dressed?"

"Absolutely."

"A lesser woman would feel embarrassed. Horrified that a man she's been with on only two occasions is cleaning up after her. I am not that woman. The dish soap is under the sink." With a flirty smirk, I squeeze past him to the bedroom.

I slip into lounge pants and a soft, long-sleeved tee and clear off my bed, which takes longer than expected. When I open the door, he's back at the puzzle. The dishes are clean and put away, and a bowl of leftover pasta salad sits next to the puzzle, along with the pistachios, which are now in a bowl.

"Thank you," I say, sitting across from him again. "Have you had dinner?" I take a bite of the pasta salad.

"I did." He lifts his gaze from the puzzle, setting aside the piece in his hand. "Is now the right time to mention I was engaged."

I pause the fork at my mouth. What? Did I hear him right?

His eyes focus as if he's visualizing something. "She left me because I enjoyed drinking until I blacked out, just like my father."

I force myself to take a bite of pasta and chew it slowly to hide any knee-jerk reaction.

A flinch.

A hard swallow.

A tiny gasp.

"I didn't help out around the house. I slept in my clothes most nights. My truck was littered with trash from takeout food and empty bottles of booze. So, order and routine have become important to me. Necessary."

Staring at my bowl, I nod several times.

"That was five years ago. And I still have to think through things. Plan *not* to drink. Walk Scrot instead of going to the bar. And if my grandfather knew I was telling you this before or even on our first date, he would clock me upside the head. But the anxiety of *not* telling you is torturous. So there you have it."

I catch myself nervously tapping the bowl with my fork. "Should I run?"

He bobs his head a few times. "Probably."

"Do you think you're unworthy of love?"

"No. But I wouldn't blame anyone for feeling worthy of someone better than me—less risky. Less fun, too, but definitely less risky."

"Well," I set my bowl and fork in the sink, "that makes you an honest man, Koen Sikes. And I'm a huge fan of honest men. Besides, I landed in a pond tonight. You might have to lower your expectations of me." I turn, resting my butt and hands against the counter.

He stands so that we're incredibly close in this tight space. My heart lurches into my throat. I've never wanted to be kissed so badly in my life. He wets his lips, and I swear he's going to kiss me. The shivers attack me for the second time tonight when he brushes his knuckles along my cheek before his palm skates down my neck.

"You've already exceeded all expectations by a landslide." He smiles. "Goodnight, Scottie."

His hand disappears. And in the next blink, he's out the door with Scrot, leaving me puddled on the floor of my trailer.

CHAPTER
seven

Dead people don't laugh.

Price

WITHDRAWAL IS A BITCH.

Six weeks ago, if someone had asked me if I had an addiction to technology, I would have laughed. I spent countless hours using technology for my job, which was also convenient for my personal life. But addicted? No.

I would have been wrong.

It's hard to go more than ten minutes without thinking about something I'd like to do that requires technology. I need something. The quietude is unnerving after a while. My thoughts aren't that comforting, and I haven't figured out how to stop thinking while I'm awake.

I consider getting a radio for music, but I don't want the commercials, news breaks, or even the weather forecast. So off to the store I go to buy a record player.

"What vinyl records do you have?" the gray-haired salesman asks, adjusting his round, black-framed glasses.

"None. Do you have any suggestions?"

"Absolutely. Vinyl albums are cool again. There's been a huge resurgence in popularity, but if you ask me, they never went out of style." He thumbs through a box of albums. "Definitely Zeppelin and The Beatles. Fleetwood Mac ... Springsteen ... The Rolling Stones ... Hendrix ... I'd get some Nirvana and throw in a little Maroon Five and Harry Styles for a nice mix."

I stare at the stack of albums in his bony arms.

"If it's too much to buy all at once—"

I shake my head. "I'll take them. Do you have some good chill albums?"

"Sure. Let's see ..." Again, he thumbs through the albums. "How about Steely Dan and Sade?"

"I'll trust you."

He laughs. "You've got a great mix. What made you want to get into vinyl?"

I follow him to the register. "I'm doing a technology detox of sorts."

"I love it." He scans the albums, slides them into a bag, and sets the bag on the box with my new turntable while I dig out cash.

"Thanks," I say.

"Enjoy."

I'm unsure how to use a turntable, but there are instructions, so I'm good. When I get home, it only takes me five minutes to set it up, and The Beatles play "Can't Buy Me Love."

For the rest of the day, I listen to music, stare at the

ceiling, and contemplate the meaning of life. I come up empty. So before bed, I break out my new journal and pen. Maybe writing my thoughts will help make sense of life.

I stare at the blank page and tap my pen on the first line until I have nothing more than a conglomerate of ink dots. Twenty minutes later, I have a drawing of a cat on a windowsill. What's most shocking is I can draw. I'm good, *really* good. How did I not know this?

But now I'm tired, so I run a toothbrush over my teeth and crawl into bed. No sooner do I shut off the light and there's a knock on the door. With a heavy sigh, I climb out of bed and head to the door, pulling a T-shirt over my head.

Scottie's smile fades when she inspects me. "Were you in bed?" She glances at her watch. "It's not even nine o'clock. Are you sick? Do you want me to come back another time? Is there anything I can do for you?"

"Do you want to come in and play something besides Twenty Questions?"

She steps inside, combing her fingers through her bangs before flipping them out of her eyes. A new mix of aromatherapy follows her. It's heavy in citrus. I like it.

"I asked you four questions, not twenty. But I could easily think of another sixteen."

I turn on the gold porcelain lamp in the living room. "I'm sure you could, but I'll spare you. I was up early this morning," (a lie), "so I decided to turn in early. You knocked on my door before I pulled the covers over my body. You didn't wake me."

Scottie turns in a slow circle, tugging on her long sleeves to ball her fists into them while inspecting my place. She's divine. Always in comfy, flowing clothes. Face makeup-less save for a hint of lip gloss or probably some sort of homemade lip balm. And her smile is content and soothing, even when she's concerned about me.

"I was going to see if you've had dinner yet, but I think I know that answer."

I skipped dinner.

"I could eat." Another lie. "What do you have in mind?"

"I don't know. What do you have? Wait ... whoa! Have you been listening to music on this?" She inspects my new turntable on the white media console below the TV, flipping through the small pile of records.

"I just got it today."

Scottie eyes me like she's seeing me for the first time. I understand. Every time I look in the mirror, I feel like I'm seeing the reflection of a stranger.

She pads her fuzzy-socked feet along the wood floor toward the fridge. Opening it, she chuckles. "You are definitely not the Price Milloy I remember."

I bought a dozen bottles of local cold-pressed juice yesterday and filled my fridge with fruits and veggies.

"I guess we're having pomegranate and..." she surveys the counter filled with fruit "...bananas."

"Do you know how long it took me to deseed that pomegranate? What makes you think I'm willing to share it?"

She plucks two slate blue bowls from the floating shelf by the stove. "I'll replace your deseeded pomegranate. I love deseeding them. It's meditative, don't you think?"

"You mean frustrating?" I hand her a spoon.

She deposits seeds into each bowl and uses the spoon to cut the banana. I love watching her do things. Her soothing motions and gracefulness have stuck with me all these years. I could watch her do anything, and it would lull me into a peaceful state.

"Can we eat on your sofa?"

I look back at the sofa as if I forgot I had one. "Sure."

Scottie plops into the corner with her feet tucked beneath her. "So I had something really embarrassing happen to me yesterday." She takes a bite of fruit and grins while chewing it.

I don't care what happened. As long as it keeps that grin on her face, that's all that matters.

"At the store?"

She shakes her head and swallows. "After the shop closed, I walked with a friend and his dog. We played fetch in the park, which can be tricky at night because the park isn't well-lit, but he had a glow-in-the-dark Frisbee. I became a little obsessed with trying to catch the Frisbee before the dog, and on the last throw, he tossed it in a different direction to give me a head start. Then he yelled for me to stop, but I was already airborne to catch the Frisbee, and I landed in a pond."

God. She's so beautiful.

I laugh because it's funny, but also because her laughter is contagious.

She shakes in a fit of giggles. "B-but I caught it."

I try to swallow but nearly choke as I picture her landing in the pond. "That's all that matters."

She tells me the rest of the story with animated expressions that captivate me, like everything else about her. By the end, she has tears streaming down her face, and I'm not far off.

I wonder if this guy, her *friend*, knows how lucky he is to experience absolutely anything with her. Countless memories of our summer together have permanent space in my mind.

Those memories are why I'm in Austin.

When the laughter dies, we start to speak at the same time. And we say the exact same words. "Remember when we—"

I grin. "You go first."

"Remember when we planned that *outdoor* surprise party for your dad, which ended in a torrential downpour?"

I nod. And we spend the next two hours reminiscing. She has no idea how much she's influenced my life.

"I should go. I'm sure you're exhausted," she says.

I stifle my yawn, but her frown confirms she doesn't miss it.

"I'll report for five o'clock duty tomorrow. Do you think I'm ready?" I ask, walking her to the door.

"Of course. You rise to every occasion like a phoenix in the Arabian Desert."

With a chuckle, I open the door.

She slips her feet into her shoes. "This was fun."

I rub my arms as the cool breeze barges into the entry. "It was."

She presses her lips together and eyes me. If I didn't know better, I'd say she's waiting for me to kiss her goodnight. But I do know better.

At least, I think I do.

While I ponder the idea, which is a bad one, she steps

toward me and wraps her arms around my neck, lips at my ear. "Goodnight," she whispers.

"Goodnight." I gently wrap my arms around her.

Scottie's hands cup my neck, and she kisses my cheek.

In the next breath, she's out the door and hustling to her red truck in the driveway.

CHAPTER
eight

If the truth is a dealbreaker, then let it break.

Scottie

"HOUSE OF CHAOS, how can I direct your call?" My sister answers her phone.

I laugh. "Hey, Steph."

"Please tell me you're calling because you're visiting Asheville, and by visiting, I mean coming to babysit while I have a spa day."

"I'm pretty sure when you were pregnant with Winnie, you said three kids can't be that much harder than two."

"I was wrong. There. Are you happy? Three kids—three *girls*—under six is the definition of an early mid-life crisis."

"Is it a bad time? I don't want you to lose one of my nieces because I'm distracting you."

She sighs. "Winnie's still sleeping, and Avery and

Mable are eating breakfast. I have maybe ten minutes of calm before the next storm. Tell me something exciting. Let me live vicariously through you. And if you don't have anything, make something up."

I open my glass jar of overnight oats and sit at my table. "Oh, I have quite the update for you. Guess who showed up at the store?"

"I slept three hours last night and said I have ten minutes tops. No time for guessing."

"Fine. You're no fun. Price Milloy."

Silence.

I'm not sure if she heard me or if she's still on the line. "Steph?"

"Are you serious?"

"Yes. I know you gave me the option to make something up, but I'm not making this up. He lives in Austin. No job. No family. And something's really off about him. I can't explain it, but it's a feeling. Kind of a dark feeling."

"Like he's up to something?"

"No. Well, maybe. I'm not sure yet. But I definitely feel something."

"You would know. I don't know how you're so in tune to people's auras or whatever you call it, but you're usually right. Have you told him?"

"No. I can't. Not yet."

"How does it feel seeing him after all this time?"

"Weird. In some ways, it feels like it's been a lifetime, but in other ways, it feels like we're back in Philly, like I should be scoping out local concerts and new restaurants to try."

"Do you think you'll develop romantic feelings for him again? I mean, is this fate?"

"Okay, this is where it's getting complicated. Yes. This felt like fate until ... I had a customer fix me up with his grandson. His name is Koen, and he's a welder. He's sexy. Steph, I'm talking about the kind of sexy that's making me think about sex nonstop."

"Now, this is what I'm talking about. Go on. I'm listening."

I giggle before taking another bite of my oats. "He has a cute little dog," I mumble before swallowing, "that he takes to work with him. And he's funny and confident. And sexy. Did I mention that?"

"Ugh, Winnie's crying. Hurry up."

"You can call me back later, but I'm in quite the conundrum because, in a matter of days, my life went from perfectly uneventful to having two guys I like. My feelings for them are quite different, but there is some overlap, and that's the part that's making this hard to navigate. But it's a good problem. I hope."

"Okay. I'm excited for you and can't wait to hear more. Go have really hot sex with one of them and tell me all about it. I can't remember the last time I had it."

I laugh. "Kiss the girls for me ... and Dax too."

"Will do. Bye, Scottie."

I finish eating and get ready to open the shop. Koen messages me several times in the process. He's been texting me while he's out of town. Sometimes, it's a simple "hi" with a goofy emoji; sometimes, it's a photo of something he's welding. In return, I send him the occasional "hi" and pictures of products I'm unloading or my progress on the puzzle.

———

On Tuesday, Herb's my first customer of the day. He's a great start to any day.

"Good morning, young lady." He tips his fedora, which covers his thick white hair, while grabbing a small cart to use as a walker. He chose a navy cardigan today instead of his usual gray. He's a dapper man at nearly six feet tall but stands closer to five-nine with hunched shoulders.

"Morning, Herb. Are you having a good day?"

"I am now."

I smile because I always ask him the same question, and he always gives me the same answer.

"The boy said I did a good job."

Refilling the soda syrups, I shoot him a curious glance. "The boy?"

"Koen. He said you two met. And you're ..." He scratches his jaw. "What was the word he used?"

I don't know, but the anticipation is killing me.

"Unethical?" He shakes his head a half dozen times. "No. No. That's not right. My brain's still asleep."

I hold back my giggle, relieved that's not the right word.

"The word's not there." He sighs, wheeling the cart toward the produce section, where he'll pick out one orange, one ripe banana, and two green-topped carrots.

He's a creature of habit, buying only what he needs for one day. I'm not sure if he likes his produce as fresh as possible or if he enjoys visiting with me. "I'm going to ask him," he says. "Otherwise, it will drive me crazy."

"It's fine. No need to check with him."

Too late.

Herb has his phone out of his pocket. "Siri, call Koen."

"I'm sorry. I didn't get that," Siri replies.

"SIRI, CALL KOEN!"

I die.

Covering my mouth to muffle my laughter, I feel my cheeks burn with embarrassment. I'm so glad no one else is in the store.

"Hey, what's up?" Koen answers.

The fact that he's on speaker makes it so much worse. I hide around the corner, shaking with silent laughter.

"It's your grandpa."

Koen chuckles. "I know. What's up?"

"What did you say about Scottie? You know, the girl from the general store."

"Uh ... what do you mean?"

"You used a word to describe her, but I can't remember. It wasn't unethical. But it started with a U-N. My brain's not working right today."

"Grandpa, what do you need to know this for?"

"I'm visiting with Scottie, and I was telling her what you said, but I couldn't remember."

"You're ..." Koen clears his throat. "You're at the store?"

"That's what I said."

"You didn't tell her I said she's unethical, did you?"

"I took the word for a test drive. But as soon as it came out, I told her that wasn't the right word. That's why I'm calling you."

"Oh, Grandpa."

I can feel Koen deflating on the other end of that call while I shake with silent laughter, trying to keep from crying.

"Unusual isn't the right word either," Herb says.

"Unexpected," Koen replies quickly—desperately. "I said she's unexpected in a really great way. But I'm not thrilled that you're sharing what I told you in confidence."

"Oh, my boy, if I don't tell the girl, she'll never know because you'll never say it."

The boy. The girl.

"Can you just get your groceries and go home? Leave the conversation to me. I'm not as inept as you think."

The door chimes with another customer. "Good morning," the young mother with a baby wrapped to her chest says before kissing the little one's head. I feel a pang of envy.

"Am I on speaker?" Koen asks.

"Yeah. It's too loud at my ear with my hearing aids."

"Jesus. I gotta go. Bye."

Herb picks out his produce and pushes the cart to the counter. "Unexpected. That's what he called you. He said you were unexpected in a really great way."

Biting back my grin, I nod. "That was very kind of him. The feeling is mutual."

"I knew you two would hit it off. Aren't you glad I set you up on a date?"

I am, even though our date isn't until Friday. "You're a good man, Herb."

———

BY THE TIME Friday rolls around, I'm a mess of anticipation. Koen ended up staying out of town longer than expected, so I haven't seen him in over a week.

"Are you sure you don't have any more questions?" I ask Price for the third time.

He grins with a headshake, making flavored sodas for a guy and his two kids. "It's my fourth day. I'm sure."

"Call me if you have any questions. My number is taped to the phone."

"Got it."

"Okay. Good. Thanks. I know you have it, and I'm not worried at all. I appreciate your help." I'm not worried about Price. It's my date that has me feeling anxious.

It's ridiculous. After all, "my date" pulled me out of a pond and stripped me down to my bra and panties. He's washed my dishes. And he's confessed to his grandpa that I'm unexpected in a really great way.

"Scottie?"

"Yeah?"

Price glances at me over his shoulder while he makes the last soda. "Go."

It takes me a few seconds to think past my nerves. Then I nod. "Got it. Yep. I'm leaving."

I change my clothes twice. I'd probably change them again, but I don't own that many things. Simplicity has been my friend, but tonight, I'd love something that feels special, not just comfortable and familiar. Settling on wide-legged jeans and a cream sweater, I slide on my Birkenstocks and recheck my hair.

I pull it back.

Put it down.

Back again.

Down again.

Then, there are three knocks on my door.

Blowing out a slow breath, I open it. "Hi."

Koen grins, giving me instant relief because he's in jeans, another flannel shirt, gray and green this time, and his brown boots. But he's not wearing a hat. His hair's a little damp and wavy around his ears and forehead like he recently showered—with a bar of his man-smelling soap.

"Ready?" he asks.

"I'm nervous."

"Nervous? Why? Did *your* grandpa call you on speakerphone to ask what word you used to describe your date? And in the process, did he reveal that the first word he used was 'unethical'?"

I glance up after sliding on my jacket. "That was the best."

"The best?" His face sours. "Complete humiliation is *the best*?"

"I might decide to date your grandpa." I grab my purse and follow him out the door.

"What do you like so much about that old man?" Koen laughs and opens the passenger door to his truck for me.

I climb inside. "I can't do this."

"Date my grandpa? God, I hope not."

I relinquish a grin. Koen has an addictive sense of humor. He has a lot of things I find irresistible, and that's why I can't do this. "I can't go to dinner with you."

His brows draw together.

"I don't want to get to the restaurant and sit across from you and suddenly feel at a loss for words. I don't want anything to feel forced or awkward. I don't want a waiter to interrupt us every five seconds."

Koen blinks a few times. "I see. So you're saying you want to go to Home Depot with me to get copper wire?"

I don't *love* him. But right now ... I love him.

"Yes. Of course. But I'm hungry."

"We'll pick up a pizza."

I shake my head. "I'm thinking falafel."

"That's what I meant. We'll pick up falafel."

My grin inflates to embarrassing proportions. "I must be back by eight to close the store."

Koen glances at his watch. "Doesn't leave much time for making out in my truck. So we'd better get going."

My jaw slowly unhinges. "Really. I don't know why Herb said you were shy."

Koen smirks. "Yeah? Well, he said I called you unethical. It's possible Herb's not that great with words." He shuts my door.

When we reach Home Depot, Koen takes my hand and leads me inside.

I feel it way beyond my hand, a fluttering in my tummy, a hitch in my breath, and warmth spreading everywhere. "Can I ask why you think I'd make out with you when we've known each other for less than two weeks?"

"That's easy." He guides me past the carts and the garden center. "Making out happens before undressing. Since I had to undress you at the park, we're now ahead of schedule. Just like babies should crawl before they walk, we were supposed to make out before getting naked. Therefore, we need to step back and hit that milestone."

The way he glances over his shoulder to grin at me while I purposely hang back a step is sexy beyond words.

"I'm hungry."

He laughs. "This won't take long."

"Yes. But you've added making out to our plans. And I won't want to make out after I've eaten falafel unless I brush my teeth."

He suddenly turns right and then left until we're in the corner of the store, by the flooring and a mammoth hanging display of area rugs.

Then ... he kisses me. It's intense yet too short. With my face in his hands, he lingers a breath away from my lips. Surely, he'll kiss me again.

"I knew it would be good," he says with a grin.

"Me too," I whisper with what little breath I have left.

"Must be that foreplay perfume."

I grin. "I'm wearing Tease Me tonight, not Foreplay."

He leads me back toward the wire. "Is there a difference between foreplay and teasing?"

"Of course. Tease Me has citrus with a hint of vanilla. It should make you curious but not ravenous."

Koen can't entirely hide his grin, but I enjoy watching him try. "Not what I meant."

"I know."

He plucks a spool of wire from the shelf, and we don't say another word while heading to the self-checkout, but we exchange plenty of sexy glances and knowing grins.

"What is falafel anyway? Isn't it like lamb balls?"

I snort while he pulls out of the parking lot. "I can't say for sure. I haven't had lamb balls. Do lamb balls taste like chickpeas with herbs and spices? Do you eat yours with tahini sauce, tomatoes, cucumbers, parsley, and onions?"

"Have you finished that puzzle?"

"So we're jumping from lamb testicles to the puzzle? You're not boring."

"You've met my grandpa. The Sikes men are never boring."

"Just awkward and creepy."

He smirks. "Exactly."

We get our lamb balls and hummus to go and return to my place with the unfinished puzzle.

I can't stop thinking about the kiss, but I also can't stop thinking about Price Milloy in the building just outside my trailer. I've been perfectly content with my stagnant love life for years, and in a matter of weeks, I have two men in my life who evoke powerful emotions.

"Is something wrong with your food?" Koen asks while I stare at my wrap.

I quickly shake my head. "No. I was just thinking about the new employee."

"Do you want to check on them?"

I take a bite of my wrap. Do I want to check on Price? No. He's fine. I know him too well. "The new employee is a man I dated years ago when I lived in Philadelphia."

Koen eyes me, pausing his chewing for a second. "Oh."

Yes, "oh" is the best response.

"Did he reply to a job listing?"

"No. I gave him a job he didn't want or ask for."

Koen continues eating. No more questions. No visible response.

"He showed up out of nowhere. We went to dinner to catch up. And when he came into the store again, I suggested he work part-time."

Koen reaches for a puzzle piece, sliding it into place.

I don't have to tell him anything, but I like him. And I don't know what Price coming back into my life means. Something's off with Price, and I think he needs something from me, but I don't know what it is, and I'm afraid to ask.

"Did you offer him a job because you need help or want to ensure you see him more often?" Koen briefly glances at me. He seems a little uneasy.

"I don't own the general store, but I run it. And I'm the only employee. So yeah, I need a little help so I can go to Home Depot with men who pull me from ponds."

A grin touches his lips before he resumes eating.

"But I'd be lying if I said I don't enjoy seeing him. He made me rethink my life when I felt conflicted. My friends were in college. And my sister was engaged. And on top of that, my parents were waiting for me to figure out what I wanted to be in life. It was just a summer but the best summer of my life."

With a thoughtful glance, Koen swallows and clears his throat. "What happened?"

That's a complicated question I don't have the answer to.

"He continued with his schooling, eyes set on conquering the world. And I ran as far in the opposite direction as possible. I didn't want to conquer the world; I wanted to exist in it as peacefully as possible. Goals felt like fifty-pound weights on my chest. I'm sure most people use goals to move them forward, but I couldn't handle the pressure of waking up each morning with the same goal. After all, what happens when you stop chasing it? Are you a quitter?"

"So if you don't set goals, you can't be a quitter?"

I laugh a little. "Are you regretting the kiss? A woman in her thirties who has no goals, doesn't own a home, has never been married, and works at a general store. Is there a voice in your head saying you can do better?"

He shrugs a shoulder. "Are you content?"

"Yes," I say without hesitation. "I like the moment. I'm passionate about the moment. And sometimes I feel like I know a secret that everyone else is working themselves to death to figure out."

"And what is that?" He stuffs his wrapper into the sack.

"We're here to enjoy life. To enjoy each other. We don't know how long we'll be here, so why chase anything? And I'm not saying that goals are bad, that chasing something is bad if you're passionate about it."

Koen eyes the door and nods toward it. "Did you have passion with him?"

So much.

"Not enough."

"No?" he asks, sliding the puzzle pieces closer to him while I continue to eat my dinner one slow bite at a time.

"At the end of that summer, we let each other go."

"Maybe this is a second chance."

I wait for him to look at me, but he doesn't. "It's not."

"How do you know?" He gives me another glance.

"Because I just do. He's ... dealing with something."

"Is that what he said?"

"No. I just know him."

Koen nods. "Why are you sharing this with me?"

"Because you kissed me tonight, and I hope you do it again. But I'm not good at lying or hiding my emotions." I check the time. "And speaking of Price, I need to close the store."

"Do you want me to leave?"

"I want you to stay."

His expression leaks vulnerability and maybe ... pleasure? "Then I'll be here when you get done."

I add my wrappers to the bag and toss it in the trash. "Thank you."

"For staying?"

"Yes. For staying." I slide on my shoes, pausing at the door before opening it.

Koen eyes me. These two men coming into my life simultaneously might seem like bad timing. But what if it's perfect timing? What if one of these men is here to give me *more,* and the other is here to give me perspective?

CHAPTER
nine

I'm right here, waiting for you to see me.

Price

I'M A NATURAL. Not to brag (okay, I'm bragging a little), but I've not had a hiccup the whole night. I've made at least twenty dollars in tips from my soda and sundae-making skills and worked the register and credit card machine like a boss.

Just as I head to the door to shut off the sign, a woman in her late fifties, maybe early sixties, slips through the door.

"Good evening," I say.

"Sorry. Are you closed?"

I shut off the neon light. "We are now, but you take your time as the lucky last customer of the day."

"Thanks. I won't dilly-dally. Where's Scottie?"

"She has the night off. I'm the new guy, Price."

"That's a unique name."

"Thanks. I'll tell my mom."

"You do that. Also, hug her and spend time with her. I wish my kids would call me once in a while." She disappears behind a display.

I don't know what I'd say if I called my mom. How would I explain something that doesn't make sense to me? How do I explain a feeling that doesn't feel definable?

"I don't suppose you know which one of these herbal creams works best for hemorrhoids." She uses her index finger, which has a pointy nail, to push her glasses up her nose.

With a nervous laugh, I drag my hesitant, clueless ass to the personal care aisle. "Being as I'm the new guy who hasn't had the pleasure of experiencing hemorrhoids yet, I can't make any personal recommendations. But I can read some labels with you, and maybe we'll find something worth trying."

She gives me a great smile. "You're a handsome man. Are you single? Do you know that Scottie's single?"

I focus on the label. "Are you trying to play matchmaker with a stranger?"

Before she can respond, Scottie peeks her head around the corner. "Hi, Evelyn. Can I help you with anything?"

"This handsome man was just helping me find something for my hemorrhoids."

Scottie's eyes widen at me. "How kind of you. Would you like my help, or do you have this?" She nods to the bottle in my hand. "Because that's a warming lubricant for her pleasure and his."

Evelyn laughs. "Oh, dear. I'm not looking for pleasure

tonight. Just something to soothe my bottom so I can sleep."

"I'll start mopping the floor." I return the lubricant to the shelf.

Scottie presses her lips together and nods.

After spending fifteen minutes chatting with Evelyn and finding the right salve for her hemorrhoids, she takes her payment and locks the front door behind her while I mop the floor.

"No 9-1-1 calls. Everything seems in order. And you're in one piece. Are you officially the newest employee?" Scottie asks, shutting down the register.

"I'm not making any long-term commitments, but I'll admit I see the appeal."

"The appeal?"

I feel her gaze on me, but I focus on the floor. "Making sodas and interacting with customers is fun. You have a fun job. I don't think everyone working in retail would say that, but this store has a good vibe, just like the people who shop here."

"Told you so."

"Everyone knows you. I'm not sure anyone walked through the door without asking about you."

She messes with the soda machine. "Well, some people think I'm unforgettable."

"Ouch. Was that a jab at me?"

"Not at all. After all, you're here."

"Happenstance."

"I'm not so sure." She tosses a white rag over her shoulder and fidgets with her gemstones and jewelry display.

"You think I'm stalking you?"

"Are you?"

"Maybe. Should I expect a restraining order?" I return the mop to the back room.

Scottie waits by the back door for me with her keys in her hand. "Thank you for helping me out. I'll write down your hours."

I pull on my windbreaker. "I don't want the money."

"Because you have more money than God?"

"Does God have money?"

She rolls her eyes.

"Why do you think I have more money than God?"

"Because I know you. I know you conquered the world."

"I conquered the world only to quit in my mid-thirties and work at a general store for no pay?" I laugh it off.

Scottie doesn't laugh. "Yes. The question is, why?" Her head tilts to the side.

"Scottie Rucker, you're the smartest person I know. If you really think that's my life, then I have no doubt you'll figure it out."

"Or you could just tell me."

I narrow my eyes. I could, but I don't know the answer yet.

"Where did this worry line come from?" I ghost the pad of my finger along her forehead. "You're not a worrier."

"It's a confusion line. Not a worry line."

"You're not worried about me?" I step closer, assuming she'll open the door so we can leave the store, but she doesn't.

So now, I'm standing too close to her, but I can't seem to make myself take a step back. I love her aura. I'd be content with her letting me stand this close to her all night.

"Do you have regrets, Price?" she whispers while her soft gaze sweeps across my face.

"I don't know yet."

There's that line again—her confusion line.

"Want to grab dinner with me?" I ask.

"Can't." She shuts off the lights and opens the door. "I have a date waiting for me in my trailer."

There's a white pickup parked next to her red one.

"You have a date waiting for you, but you spent all that time talking to Evelyn and now me?"

"He's working on a puzzle. I bet he hasn't missed me." She saunters toward the Airstream.

"I bet he has."

Scottie stops at the door, turning her head and resting her chin on her shoulder. "Who do you miss?"

I drop my gaze and shake my head. "Goodnight, Scottie."

CHAPTER
ten

If in doubt, kiss it out.

Scottie

"WHOA! SAVE SOME PUZZLE FOR ME."

Koen smirks while he slides the last two pieces into the puzzle. He lights up with satisfaction. "I'll buy you a new puzzle."

"Says the guy who said puzzles are not good gifts."

He stands, his hands parked on his hips, admiring his work.

"You might as well go home now since we have nothing to do."

"Do you want me to go home?" He turns toward me, tucking his hands into his pockets.

"No." I deposit my shoes by the door and step in front of him. I think about Price, and it takes a little joy from this moment. I hate that. But I wouldn't change the situation. My life feels more pivotal now than it's felt since ... well, since I left Price Milloy twelve years ago.

"We could kiss." Koen smirks.

"We could." I take another step, resting my hands on his chest and curling my fingers around his shirt.

Koen ducks his head and kisses me, keeping his hands in his pockets until I take another step toward him, forcing him to step backward and use his hands to frame my face so the kiss doesn't end in us falling.

He teases my tongue with the tip of his. It's a moan-worthy kiss, but I control my urge to sound desperate despite my fingers unbuttoning his shirt.

"We ..." he breaks the kiss. "We shouldn't do this."

My hands stop with half of his shirt unbuttoned. "You're saving yourself for marriage."

Koen eyes me without blinking, without a single tell in his expression. I'm joking, but I now think I hit it on the nose.

"No," he says slowly. "I was just being considerate. I didn't want you to think I stayed and finished the puzzle just to have sex with you."

"Then why did you stay?"

His neutral expression morphs into an incredulous one. "I ..." he twists his lips. "I was staying to ..."

"You just wanted to finish the puzzle."

"No. I stayed to be with you."

"Well, here I am."

"Fine. I stayed to kiss you."

Oh my god. He's a gentleman at heart, but I'm not sure he's proud of it. Or maybe he's not proud of the other part who wants to kiss me so badly.

It's that part that wins.

His expression relaxes, and he cups my face again, pressing his lips to mine. Then he takes the deepest inhale through his nose. As he exhales, our lips move together, and his hands slide up the back of my shirt, unhooking my bra.

Dear God ...

He's such a good kisser.

His lips skate along my jaw to my neck while one of his hands cups my breast, teasingly pinching my nipple. Need explodes inside of me. My eyes close, and my lips part for an audible breath.

As my head begins to spin, there's a knock at my door.

Koen releases my lips, but just barely. We breathe heavily together.

"Shh ... maybe they'll go away," he whispers, circling the pad of his thumb over my nipple.

I grin against his lips. "I doubt it's someone selling cookies."

He drops his head in defeat to my shoulder while adjusting himself and grumbling something inaudible.

After hooking my bra and rubbing my lips together, I open the door.

Price cringes. "My car won't start. And I don't have a phone. Can I borrow your phone to call for a ride? Or do you have jumper cables?"

I nod, then quickly shake my head. "Yes. You can borrow my phone. No, I don't have jumper cables." When I step away from the door to grab my phone, Price follows me, stopping when he sees Koen.

This is a new level of awkwardness, even for me.

"Koen, Price. Price, Koen," I make a speedy introduction while snagging my phone from the table. "Price's car won't start; he's going to call for a ride."

Koen buttons his shirt.

So awkward...

"I've got jumper cables in my truck," Koen says.

God!

Why am I so embarrassed that Price knows exactly what we were getting ready to do? I feel like my parents caught me in the basement going to second base with my homecoming date.

There's not enough room in here for the three of us, so I nudge Price toward the door with Koen behind me.

"I really appreciate it," Price says.

"No problem." Koen heads toward his truck while I hug myself to keep warm and look at anything but Price as the night air fills with a smoky smell like someone's burning something not too far from here.

The two men try to jump-start Price's car with no luck.

"You need a new battery," Koen informs Price while disconnecting the cables.

"Thanks for trying. Sorry to have disturbed your date. I'll make a quick call and wait for my ride."

"I'll drive you home," Koen offers, storing the cables under his back seat.

"No. I'll wait for a ride. But thanks."

"It's no problem. Get in."

Price looks at me. What am I supposed to say?

With a tight smile, I shift my gaze to Koen. "Thanks."

"Yeah, thanks," Price echoes, climbing into Koen's truck.

I give them a tiny wave. "Goodnight."

Price returns a wave, but Koen just gives me a half smile that I can't decipher. Is he mad? Relieved? Indifferent?

Thirty minutes later, I'm perched on my bed, working on a new bracelet, when I get a text from Koen.

I had a great night. I hope we can do it again

I laugh. Yes. Minus the interruption.

Thanks for taking Price home

UR welcome

CHAPTER
eleven

I don't need you to be mine; I just need you.

Price

SLEEP EVADED ME LAST NIGHT. I couldn't shake the feeling I had when I saw Koen in Scottie's camper, buttoning his shirt. There wasn't enough time for them to have sex, but I walked in on something. It was all over her face.

Guilt.

I don't want her to feel guilty, and it's not my intention to interrupt her life. Last night's incident reminded me that I need to tread more lightly.

After drawing another picture (a bouquet of wildflowers), I take a much-needed nap. Then I grab a juice and return to my journal, determined to write actual words today.

When I decide to write about her, the words flow; my hand can't keep up with them.

Her smile.

Her laughter.

The way she watched me work at my computer while sipping her wine. And when I wouldn't acknowledge her, she'd stand behind me and tickle the nape of my neck before bending over to kiss my ear. She never played fairly. I'd turn in my swivel chair and plead my case for why I needed thirty more minutes to work. She'd unfasten my pants and straddle my lap with no underwear beneath her dress, making her case for why she only needed five minutes of my time. I never took for granted just how lucky I was to have someone who needed to be intimate with me before she could go to sleep.

When I shut my journal, I attempt yoga for the first time. It's harder than it looks. By two in the afternoon, I get a delivery—an infrared sauna that fits nicely into the spare bedroom now that I've disassembled the bed and shoved it against the wall.

I sweat my balls off for thirty minutes, hydrate, and shower. Then I order a ride to the gas station to pick up my car with its new battery—just as Koen suspected. The general store is on my way home, so I stop to visit Scottie.

"Showing up at work on your day off makes you look like a loser with no life." She grins while climbing down the sliding ladder on the wall of canned goods.

"Guilty." I tidy up the produce area, restacking the sweet-smelling apples before they tumble with the next customer who decides they want one from the bottom of the pile.

"I saw your car got towed this morning. Is it fixed already?"

"It is. I just picked it up. I'm really sorry about interrupting your evening. I clearly walked in on something, and I felt like a total ass."

Her face turns pink as she slides the ladder into the corner. "We just started seeing each other. It's no big deal. He finished the puzzle, and well ..." She curls her lips between her teeth.

"That blush looks stunning on you. I'm glad you've found someone who does the impossible by making you look even more radiant than you already are."

She messes with her hair before flipping her bangs away from her eyes. I've made that blush a few shades darker. "This ... you ... him ... it's all unexpected and a little weird."

I organize the mangoes and fix their crooked sign. "You make us sound like a threesome."

Scottie coughs a laugh. "That's not my style."

"No? A shame. I've heard they can be fun."

"Price Milloy."

I chuckle.

"What did you two talk about?" She steps beside me, picking out the stray pieces of lettuce and kale that have fallen into the bottom of the cooler.

"I never kiss and tell."

She shoulder-checks me. "Stop. You're so ornery today."

I glance at her. I've missed her, even when I didn't know what I was missing. "We stuck to first-date conversation. He asked me about my job. I asked him about his. He asked me about my relationship with you. I asked him about his relationship with you. And when he pulled into my driveway, we compared dick sizes and called it a night."

"Who had the bigger dick?"

"You tell me."

She shakes her head. "Can't. *Someone* needed a ride last night, so I got no D."

I bark a laugh. "I'm an asshole. An unsuspecting cock-blocker."

Scottie eyes me while trying to look upset, but I see through her facade.

"I didn't allow Koen to ask me much of anything. I grilled him. Your father would be proud of me."

She heads behind the counter, depositing the leaves in the trash. "What did you find out?"

"That's confidential. If you're too busy trying to get into his pants to take a few seconds to get to know him, then that's on you, Scottie Rucker."

She rests her arms on the counter. "Is this weird?"

"This conversation?"

"You and I talking about my sex life with another man."

"I think it would be weird if we talked about our sex life." I meet her at the counter, leaning onto it, mirroring her pose. "Even though it was really good. At least I know I was good. I don't remember your part that much. You pretty much just laid there."

Scottie glares at me but loses, covering her mouth to muffle her laughter. She'll never know what this means to me.

The smiles and laughter.

The banter.

The tiny nudges.

The chance to live in her world again.

Her budding romance complicates things, but I see it

in her eyes. She's happy I'm here. I like to believe that, in some small way, I'm something positive in her life, too.

The door chimes, and I glance over my shoulder at the two teenage girls, taking a quick right toward Scottie's gemstone and jewelry display.

"I noticed you've been wearing your bracelet," she says.

I pull up my sleeve. "I wear it every day. It's magical."

"Ya think?" Her eyes widen.

"I do." I knock twice on the counter. "I'll let you get back to work. I just stopped by to …"

"Tidy up the produce?"

"Exactly."

"Have you been to the salt room?"

I shake my head.

"It's a little pricey." She shrugs. "But we should go."

This feels like our summer together. Scottie would find something new to do, and we made Philly feel new again, despite having lived there our whole lives.

"Funny you brought it up," I say. "I was planning on going to one this week."

"Let's go after work tomorrow. Are you still working?"

I twist my lips. "I suppose."

"Do you have this with tiger's eye?" one of the girls asks.

"See you tomorrow then."

"Bye, Price."

CHAPTER
twelve

I don't need butterflies, but I'll take them.

Scottie

FIFTEEN MINUTES BEFORE CLOSING, I message Koen.

> You should invite me to your place tonight :)

Less than ten seconds later, he calls me.

"Hey. Did you get my message? Or is this just a lovely coincidence?"

"Got your message. I was going to call you, but I wanted to wait until you were done working."

"Nobody's here, so I'm not doing much."

"Don't tell your boss."

I laugh. "I won't. He's itching to close this joint, but his wife likes me, so they keep it open for me."

"Dang. You must be special."

"I do my best."

He hums as if he agrees, and it feeds my giddiness.

"Well, I'm on my way out of town. I took on a last-minute job that's three hours outside of Austin. I'll be gone for two weeks, give or take."

"Work is good. So that's good. Right?"

"No. I mean, yes. Work is good. Having work is good. Leaving town for two weeks after what happened last night feels like a special kind of torture."

"Is it an emergency? Did you really not have time to stop by on your way out of town for a quickie?"

"A quickie at the store?"

"Yes, at the store. There's a back room with a stainless steel bench or the washer and dryer they installed, so I don't have to go to the laundromat. We could have worked something out."

"You're killing me, Scottie."

I walk the store's aisles to release some tension—the good kind that Koen elicits every time we talk. "What you did last night was very kind. I can't thank you enough."

"You're welcome. I'm a breast guy, so nipples are my specialty."

I bite my bottom lip, but it doesn't suppress my laughter. "Stop. You know what I mean." These two men in my life are not so different. Humor is their favorite form of flirting. "Taking Price home, that was kind."

"Oh, that? No problem."

"What did you two talk about?" I try this from a different angle.

"He asked me about my job and my family. Then he asked me about my intentions with you."

"Are you serious?"

"Yeah. Why?"

"Nothing. What did you say?"

"I said I'm a welder—"

"No. What did you say your intentions were with me?"

"I said my intentions were none of his fucking business."

I start to speak, but I don't have a follow-up to that. "Um ..." I clear my throat. "And what did he say?"

"Nothing."

I nod to myself several times.

"Until we got to his house. Then he said he'd end me if I hurt you. And in the next breath, he asked me if I belonged to a gym because he needed a workout partner. So now we're BFFs, and when I get back in town, we're working out together three nights a week."

I chuckle. "Wouldn't that be something?"

"I'm not joking."

"What?" I hold my phone out and stare at it, but I'm unsure why.

"I don't belong to a gym, so he's paying for my membership. I have weights in my garage, but I felt sorry for him, so I agreed to be his gym partner."

This isn't happening. It's a joke. Right?

"Why did you feel sorry for him?"

"Because he let you go."

Did he?

"Koen?"

"Yeah?"

"Hurry up and come back home."

"That's the plan."

———

I feel sorry for Price, too, but for different reasons. Every time I start to ask him what I need to ask him, everything in my chest constricts clear up to my throat, and I suffocate.

He didn't tell me about his new gym partner, so I don't mention it when he comes into work the next day or when we go to the salt room, where I discover he's bought us memberships.

Over the next two weeks, I spend many evenings with Price, sitting in the salt room, grabbing a healthy dinner, harvesting his sprouts, and listening to his growing collection of vinyl records while watching him work on his Lego projects.

It's incredibly soothing.

One man loves puzzles, the other loves Legos.

As soon as I'm not with Price, I call Koen, and we spend over an hour on the phone.

"What's a salt room?" he asks.

"It's a room where you sit on lounge chairs and breathe in micronized salt particle air. The salt particles absorb toxins in your respiratory tract, and there's a long list of potential benefits."

"Are you serious?"

"Dead."

He chuckles. "Okay. I guess I should be glad he asked you to be his salt room buddy instead of me."

"I'm still shocked that you said yes after having known him for ten seconds." I put him on speaker while folding laundry on my bed.

"You know what they say: Keep your friends close and your enemies closer."

"Price is your enemy?"

"We're going to find out."

"Just hurry up and come back to Austin. We have unfinished business."

"I'm doing my best."

"Do you want me to give Herb a hug for you or anything like that?"

"I don't want you hugging anyone until I get home. Herb can be a little handsy."

"Like his grandson."

"He's more of an ass guy. Don't say I didn't warn you."

"Herb is the nicest guy I have ever known." I slide my clothes into the drawers.

"Ouch. I'll pretend I didn't hear that."

"I've known him much longer than I've known you. Why do you think I agreed to our blind date? I hoped Herb's grandson would be like him."

"Are you talking about the date we never went on?"

"Yes. That one." I grin, plopping onto the bed and leaning back. "Can we FaceTime? I need to see your face."

He doesn't answer. Instead, the call ends, and he's FaceTiming me a second later. He's all grins when I answer, as am I.

"Hi," I say.

"Hi. Are you in bed?"

"Technically, yes. I don't have a lot of sitting options. Do you?"

"Nope. I'm at a cheap motel in its cheap bed."

"I mean at your place. I know you have weights in a garage. I assume that means you live in a house."

"I do. I live in a house that I built."

"Really?"

His grin swells with pride. "Really. I lived out of a dinky trailer while building it."

"Are we boxing or talking? I wasn't expecting that trailer jab."

"I'm kidding. I love how content you are with your life. It's refreshing."

"Because I set the bar so low."

"The lowest."

I roll my eyes.

"It took me a year to build my house. I'm surprised Herb didn't mention it. He checked on my progress every day without fail. He used to be a contractor."

"I didn't know that."

"That's odd since you've known him for *so long*."

"Koen, I'm ready to crawl through this phone and strangle you tonight."

"If you crawl through the phone, I can think of better things we can do that don't involve you strangling me, unless that's your kink." He waggles his eyebrows, and they look extra goofy from his reclined position.

"Can I ask you a personal question?"

"I thought sex was personal, but sure, whatcha got?"

"Do you still get help for your drinking issues?"

"You can call me an alcoholic. I take responsibility and own it. And, yes, I go to meetings. If I feel like I'm struggling, I have someone to call. And I have friends and family who support me. That's why I don't try to hide it, even when I probably should at least hold off on over-sharing too soon. When people know, there's accountability. Does it suck when I think someone's judging me or having trouble trusting me? Of course. But I did this.

And I hurt a lot of people in the process, so I take full responsibility."

"You're a good man, Koen."

He yawns. "Thanks. I appreciate you saying that. I'd better get to sleep. I start early in the morning. Long days mean I get home sooner."

"I like that plan. I'll let you go."

"Goodnight, Scottie."

"Night, Koen."

CHAPTER
thirteen

If I give you everything, will you break it?

"LISTEN, I'm against body-shaming. So please know that I'm not body-shaming you when I say this, but you're too thin."

Price glances up from the instructions to his newest Lego set while I eat alone on the other side of his kitchen table. These days, it's hard to see the old version of him where he always wore suits and tamed his waves with hair gel. The man, gazing back at me, drinking his juice, has wayward hair, a wrinkled gray T-shirt, and sweatpants. I have never seen Price Milloy in sweats. Designer activewear? Yes.

All he does is drink juice and look like an imposter. And it feels unbearable keeping my mouth shut, but it's just as unbearable to ask him the question I don't want the answer to.

Price blinks several times before returning his attention to the instructions. "You've mentioned this before now. I agree. But I feel better than when I was twenty pounds heavier."

Swallowing past the lump in my throat, I nod. "That's good, I suppose."

"Yeah," he mumbles absentmindedly, "I think so too."

"How would you feel about me fixing you up on a date?"

He stops stone still.

Despite my instinct to give him an out, I wait to say I'm kidding.

"According to you, I'm too thin. Do you think it's a good idea for me to date when I'm too thin? Perhaps we should hold off on double-dating until your boyfriend helps me get buff."

"What makes you think Koen's my boyfriend?"

"The way you look at him."

I finish the last bite of my pasta salad. "How do I look at him?"

"The way you used to look at me." He waves a hand in the air without looking up at me. "You know. All doe-eyed and flushed with uncontrolled desire."

I cough and take a sip of water. "That's ridiculous."

"I agree. You shouldn't be so obvious, but I know you can't control it."

"Price Henry Milloy, you are so full of shit."

He chuckles. "I'm not. I went poop less than an hour ago. I'm a six on the Bristol Stool Chart, but I was a seven last week, so I'm making progress."

"Look at me."

He glances up.

I point to my face. "See? No doe eyes. No flushed face. Discussing where you are on the Bristol Stool Chart is not sexy."

His brow furrows. "Do you want me to be sexy for you? Are you rethinking the threesome?"

"Play with your Legos, little boy. I have to head home." I stand and pull on my hoodie.

Price grins. "See you tomorrow, boss lady."

"Mmm. Good luck with your next bowel movement." I head toward the door.

"If I had a phone, I'd send you a picture."

"Do I want to know why you don't have a phone?" I slip on my shoes.

"Probably not."

I hold my breath while quickly wiping the corners of my eyes. All these years later, Price Milloy is still my biggest weakness.

———

A LITTLE BEFORE ten that night, I pull around the corner to the back of the general store. A white truck is parked next to my trailer. He said he wasn't coming home until Saturday.

I barely get my truck in *Park* before leaping out and running to his driver's door. As I reach for the handle, he opens it and slides out of the seat.

Too cool.

Too slowly.

Too basically everything that I am not.

I throw my arms around him.

"Whoa!" He laughs, hugging me.

A tiny voice in the rational part of my brain tells me to slow it down.

"Where were you?"

I give the middle finger to that tiny voice while I kiss his neck up to his ear. "Watching Price put together a Lego set."

Koen stiffens.

"Don't," I say with a heavy breath. "We're just friends." I kiss him.

He hesitates for a second until my tongue slides along his lower lip, and he opens his mouth to give me a real kiss.

I unbutton his jeans and slide down his zipper.

Holding my face, he breaks our kiss and tips his chin, watching me tease my fingers over his briefs. "Are we doing it here or going inside?" He lifts his gaze along with a questioning eyebrow.

The string lights along the trailer's retractable awning illuminate the area quite well. And the store has a security camera at the back door that comes close to catching where we are.

"We'd better go inside," I say just before kissing him again as if I don't mean it.

He hikes me around his waist and carries me toward the trailer while I fish the key from my pocket. We stumble through the open door, and my butt hits the counter, knocking a few dishes into the sink.

"Looks like I need to clean your kitchen again," he says between labored breaths while shrugging off his shirt and ridding me of my shirt and bra.

"Shut up," I mumble, curling my fingers into his hair

and tugging it until he ducks his head and gives my breasts the attention they need.

He chuckles, teasing my nipples with his teeth before sucking so hard I nearly orgasm.

"Goddamn ..." I arch my back.

Again, he chuckles.

"Stop laughing," I say ... while laughing.

He lifts me off the counter and turns me so my hands press against the cabinets.

"Baby, if I don't laugh a little," he pulls my cotton joggers and underwear down my legs, "I'll fucking come before I get my dick out of my pants because you're so damn sexy." He sinks his teeth into my bare ass.

I jerk my hips.

Koen's mouth devours my skin, kissing the entire length of my body. When he stands, kissing my shoulder, the bulge in his briefs rubs along my backside. His hands claim my breasts for a moment before one hand slides down my belly between my legs.

I release a soft moan as his finger glides along my sensitive flesh.

His hips rock into me several times, and I push back against him, turning my head and kissing him. Then I turn my whole body, and we make a clumsy retreat to my bed.

"Scottie," he murmurs, dragging his lips at my neck.

Raw need hijacks my body's ability to see or hear clearly. "Huh?"

"Your bed."

"What?"

"Your bed is ..."

I crane my neck, glancing over my shoulder.

Oh my god.

It's covered with materials and supplies for making my jewelry.

"Uh ... just give me one sec." I snag containers from the floor and grab fists of stones and beads.

Koen sits on the edge of the bed and rakes his fingers through his hair.

"I'm so sorry." I don't want to throw everything in the same container. Yes, I'm a mess, but I'm an organized mess.

After I clear half the bed, he plops back and tosses an arm over his eyes.

I cringe. How sexy am I? Flailing around naked in a panic to get my bed clean before the mood is lost.

As soon as I get the stones in their containers, I slide the rest of the supplies into a shoe box and nudge it with my foot into the cubby under the bed. And then it's quiet, save for Koen's steady, audible breaths. I can't see his eyes, but he's asleep, shirtless with his jeans unfastened, and the erection behind his briefs looks to be relaxing into a slumber as well.

I cover my face with my hands and contemplate crying. Then I consider waking him up. Finally, I slip on his discarded shirt, turn off the lights, and curl up beside him on the bed.

Hours later, I wake with a tiny gasp, feeling a little disoriented and a lot ...

Oh god.

Aroused.

My hips adjust to the calloused hands, spreading my bent knees a little wider. The warm, wet tongue teasing between my legs pulls a tiny gasp from my open mouth.

Silky strands of hair tangle with my fingers when I reach for Koen's head between my legs.

My other hand grips the sheet as he hums. When he crawls up my body, he takes the T-shirt with him, drawing it over my head and tossing it onto the floor. My hands skate along his back, soft skin, and hard muscles to his butt.

He's naked.

Our gazes meet in the dim streetlight that's made its way through the gap between the shades.

"Hi," he whispers with that irresistible smile.

"Hi." I grin just before he kisses me while lowering his body until his hips are cradled between my legs and the head of his erection slides across my clit. He repeats this over and over while we kiss, his tongue becoming more demanding with each stroke and each tiny lift of my hips off the mattress.

"Is this okay?" he asks in a restrained voice.

I nod, and he fills me.

This is living. Euphoria is my drug of choice.

"God ... that feels good." I close my eyes.

Sex is a basic human instinct. Why do we complicate life?

Good food.

Good friends.

A sunny day.

Mind-blowing sex.

Koen's lips bend into a smile when he kisses me. My fingers dig into his flesh because I want him to know how much I love this. This is a moment—a really good one. Our bodies search for pleasure, moving together like we were made to do. My lips part with unrestrained moans until I release, drowning in endorphins. Koen quickly follows and collapses on top of me.

"So ..." I pant. "So, so good ..."

He rolls to his back with a chuckle as we catch our breaths.

After a few minutes, I lean to the side and kiss his chest. "Be right back."

When I return from the bathroom, Koen sits up, legs hanging over the side of the bed. He pulls me between them and kisses the swell of my breasts while his hands skate up the back of my legs to my butt.

"Wanna do it again?" I ask, teasing the hair around his ears.

"Hell yeah."

CHAPTER
fourteen

Love is complicated, as it should be.

Price

THE REFLECTION in the mirror is orange. *I'm* orange. Cheap spray tan orange.

Have I over-juiced on carrots? Is that possible?

I feel pretty good today, so I ignore the orange guy in the mirror, grab a juice, and sit down with my journal. Today's a little harder for me. I don't have the emotional capacity to write about her this morning, so I draw a picture instead. When I'm done, I stare at it.

Of course, I drew her.

Moving on ...

Yoga. (I'm still flexible as a board.)

More juice.

Sauna.

Shower.

After I'm dressed, there's a knock at my door.

"Koen," I say with a hint of shock. "Don't you have to work?"

"You need a phone. How are we supposed to work out together if you don't have a phone? And yes, I have to work today, and we should be having this conversation via phone, but you don't have one, so here I am. What time are we meeting at the gym? And really, why don't you have a phone?"

"Do you want to come in and have a juice?"

His face sours. "No. I just need a time."

"You tell me. I'm open. My job is flexible."

"You said you didn't have a job besides helping at the store."

I take a big breath and hold it, cheeks puffed out before releasing it. "True. But I still have work."

"What work?"

"Where to begin? I make Lego constructions, juice, yoga, sauna, walk, nap, listen to music, journal ... I haven't mastered meditation, but I'm working on it."

Koen blinks slowly. "You're a weird guy, Price."

"And I take it you've *bedded* Scottie."

His jaw tenses for a second.

Anger? Confusion? A bit of both?

"Why do you say that?"

I shrug. "Because you're here, which means you feel secure enough in your relationship with her to befriend *the other guy*."

"My relationship with her is none of your business."

I slide my hands into my pockets. "I wasn't asking for details or clarification, for that matter. It was an observation. That's all. So what time can you be at the gym?"

Koen eyes me with suspicion, as he should. Not only am I using a medieval term for sex, I'm orange.

"I can be there by seven," he says.

"Make it eight thirty. I have to work until eight."

Koen continues to eye me. "You said you were flexible."

"I usually am. But I work tonight."

He shakes his head while pivoting and stalking toward his truck.

"If she had sex with you, she's going to fall in love with you," I say.

He glances over his shoulder.

"I'm not your competition, but I'm the guy you'll answer to if you break her heart."

Koen raises an eyebrow as if it's preposterous that this skinny orange guy could land a punch. And it might be inconceivable, but I love that woman too. And love is pretty damn powerful.

"Have a great day, buddy!" I wave and shut the door.

———

"I HEARD you're meeting Koen at the gym tonight," Scottie says the second I arrive for my shift. "And you're orange. What the hell, Price?"

"I heard you got laid."

Her mouth falls open. "He told you that?"

"Sure did. He said you were a little *looser* than he expected, but he made me promise not to tell you. So, whatever you do, keep your mouth shut. I don't want to lose my new BFF."

Her nose crinkles. "He said I'm ..."

"Loose." I shrug while peeling a banana that I haven't paid for yet.

She swallows hard. And I can see the sparkle in her eyes slowly die.

"Scottie, I'm kidding."

That dying sparkle turns into red rage, and she punches my arm. "You are a terrible man, Price Milloy. And I'd fire you if I didn't need you to work so I can clean my trailer."

I snicker over my bite of banana. "I'm not sure whose chain I enjoy yanking more, yours or his." I make a shooing motion with my hand. "Go clean."

We have a stare-off.

She loses, averting her gaze.

"What?" I mumble over the banana in my mouth.

"Nothing."

"It's something. Out with it."

Her lips twist for a beat. "Since you first came in here and saw me after all these years, has there been a time when you've imagined us being more than friends again?"

Well, shit. Can I withdraw my plea for her to answer me?

Her question takes me aback. "Have you?"

"I'm with Koen."

"You didn't answer my question."

She shrugs. "Neither did you."

A customer comes into the store, saving us from each other.

"I'm off to clean," she murmurs.

I nod several times.

———

THREE HOURS LATER, Scottie returns to close the store after a slow night.

"You sidetracked me earlier. Now, will you tell me why you're working out with Koen?" she asks while shutting down the register.

I restock the soda glasses behind her. "I need a spotter. He looked capable and proved himself helpful by taking me home the other night."

"I like him, Price."

"That's good to know. At the very least, you should like someone before sleeping with them."

"You're mad that I slept with him."

I chuckle. "I'm not mad or jealous. I'm happy for you."

"Liar."

Yes, I'm a liar, but I don't think I'm lying about this. Am I? Is it possible that I'm jealous on a subconscious level? That would be an unexpected and interesting revelation.

"Scottie, why do you think I'm lying?"

"Because I think I would have complicated feelings if I were in your shoes."

"Complicated feelings?"

She turns, leaning against the counter. "Price, we weren't just friends. We went from strangers to something intense in a matter of days. And we had an unforgettable summer together. I don't have memories of us being anything *but* lovers. And now you're here, and I'm single. But this other guy just walked into my life. So yeah, I think it would be fair for you to have complicated feelings about us."

"Do *you* have complicated feelings about us?"

"Stop deflecting." She crosses her arms.

"I'm not deflecting."

"Then answer the question."

I shrug. "You didn't ask me anything."

"Do you have feelings for me?"

"Yes."

She presses her lips together.

"But I'm not saying they're romantic. They're ..."

She eyes me. "They're complicated."

With a sad smile and a tiny nod, I accept her assessment of my feelings for her. "But the dominant feeling I have is bliss. Being back in your life in any form is unexpectedly amazing." Lie. Lie. Lie.

I one hundred percent expected it to be amazing.

"I like Koen *so* much," she whispers.

"Scottie, I'm not asking anything of you. I'm not asking you to love me. I'm not asking you to choose me. I'm not even offering myself up as a choice. So by all means, feel free to like whomever you want."

After a breath, she glances at her watch. "You better get going."

"Are we good?"

Her expression cuts me. It's so sad. "We're good."

"Goodnight." I head toward the back door.

"Price?"

I turn.

"I will always love you."

I know. That's why I'm here.

I return my most sincere smile. "And I you."

CHAPTER
fifteen

He was the exception, but you are exceptional.

Scottie

I SPREAD my new puzzle onto my table and sort out the edges—one thousand pieces to distract me from thinking about Koen and Price spending the evening together.

I brush my teeth a little after ten, feeling disappointed that Koen didn't stop by after his workout. He left so early this morning we didn't get a chance to talk.

As if he knows I'm sulking, I get a call from him, so I quickly spit the toothpaste into the sink. "Hey!"

"I'm texting you my address if you want to see my Scrotum."

"You could get arrested for that kind of proposition."

He laughs.

"But yeah, I'd love to see your dog, and I wouldn't mind taking a gander at your scrotum. It was dark last night. I didn't get to inspect much."

"I'll unlock the front door. I'm going to jump in the shower. Come on in when you get here."

"Okay. See ya soon." I end the call before squealing like a little girl. Then, I shave everything but my head before applying lotion and my Foreplay essential oil blend.

To my surprise, Koen lives less than fifteen minutes from my place. He has a sprawling lot covered in trees, and his house isn't just any house. It looks like one shipping container stacked onto another with massive windows and a detached garage.

"Hello?" I call, cracking open the door.

Scrot barks and greets me the second I step inside.

"Hey, buddy. Oh, you're such a good boy." I squat and give him the attention he's craving. "Where's your daddy? Is he still in the shower? Should I get naked and join him?"

"Fuck. Hold that thought. I'll head back to the bathroom," Koen says, descending the last few steps, wearing jogging shorts and nothing else. A few drops of water still cling to his torso and damp hair.

I grin. "You live in shipping containers. This is very cool." I glance around the open space with only a few walled-off rooms. A wide steel split staircase leads to the upper level.

"I think your friend is loaded," Koen says.

I give Scrot one more scratch behind his ears and stand. "Price?"

Koen leans against the railing. "Yeah."

"Why do you say that?"

"Because he spent the entire time giving me tips on investing. He knows his stuff. When someone knows that much, they've used that knowledge to their benefit. So I have to wonder why he's living where he lives, driving a Honda, and working at the general store."

"Did you ask him?"

"No."

"Why not?"

"Because I just met the guy. I didn't want to pry or sound like a dick putting down his lifestyle. I think being rich but living a modest life is pretty admirable."

"Is that why he was giving you advice? So you could be rich and live a modest life?" I pad my way to him.

"No. He wants to ensure I can care for my wife and kids."

My eyebrows shoot up my head as I wrap my arms around his neck. "You have a wife and kids? Do they know where you were last night? When will they be back? How much time do we have?"

Koen ducks, kissing my neck. "He loves you. It's painfully obvious." He kisses my jaw before finding my mouth.

I don't want to talk about Price. It's too heartbreaking. And a little heart-confusing. So I press my hands to Koen's face, kissing him deeper until I need a breath. "Did you clean off your bed for me?"

He grins. "Clean sheets, too."

"Why? We're just going to get them dirty."

"Careful." He pulls off my sweater, eyebrows peaking in approval when he discovers I'm not wearing a bra. Again, he kisses me.

So, this is what addiction feels like. My head swims from his touch.

"I will not give you back to him if you keep saying

things like that," he whispers, one hand cupping my breast, the other sliding down the back of my linen lounge pants. He moans when he's greeted with flesh, no underwear.

I packed light.

Koen squeezes my butt, claiming it, and I gasp. If I could catch my breath, I'd tell him I'm not Price's, but even as I think the words, my heart feels a slight objection.

"We're not going to make it to the bedroom this time. Sorry," he mumbles between kisses, walking backward to the sofa. The second he unties my pants, they fall to the floor, where he quickly adds his shorts and briefs.

As soon as my ass contacts the cool, soft leather, he's inside of me. It's slow and hard, with an occasional kiss, but mostly, we look into each other's eyes. I feel like he's making a statement that I'm his.

I wouldn't be here with him like this if I didn't feel the same way.

———

"I TAKE it you don't eat meat," Koen says as I politely decline the leftover rotisserie chicken and stick to the mango and trail mix as we refuel in his kitchen just after midnight.

"Is that a blowjob reference? Because you haven't—"

"No." He grins before licking his fingers, legs dangling from his perched position on his concrete counter. Tempting me in nothing but his boxer briefs.

I lean against the opposite counter, swimming in his tee. "My mother's a cardiologist. My father's a horticulturist. I was raised on veggies. Please don't ask me where I get my protein."

He slowly chews and inspects me with a hint of mischief tugging his lips. "I won't ask you where you get your protein if you don't ask me where I get my veggies."

I slide a chunk of mango into my mouth. "Deal."

"Has that question ended a lot of relationships for you?"

"All of them." I smirk.

"What about Price?"

I stare at the bowl of trail mix, sifting through the raisins and sunflower seeds to retrieve a cashew. "Price was the exception to everything."

"That's not very comforting."

I try to reassure him with a slow headshake and a soft smile. "You shouldn't feel threatened by him."

"When you're wearing nothing but my shirt and standing in my kitchen, I don't feel threatened by him. But I can't say the same when I'm out of town, or you're hanging out at his place."

I absentmindedly tug at my bottom lip and stare at the floor. "How honest do you want me to be?"

Koen's gaze lifts to the ceiling, and he shakes his head with a shrug. "Rip off the bandage."

"We were opposites in every way. In a good way. And he would tell you that I broke it off. I did, but only because I felt intimidated by his big dreams. I was younger, with no direction. Still, it was a perfect summer that didn't feel real. *He* didn't feel real. I was the girl in Birkenstocks and braids. He was the guy in a suit and tie. He taught me how to taste wine before I was old enough to drink it. I taught him how to lie in the grass and stare at the clouds."

When I glance up, Koen gives nothing away.

"At the end of summer, I told him to go conquer the world, and if we were meant to be, we would be." I grunt a laugh. "I told him so many things that made no sense, but I did it with such fake confidence and conviction that he bought it. He trusted me. Who trusts a nineteen-year-old girl working in a store filled with stones and essential oils? A girl who walked away from the chance to go to college with her parents footing the bill. A girl who lived in a dinky studio apartment rather than at home to save money for something better."

Koen covers the rest of the chicken and rests his hands on the counter's edge. "It would seem he conquered the world, and now he's here for you."

I shake my head. "I thought he'd call me out on my bullshit. I thought he'd tell me how ridiculous I was being. When you find that kind of love, you don't walk away. You don't treat that kind of love like an option. It's everything, and all the other stuff takes a back seat." I run my hands through my hair. "He returned to school, but I knew he'd call. Or he'd come back for Christmas and tell me what an awful mistake he made letting me walk away. But he didn't."

Life happened instead.

"Why didn't you go after him?"

I don't want to lie. I'm not that good at it, but some lies are easy if the truth feels like torture. So I shrug and give him what I can without the pain making a jagged incision on my fragile scars.

"Because," I say, "although I'm still single, I'm a sucker

for romance. And when he walked into the store a few weeks ago, I felt all the things I felt that summer, including the heartbreak. He broke my heart. I wanted him to need me more than anything, but he didn't. And that feeling doesn't go away. All I can say for sure is I'm happy he's back in my life, but I don't think he can ever *be* my life."

"Because he didn't fight for you?"

I meet Koen's gaze, heart heavy with melancholy. "Yeah," I whisper. "And now I've met this guy. And I like him so much I can't think straight."

This elicits a tiny smile from him. "Don't ask you where you get your protein. And fight for you. Got it."

"Are you taking notes?"

He hops off the counter. "Diligently."

I step into his embrace. "You need to get some sleep. You get up way earlier than I do. I should go." I kiss the middle of his chest.

His lips press to the top of my head. "You should stay. And help yourself to breakfast in the morning. Stay as long as you want. But just … stay."

I tip my head back, and he slides his fingers into my hair. "Koen, if you don't stop touching me like this, we won't sleep tonight."

He grins, lowering his lips to mine. "Fuck sleep."

CHAPTER
sixteen

Inclusion is sexy.

AFTER A WEEK OUT OF TOWN, Koen returns on Valentine's Day. We're five weeks into this relationship, and my sex drive rivals any man's. With some extra lip gloss, rose-water body spray, and a red V-neck sweater and dark jeans, I meet him for dinner at his place.

However, there are two vehicles in his driveway that are not his. The open blinds on the main floor give me a clear view of his kitchen. I recognize Herb, but not the other guy or the woman.

When I knock on the glass door, all heads turn. Koen heads in my direction just as I open it.

"You don't have to knock." He hugs me and drops a quick kiss on my lips. "Happy Valentine's Day."

With a stiff smile, I nod. "Thanks," I mumble. "Uh ..." I glance past him.

"Listen," he says, keeping his back to everyone gathered around his kitchen island. "I didn't know they were going to show up."

"They as in?"

"My family. They arrived ten minutes ago with food and cake. I knew you were already on your way, so I didn't want to scare you off by giving you a heads-up."

"Wow. Your family goes all out for Valentine's Day?"

"No. It's my grandpa's birthday. He's eighty-nine today. I'm sorry. I'll make this up to you."

I shake my head. "Make what up? I adore your grandpa."

Koen sighs with a smile. "Thank you. Let me introduce you to my family." He takes my hand and pulls me toward the kitchen. "Hey, everyone, this is Scottie. She works at Drummond's, Grandpa's favorite store."

"Happy birthday, Herb." I rest my hand on his shoulder.

"Thank you, young lady," he replies, perched at the counter while arranging cheese on a cracker.

"Scottie, this is my mom, Shelly, and my brother, Kaleb."

"Hi." I hold up my hand in a friendly wave as they greet me.

Kaleb's gaze drops a few inches.

Shit.

My V-Day sweater is not only red for the occasion but also thin and almost sheer from the loose knitting. And ... I'm not wearing a bra or underwear, for that matter. I saw the evening going in a different direction, and I dressed for not wearing my clothes.

"How long have you worked at Drummond's?" Shelly

asks, sipping a bottle of green tea with one hand while tucking her flaxen curls behind her ear with her other.

I melt from her smile that's as genuine and unpretentious as her pink pilled button-down and relaxed jeans on her curvy body.

"Ten years. I love Austin, the neighborhood, and the people who shop there." I wink at Herb.

Again, when I glance at Kaleb, I catch him staring at my chest. I turn toward Koen. "I need to go upstairs for a minute," I whisper, offering him a tight grin.

He narrows his eyes before nodding.

"I uh ... need to make a quick call," I tell his family. "So I'm going to run upstairs for just a few minutes if you'll excuse me."

I don't wait for an answer before hightailing it up the stairs. After turning on the light in his closet, I riffle through his clothes.

"Forgot your phone," Koen says.

I glance over my shoulder while he holds up my phone.

"Is there something I can help you find?"

"You don't happen to have a bra, do you?"

He squints with a headshake. "Did yours break?"

"No ..." I say slowly, eyes wide. "I thought it would be just the two of us, and it's fine that it's not, but I wore the bare minimum." I lift my sweater.

Koen's eyes flare, lips part.

I lower my sweater. "Your brother keeps staring at my chest. I'm sure it's because he can easily see my nipples, which means your mom can too. This isn't the first impression I want to have on her."

Koen slides the pocket door shut behind him and steps toward me.

"What are you doing?"

"Did you miss me?"

With a nervous laugh, I avert my gaze. "Stop."

"Because I missed you." He takes a step closer.

I have nowhere to go with a full-length mirror at my back.

"Lift your sweater again." He wets his lips.

Again, I return a shaky chuckle. "Your family is downstairs. You're teasing me. That's not nice."

"Why would I tease you? If I'm teasing you, then I'm torturing myself. Want me to make you come?"

"Stop. It." I press my lips together to keep from grinning.

"Lift your sweater."

He could lift it, pull it over my head ... rip it off my body if he wanted. But this is a game.

Do I want to play this game? Is this the time to play games?

Of course not.

But the way he says, "Lift your sweater," in a deep voice, has the same effect as "Spread your legs."

Sometimes, living in the moment isn't the responsible decision. Now is an example of that. Yet, I *really* love to seize the moment.

I pull my sweater up past my breasts.

Koen palms both breasts, keeping his eyes on me while he ducks his head to flick my nipple with his tongue and suck it.

I hiss, feeling a jolt of pleasure shoot between my legs.

He does this over and over, gazing at me the whole time. I begin to squirm, hands in his hair, heart racing.

His fingers work the button to my jeans and slide down the zipper. "Fuck me ..." He moans and drops to his knees as he discovers my lack of underwear.

When my jeans hit my ankles, I step out of them. "Koen!" I yell while his mouth dives, eager and hungry, between my legs.

While my knees fight to keep from buckling, I wrestle with my sweater to shrug it off. Koen unfastens his jeans and strokes himself several times before standing and discarding his shirt.

With his jeans and briefs barely past his butt, he lifts me and presses my back to the wardrobe door. I bite his shoulder and pinch my eyes shut to keep from making any more noise while he relentlessly pumps into me.

Embarrassment awaits us downstairs when we're done, but I don't care because I'm too busy reveling in the moment. I've missed him and *this* so much. There's nothing better than being so horny that your mind loses all ability to make rational decisions. Wanting (needing) this orgasm trumps *everything*.

"I love ... you ... Scottie Rucker. So ... fucking ... much."

I open my eyes and press my hands to his cheeks so he looks at me. But he doesn't stop moving, and my need to orgasm doesn't lose momentum.

I grin.

He grins.

We release, kissing hard to mute the moans until he drops his head to my shoulder, breathless.

"I love you, Koen Sikes." My fingers tease the nape of his neck. "My heart is all-in."

After we put ourselves together, including his black tee that I have to shove way down into my jeans, we head down the stairs hand-in-hand.

"Gettin'er done, son. Good for you." A man in a cowboy hat chuckles, lifting a beer bottle toward us. He wrinkles his veiny nose and sniffles before taking a long swig and wiping his mouth with his denim shirt sleeve.

Shelly cringes, eyeing Herb, who smacks his hand on the barstool beside him. "Have a seat and leave him alone, Russ," Herb says.

Kaleb's jaw clenches while he glares at his dad, but Koen just leads me to the other side of the island and hands me a plate. "Dad, this is my girlfriend, Scottie."

His dad leans over the island, letting his shirt fall into the dip while offering me his hand. "I'm Russ. Nice to meet such a pretty little thing."

I glance at Shelly, but she keeps her head bowed.

"Nice to meet you," I say, shaking it.

"Bout time you got back on the horse," Russ says. "Maybe you can keep this one if you stay sober. Ain't that right, honey." He eyes Shelly, but she slides a chip into her mouth and ignores him.

"Why don't I drive you home, *Dad*?" Kaleb suggests, tossing his empty plate into the garbage.

"I just got here. We haven't even cut the cake."

"You're right." Herb slides the round cake with chocolate frosting toward him and cuts a piece with a flimsy plastic knife. Then, he deposits it onto Russs's plate and hands him a fork. "Eat up, son."

After I absentmindedly fill my plate with food, Koen

steps behind me, arm around my waist, hand splayed on my stomach, and walks us backward until he's leaning against the opposite counter, sipping water while I pop grapes into my mouth.

This is the most awkward situation I've been in since ... well, maybe ever.

Russ eats his cake and drinks his beer while everyone watches in silence.

When he finishes the last bite, Kaleb snatches the plate and empty bottle and drops them in the trash. "Let's go, Pops." Kaleb not so gently grabs Russ's arms and forces him off the stool. "Can you take Grandpa home?" he asks Shelly.

She gives him a sad smile and nods while sliding her plate away from her and dusting off her hands.

Still, Koen says nothing.

As Kaleb and Russ head toward the white Toyota 4Runner, Herb slips on his gray cardigan, and Shelly tidies up the food. "Will you and Scottie eat this if I leave it here?" she asks.

"Sure," Koen says calmly as if nothing has happened.

"I'm sor—" she starts to apologize.

"Don't." Koen releases me and steps toward his mom, hugging her. "Don't ever apologize."

She releases him and finds a more believable smile for me. "It was a pleasure meeting you, Scottie. I hope next time we can chat more."

"Nice meeting you as well."

"All right, boy, take care of that girl." Herb winks at us.

"Happy birthday, Grandpa." Koen hugs him, and I smile when Herb gives me his conspiratorial grin.

After the door closes, and it's just us, Koen turns,

sliding his hands into his front pockets. "My dad's an alcoholic."

"Yeah? Well, you were quite patient with him compared to your brother."

His gaze drops to his feet. "Kaleb's never had an issue with alcohol. I have."

"Is your dad's drinking the reason why your parents got divorced?"

"Yes."

I set my plate aside.

He shakes his head in regret. "I will never drink a drop of alcohol. I need you to know that. I was him. I was my dad. The fucking life of the party who had to be escorted out before I further embarrassed myself. And I'll never go back."

I resist the urge to hug him. Given the words exchanged upstairs earlier, this is a conversation we need to have.

"How did your drinking get out of control?"

His forehead wrinkles, but he doesn't bring his gaze to mine. "I got too far into a relationship that wasn't right, but I felt like a dick trying to get out of it, so I ... coped."

"Well," I laugh despite nothing being funny, "I feel like we're in a relationship. And it's starting to feel serious."

This brings his gaze to mine. "I won't let it go too far unless I know it's right."

"What was wrong with the last one? If I can ask."

His lips twist, gaze intensifying. "I thought love was enough, but then I realized she had a different view of married life." He grunts a laugh, slowly shaking his head. "She didn't want kids, and instead of walking away, I thought I could drink my way through it, and then I wouldn't have to disappoint anyone. Turns out, I disappointed everyone." Finally, he looks at me. "Do you want kids?"

I shrug. "I don't *not* want them. I haven't needed to give it much thought." That's not entirely true. "In case you haven't noticed, I'm not a planner or overachiever. I live in the moment."

"I'm not asking you to have my babies; I'm just ..." He eyes me as if expecting me to finish his thought.

I don't finish it. There's no need. Instead, I push off the counter and slide my arms around his waist, tucking my hands into his back pockets and squeezing his ass until he relinquishes a grin.

"I have an idea."

He presses his lips to the top of my head. "Hmm?"

"Do you have a tent?"

"Of course."

"Great. Let's set it up in the backyard, open the top flap, and stare at the stars."

Koen chuckles. "You want to stargaze with me?"

"I do."

He eyes me with wonder, the good kind, where I can imagine great possibilities running amuck in his mind. And I know this because it's how I look at him.

CHAPTER
seventeen

It's enlightening to realize that controlling nothing is the most empowering feeling in the world.

Price

ANOTHER DAY, another journal entry. I've been in Austin for almost two months.

Two months of watching Scottie fall in love with Koen.

Two months of befriending the man well on his way to having the life I gave up twelve years ago.

Two months of seeing that look of distrust in his eyes. When will he give me a break and settle into our bromance?

My pen taps on the paper. Is today a sketch or words?

Words. I have a lot of feelings today. But where do I begin?

How did I become an expert on women? How can I make them fall in love with me and disappoint them beyond words? I loved her as much as a man could love a woman, but even that most coveted emotion has limits. Being someone's "everything" holds a power that's too great for any human being. She wanted me to be her "'til-death-do-us-part" person, and so did I.

But nobody thinks that through.

For richer or poorer. Define poorer.

In sickness and in health. Define sickness.

In good times and in bad. How bad is bad?

Love isn't everything; context is.

Is the ultimate sacrifice the only kind? Or are there degrees to which one person sacrifices themselves for another? She may never know that I saved her from the worst kind of grief.

I hope I did.

And in the process, I've made some valuable progress in my life.

Today, I can touch my toes. When I started this journey, I could barely reach past mid-shin.

Today, I made it twenty minutes with my meditation. I think I get it. For twenty minutes, I rest and exist in the moment. All thoughts and physical sensations drift in and out of my moment. I don't grab them, nor do I chase them away. I control nothing.

It's enlightening to realize that controlling nothing is the most empowering feeling in the world.

The sun is out after a spell of rain, and it's seventy degrees in March.

What are my thoughts on earthing? Do it.

I've had some funny looks from the neighbors, but I don't care. For thirty minutes, I walk barefoot in the yard, feeling like a new person, or at least a renewed person.

"Do you know how often my dog has peed in your yard?" a man in a tweed flat cap, probably in his mid-sixties, says while strolling past my front yard with his white Shih Tzu's nose to the ground.

I smile, hands in my pockets, gaze affixed to the grass. "Probably not as many times as I've pissed in yours." Glancing up at him, I wink.

He barks a laugh. "Good response. I'm Ed. Welcome to the neighborhood."

"I'm Price. It's nice to be here."

"Enjoy it. I'm gonna be out before too long."

"Where are you going?"

He stops and shrugs while his dog sniffs around the mailbox. "No clue. My wife died last year. She took care of our finances. I don't know how she made ends meet, but I can't." He continues down the sidewalk.

"I'll be done walking in your dog's piss in fifteen minutes. Bring me your bills and banking information."

He chuckles. "Why?"

"I'll show you how your wife did it. I might even help you do it better."

"I'm good. But thanks." He continues onward.

An hour later ...

Ed knocks on my door, holding a cardboard box. "Janice had a better filing system."

I grin, taking the box from him. "I do not doubt that."

———

LATER THAT EVENING, I meet Scottie at the salt room.

"You're late, Milloy," she whispers from her zero gravity chair when I sit beside her.

131

"Community service took longer than expected," I say, leaning back.

When I roll my head toward her, she grins without opening her eyes. The salt is good for me; Scottie is better.

Forty-five minutes later, we exit the building together.

"Tell me about your community service." She retrieves her keys from her bag.

"Can't. It's confidential."

"Pfft." She heads toward her red truck. "Liar."

"When's Koen coming home?"

"Sunday." She opens the door and turns. "Why? Do you need me to spot you at the gym?"

"Just making conversation."

She nods slowly, eyeing me with that look of equal parts concern and distrust.

"I think we should go to a comedy club tomorrow night. I found one that starts at 8:30, so we could make it after the store closes."

She frowns.

"If you need permission, ask Koen. Tell him I promise to stop at second base."

"You've never stopped at second base." She blows her bangs away from her face. "And I love him, so there's that little hiccup in your plan."

Of course, she does. It's been eight weeks. She loved me in less than two. Scottie's heart doesn't know how to do anything but love.

It's why I'm here.

"I love him, too. He's not failed me once. Last week, I tried lifting more than I should have, but he swooped in and saved me. It made my skin tingle when his biceps bulged, and he made it look so easy." I pull my T-shirt away from my chest to fan myself.

Fighting her grin, she shakes her head and glances over my shoulder. "Pick me up at 8:10."

I feel joy down to my fucking soul. "Goodnight, Scottie Rucker."

CHAPTER
eighteen

I always knew he would never stop breaking my heart.

Scottie

"TELL ME SOMETHING GOOD," Koen answers his phone a little before ten with a heavy sigh punctuating his plea.

"Oof! That's a lot of pressure. Do you believe in God?"

"Yeah."

"Well, I've heard he's good."

He sighs. I don't read into it. Vague sighs are not my specialty.

"Sorry I'm calling so late."

"I figured you were at the salt room. Do you ever think, 'What if this salt room thing is a big hoax? A scam'?"

I grin, rubbing Scrot's belly as he lies spread eagle on the bed. When Koen's out of town, he leaves Scrot with me instead of asking his neighbor's sixteen-year-old son to watch him. "I think, what if this salt room is not a big hoax? What if it's not a scam? What if the benefits are real?"

Again, he sighs. It's so heavy that I feel the weight of it on my chest.

"Bad day?"

"Everything that could go wrong today did go wrong."

"You didn't die. Did you take a drink?"

"What? Fuck, no. *Please* don't do that."

I pause, not expecting him to sound upset with my reply.

"I hate it when people try to fix shit that can't be fixed and assume the worst. I can't undo my day. It happened. I'll get over it. But right now, I'm still feeling the effects. And I can have a bad day without falling off the goddamn wagon. But thanks for your trust."

"I'm sorry. I don't know what to say."

"You don't have to say anything. I just ... I had a bad day. Hearing your voice makes it a little better, but so will a good night's sleep. When I vent, I don't expect you to make it better. Haven't you felt the need to vent without expecting someone to make it better? And isn't it nice when people think the best of you?"

"Koen, I'm sorry. Truly."

I wait.

And wait.

"I'm going to bed. I don't feel like talking. I feel like an asshole tonight, and I don't like exposing you to my lack of charm. It's not your job to cheer me up."

"You're not an asshole, but sleep is a good idea. I'll talk to you later."

"Bye—"

"Koen?"

"Yeah?"

"Your Scrotum's on my bed. And he's the cutest Scrotum I've ever seen. I like to nuzzle my nose into your little Scrotum, don't you?"

Koen laughs. It's reserved, but it's a real laugh, nonetheless. "Thank you, Scottie. I hope you like me half as much as you like my Scrotum."

I giggle. "I *love* you."

"I love you too. So much. I'm sorry I snapped at you. I'm just ..."

Well, damn.

Now he's making me cry.

"You're just human. Goodnight," I say with my emotions in a chokehold.

———

"Are you wearing skinny jeans?" Price's jaw hangs in the air when I climb into his Honda.

"I'm giving them a test run."

He laughs. "Why?"

"I decided it's time for a change. I've had them for years. My sister got them for me, and I've never had the heart to get rid of them. So here they are, making their uncomfortable debut on my ass. I hope this comedian is funny because I need something to take my mind off my visible panty line."

"I was joking about second base. You know that, right? You didn't have to wear these for me." He shoots me a quick glance after pulling onto the main road.

"Do you think Koen will like them?"

"What I think is that I need to have a talk with him if

your relationship has made you think you need to be something different than exactly who you are to impress him, to keep him."

"I clearly needed to be someone different to keep you."

He lets up on the gas and pulls to the side of the road. "Excuse me?"

I cross my arms, but I don't look at him. "Just go. We're going to miss the show."

"All of a sudden, I don't care about the show. Scottie, I didn't leave you. You let me go. You made the world's best case for why it wasn't our time. And I trusted you because I thought you were emotionally more mature than me."

"You didn't look back."

He stabs his fingers through his hair. "I-I was driven, and you were grounded. In hindsight, I needed you. But I wanted something else more. And I thought you wanted your path as much as I wanted mine."

The second my tears release, I bat them away.

"But, Scottie, I wouldn't have ended us. Everything with you felt perfect. And when you broke up with me, I realized how distorted my perception of perfection was. After all, who walks away from perfection?"

I sniffle, but I still can't look at him. "Loving you made no sense. We could not have been more opposite. But it just felt ..."

"It did," he whispers.

Finally, I turn to him, slowly nodding.

"I would have destroyed us," he says.

I try not to react, but my brow twitches anyway.

He rubs the tension from his neck. "My dreams were too big. I would have tried to make my dreams your dreams, and I would have crushed your soul. I would have taken everything that made you ... you. And I would have turned it into dust. But you would have loved me enough to let it happen. When you broke up with me, I was heartbroken, but I was so proud of you for not compromising. You were nineteen. That was way too early to compromise, to bargain for a lesser life."

"Jesus, Price." I stare out the window. "I hardly think you've lived a lesser life."

"I gave up what mattered most. And now I'm paying for it."

Did I matter most?

"We're going to miss the show."

He looks at his watch. "Too late."

"I'll walk back home." I open the door.

"Scottie?"

Nope. I can't do this. Speed-walking down the street, I wipe more tears.

"Scottie!" He jogs after me.

"Go home, Price."

"Let's grab dinner. I know you haven't eaten."

"Dinner?" I whip around. "What are you going to have? Juice? Are you going to share your juice with me? I haven't seen you eat solid foods in weeks, and you're orange. You're goddamn orange!"

He deflates.

I shake my head a half dozen times. "I don't want to know." Pivoting, I jog.

He jogs.

So I run.

He runs.

My vision blurs behind the tears. No matter how hard

I run, I know I can't outrun this, but it doesn't stop me from trying. When I reach my trailer, I stop at the door, feeling him a few feet behind me, hearing his labored breaths chasing mine.

"You're sick," I whisper with my back to him.

There's a long pause.

"Yes."

I've known it since the day he came into the store. But Price is the one person who makes me question my feelings, my instincts, my intuition. Nobody likes to be wrong, but I've wanted to be so wrong about this.

"Cancer?" I barely get the word out before my heart lurches into my throat.

"Yes."

My eyes pinch shut, and my body shakes in silent sobs. This isn't happening. No. It's not right. It's not fair.

Slowly, I turn around, hand cupped over my mouth. Tears spring from my aching eyes. "Oh god, Price ... w-what am I s-supposed to d-do?"

His arms slide around my waist, holding me to him, lips pressing to the top of my head. "Burn the skinny jeans."

Why is he making me laugh through my sobs?

"Be your beautiful, inspiring, kind, exquisite self. Radiate that unmatched light of yours. I need your light, Scottie. I truly *need* it."

I hug him harder than I've ever hugged anyone.

Fuck cancer.

CHAPTER
nineteen

It's not mine to share, even if it's mine to bear.

I SHUT off the shop lights for the night and lock the door. Koen's pickup is parked beside mine, and the kitchen light is on in my trailer. Each step feels unbearably heavy.

When I open the door, he drops the puzzle piece in his hand and sits back. "Hi," he says cautiously.

"Hi." I close the door and toss the store keys onto my counter as Scrot greets me. I reach down and give him a quick scratch under his chin.

"Are we good?" Koen stands.

He's talking about our minor argument on the phone, but I can't think about that right now.

I shake my head. Seeing him brings everything to the surface again. The tears win. And I break down. "I h-had a b-bad day." My body shudders with sobs.

As I melt into his arms, he holds me together. "Scottie? What happened?"

I can't talk, not yet, so I cry until I can catch my breath.

Koen kisses my head. He cradles my jaw and deposits endless kisses all over my face. "It's okay. I've got you."

His words pull a few more tears from my swollen eyes.

"You ... you're right." I close my eyes, letting him continue to kiss my face. Then I blow out a slow breath. "You can't fix a bad day. Not with a hundred positive affirmations. Not with anything." Before opening my eyes, I replay my conversation with Price.

"Scottie, you can't tell Koen."

"Why not?"

"Because it's not real if we don't make it real."

"Price—"

"Please."

Price has put me in a terrible position to keep this from Koen.

"Do you really love me?" I whisper.

He narrows his eyes. It's unfair of me to ask him this on the heels of an emotional breakdown, but I'm in an awful situation. I need him to understand something—something I can't tell him.

"Because I love you. I'm so in love with you, Koen Sikes."

The muscles in his face relax. "Of course, I love you." He presses his lips gently to mine.

I smile. It's a sad one, but it's also honest and raw. And it's killing me to keep this from him. "I can't tell you why I'm so emotional. It's not mine to share, even if it's mine to bear. And the reason isn't selfish or petty. It's the right thing to do. And I need you to love me and *trust* me."

His hands slide from my face, landing idle at his side. "Scottie."

"I wouldn't ask this if—"

"Then don't." He shakes his head, taking a step away from me. "Please tell me you see how rich this is? You're asking me to blindly trust you after your bad day, but when I had a bad day, you right away assumed I was drinking."

I start to plead my case, but I close my mouth before the first word escapes. "What I did was defenseless. That was terrible of me."

He stares at me as if he's waiting for me to elaborate.

I shrug. "I'm sorry. I don't know what else to say."

"I don't know how to deal with this. I've been transparent with you about my life. I need that in return."

"I want to tell you."

"Then tell me."

"I can't."

"Is it a life or death situation?" he asks, each word bleeding sarcasm.

"Yes," I whisper.

Koen rubs his hands over his face. "Christ, Scottie. I need a minute. I can't even think right now. Come on, Scrot." He slips past me toward the door.

I grab his wrist.

We have a stare-off. The pain feels like quicksand. And I don't know who's saving who or if we're both destined to go under.

"Don't go."

"I need space."

"I need you."

He shakes his head, pulling out of my hold. The door clicks shut behind him, and he treks toward his truck with Scrot behind him. A few feet from the front bumper, he stops, dropping his head for a few seconds before pivoting. He's coming back.

I can't move. Everything hurts too much.

Koen opens the door. "Come with me."

"Why?"

"Because I need more space than this trailer gives me, but the distance from my place to yours is too much."

He. Came. Back.

Maybe not with a bouquet and a big smile, but he came back. I grab my bag and keys and follow him. He doesn't give me a second look before hopping into his truck and backing out of the lot while I climb into my truck and follow him.

When we get to his place, he heads straight into the bathroom to shower. I steal a T-shirt and slip it on, then I brush my teeth in the half bath on the main level. By the time he exits the bathroom, I'm in bed with my back to him and my heart in my throat. He slides into bed and shuts off the lights.

The silence haunts me.

The fear of losing Koen haunts me.

Price Milloy ... he guts me.

My heart thumps to the point of a dull ache in my chest before I drift off to sleep.

In the middle of the night, Koen's arms wake me, wrapping around my waist and pulling me into his body. "I can't sleep," he whispers. "The distance is too much."

I roll toward him, nuzzling my face in his neck.

"I'm sorry you had a bad day," he says.

Words die deep in my throat behind a mass of swelling emotions. Tears fill my eyes. And I hold still, willing them away.

He's the one. The person who becomes everything you never knew you needed.

"Scottie?"

"Hmm?" It's all I can manage.

"Move in with me."

What?

Forcing my breaths to slow and my heart to calm, I let those four words play in my head until I can form actual words. "I need to think about it."

"Take your time."

One breath.

Two breaths.

Three breaths.

"I'm done thinking. I'll move in with you."

His chest vibrates with a chuckle, which steals some of my pain and replaces it with hope.

"But I must warn you, I'm a little messy."

"Ya don't say?"

"Can you love the messy parts of my life?" I kiss his shoulder.

"No. But I can love you and deal with your messiness."

I grin, closing my eyes. What a life this is.

Until ... hours later, I awaken alone in bed and am filled with unease because I had the most vivid sex dream, but I wasn't having sex with Koen.

CHAPTER
twenty

What if there's a third kind of love?

Price

I'VE UNINTENTIONALLY MADE a new friend. Ed's back on track, and we figured out the best way to keep him in his house. In return, he's insisted on fixing my fence. I had no idea the fence needed fixing.

"Got any coffee?" he asks, pulling a hanky from his pocket to wipe his brow when I offer him a glass of water.

"I don't. I have juice."

"Orange?"

I shake my head.

"Apple?"

Again, I shake my head. "Carrot, beet, and ginger."

His nose wrinkles. "You one of them health nuts?"

"Guilty."

He grumbles, nodding to the door, inviting himself inside after working for only thirty minutes. "I suppose your concoction won't kill me." He starts to follow me then stops. "Grab that bag."

I glance to my right at the worn brown briefcase on the deck beside his toolbox. "This?"

He nods.

I carry it inside, and he takes it from me while I get his juice.

"I noticed you didn't have anything from The Righteous Brothers." Ed pulls his vinyl record from its cover, blows on it, and plays it on my turntable.

It's impossible not to grin as Ed snaps his fingers and sways his bony hips in the middle of my living room.

"You think I've lost that lovin' feeling?" I ask, handing him a bottle of juice.

He takes the juice and sits on the sofa while I inspect his small stack of records in his briefcase.

"You're living by yourself, young man. Either you've lost it, or you haven't found it. Which is it?"

"Maybe both," I mumble.

The Four Seasons.

The Coasters.

Brenda Lee.

He's an oldies guy.

"Divorced?"

I shake my head.

"Widowed?"

Another headshake.

"Gay?"

I grin. "No."

"What's your problem?"

His directness is refreshing.

"Haven't you heard of a straight male being single by choice?"

"No."

I laugh, and it feels so good.

"But I don't understand your generation, so forget I asked." Ed has a beet-red mustache, and from the look on his face, I'd say he's not a fan of my juice, but he slowly sips it anyway.

"How did your wife die? If you don't mind me asking."

"Cancer." Ed slowly shakes his head. "Just between us, I think it might have been the chemo that killed her. That stuff's poison."

"I'm sorry for your loss."

"It was quick. She didn't even make it through one round. Diagnosed and gone in less than six weeks." He gives me a sad smile. "Took me a long time for everything to register. Sometimes, I still forget she's gone. I'll be watching TV and yell for her to bring me something." He stares at his juice. "I bet she's up there laughing her ass off."

I sit in the armchair adjacent to the sofa. "I bet she is too."

Ed tosses me a wry grin, but it quickly fades when he sighs. "Cancer's gonna take all of us. Or a heart attack. Strokes are up there, too."

"Accidents. Chronic respiratory disease. Covid. Alzheimer's. Diabetes," I add.

Ed eyes me like I'm the morbid one, but in the next breath, he takes another swig of his juice. "Suicide, homicide."

I nod, fighting my grin. "Lightning strike. Shark attack."

"You need to get laid, young man."

I chuckle. He's not wrong.

———

I'VE MOVED my bedtime to nine instead of ten. Sleep is my friend. Just as I fall into a peaceful slumber, there's a knock at my door.

Opening my eyes, I wait. Maybe there wasn't a knock. Maybe it was a dream.

Tap. Tap. Tap.

With a sigh, I sit up and pull on a T-shirt. The wood floor creaks as I approach the door, turning on the entry light.

Scottie's nose wrinkles. "Shit. You were asleep. I'm sorry. Go back to sleep."

I nod at the big bag in her hands. "Whatcha got?"

"Things to make you better."

"Better than what?"

Her crestfallen face doesn't appreciate my humor.

"Come in." I step aside.

"I really need to find another employee." She slips out of her Birks and carries the bag to the kitchen.

I flip on the light over the sink. "Are you firing me?"

"No. I need someone to work so I can check on *you* before your bedtime."

"Scottie," I scratch my head, "I don't want you checking in on me."

"Someone needs to." She pulls smaller bags and bottles of supplements out of her big bag.

"Why?"

"Because you live alone."

"Did it ever occur to you that I live alone for a reason?"

She looks up at me. "You don't want me here." Her lips twist. "That's rude."

"No. That's not it. I want you here. I want you here in ways you can't understand. But I don't want to be your pet project, patient, or burden." I shake my head. "A job. A distraction."

"You're not."

"Can we just go back to you knowing about my cancer but not telling me that you know, and I'll pretend that you don't know even though I know you know? Ya know?"

That line forms at the bridge of her nose, but it falls victim to her giggles.

I don't care what she has in that bag; it can't begin to heal me like the beautiful sound coming from her right now.

"Price. It's not a coincidence that you came into Drummond's when you did. It was fate. You needed me."

More than you know.

But it wasn't fate.

"And I have to believe that I need to do this, not only for you but also for me. I need something to keep me from losing myself in Koen."

"Losing yourself?" I fill my water glass.

"He asked me to move in with him. And I didn't think. I just said yes."

"If his house is bigger than your trailer, I can see how you might get lost."

"Har har."

I pull out a chair, straddling it backward, and inspect

149

the contents of the bags. "What do you mean by getting lost?"

She sits next to me. "The way I got lost in you."

Glancing up from the bottle of nattokinase, I narrow my eyes. "You felt lost in me?"

She nods. "I spent entirely too much time thinking about you when we weren't together. And when we were together, I resented the passing of time."

I try not to react, but it's a terrible feeling to think of how oblivious I was to her emotional state. "I was a terrible boyfriend. And don't try to convince me otherwise. Just let me own this."

"You *were* the worst."

"Thanks."

She laughs.

"Scottie. This stuff had to cost a lot. I'll get you some cash."

"Don't. I'm not your level of wealthy, but I've lived a frugal life and saved almost everything."

I lift an eyebrow. "What is my level of wealth?"

"Filthy."

With an easy nod, I hum. "Filthy, huh? Sounds exorbitant."

Her grin slides off her face, replaced with a tiny frown. "Why didn't you do chemo?"

"Because what I have is a death sentence, and palliative chemotherapy can do more harm than good. I fell into a rabbit hole of stories from people who beat the odds by lifestyle and diet changes. And by beating the odds, I mean they lived longer than expected, and some are still alive. I had nothing to lose and everything to gain. It's not death.

I'm not afraid of dying, but I'm really fucking terrified of suffering. If staring death in the face isn't life-changing, then I don't know what is. So here I am ... changing my life. And if I don't live, I want to go out on my terms."

Tears fill her eyes, but she manages to keep them from escaping. "Your parents have to be beside themselves."

"They are. But there's nothing they can do."

"Well," she says, putting on a brave face and blotting her eyes, "you're going to live."

"I am."

"But let's continue to tip the scale in your favor." She goes through the supplements, healing stones, essential oils, flower essences, non-toxic deodorant, and other safe body products.

When she pulls out the enema bag, my eyes widen, but she ignores me. Scottie knows her stuff. She's lived this life, and maybe that's why she's single. But I'd rather she honor her true self than bend to anyone.

"Dry brush before you shower. Make sure your strokes go in the direction of your heart. And you really should look into a sauna and red light therapy."

I stand, jerking my head for her to follow me.

She grins when I show her my red light and sauna in the spare bedroom, along with my rebounder and meditation pillow. After scanning the room multiple times, she faces me. "You don't have internet."

I shake my head.

"No cell phone."

She already knows this, but I affirm her statement anyway.

"Who are you?" she whispers through her grin. "An outcast?"

Scottie's proud of me. And while I don't need that from her, it's still nice not to feel judged.

"I love you, Price. In a purely non-sexual way."

I twist my lips for a few seconds. "I think outcasts rarely get laid anyway, so I'd expect you to love me in a purely non-sexual way."

She rolls her eyes before pivoting and returning to the kitchen. "If you need to get laid, I can find you a nice girl."

"You *marry* nice girls. You get laid by dirty girls."

Her face flushes. "Fine. I'll find you a dirty girl."

"As dirty as you used to be?"

She curls her hair behind her ear and averts her gaze. "I was a virgin. You were the dirty older man who made me unclean."

I finish my water and set the glass by the sink. "It would have been nice to know about your virginity before I was in the process of *unknowingly* taking it."

Scottie fiddles with the empty sacks, folding them and sliding them into the larger one. "In other news ... I couldn't control my emotions when Koen came home. And when I told him I couldn't share why I was so upset, it didn't go over well."

"Yet, you're moving in with him even though you're scared of getting lost in him."

She eyes me, teeth trapping her lower lip. "Bad idea?"

"Scottie," I cross my arms and lean against the counter, "if you find someone who loves you for you, and you love them for who they are, then you've found what everyone else is looking for."

"Are you looking for that?"

"Okay, maybe not *everyone*, but a lot of people. Outcasts battling life-threatening illnesses are exempt."

"Exempt from happiness?"

"Exempt from caring about the needs of others."

Her head juts backward. "That's harsh."

"But true."

She doesn't argue. "What kind of cancer?"

"The kind you don't need to know. The kind that you don't need to research. The kind you don't need to obsess over."

Scottie returns a pouty face. It's irresistible, but I manage to resist.

"How can I help you—"

"Stop. I don't need your help. I just need you."

"Price, you can't have me."

"I already do." I push off the counter. "Go home. Drive safely. I need sleep."

She follows me to the door and slips on her shoes. She doesn't hesitate for a second when she glances up at me. Her arms encircle my neck, and she hugs me with all she has to give.

"Red blood cells," she murmurs. "Hugging builds red blood cells. Make sure you hug everyone you see." Her lips press to my cheek, and it's more than a friendly gesture, but it's not romantic either.

I don't know what we are, but it's all I have, so I don't try to define it because the easiest way to lose things is by labeling them—devaluing them with the simplicity of a word.

She steps outside.

"Scottie?"

"Yeah?"

"Don't lose Koen because of me. Keeping him is more important than keeping my secret."

I can't read her expression, but it softens after a few seconds. "I really do love you."

I've heard people say that cancer is a gift. I never understood it until now.

"And I you."

CHAPTER

twenty-one

Marry the man who treats you like a cow.

Scottie

"ARE you going to be my granddaughter-in-law?" Herb asks, pushing his cart of fruit to the counter.

I didn't think anything could beat the phone-on-speaker conversation. I was wrong.

"Uh ..." I laugh nervously, weighing his produce. "Not to my knowledge."

"Oh. The boy said you were moving in with him."

"I am."

Herb inspects me through narrowed eyes. I've never seen him be anything but jovial and full of smiles. Even a little flirty. This is the opposite of all those things.

"Surely not out of wedlock."

Uh-oh ...

"We haven't ironed out all of the details. It's not happening today or anything like that."

Tomorrow.

Koen took tomorrow off to help me move my things. I told him I didn't need help. I have limited belongings. But I think he's a little anxious about me messing up his organization, hence the "help."

"Phew." He relaxes. "You had me going there for a minute."

With a nervous "tee-hee," I slide the produce into his reusable bag. "Sorry. I didn't mean to worry you."

"His grandma, God rest her soul, would turn over in her grave if the boy didn't first make you an honest woman." He holds up his index finger and waggles it at me. "Don't let him have the milk before he buys the cow."

I choke on a bit of saliva. Is this really happening? Did he not hear us upstairs on Valentine's Day? "No," I say. "Uh ... of course not. But I don't think of myself as a cow."

"It's just an expression. But really, cows were once sacred. Think of it as a compliment."

"Mmm." I nod with a tight grin. "Well, it's always nice seeing you."

"Have a lovely day, Scottie."

After he exits the store, I grab my phone.

> Scottie: Your grandpa doesn't want you to have free milk!

> Koen: I'm lost

> Scottie: He thinks we need to be married before we live together!

> Koen: Lol

Lol!

That's his response.

After the remaining two customers check out, I call him.

"Hi." He sounds cool and calm.

"He's not joking, Koen. I have never seen him look so disappointed as he did when I confirmed we were moving in together. He said your grandmother would roll over in her grave."

"Don't worry about it. That's not even possible. She was cremated."

I cover my mouth to muffle my snort. "I'm serious, Koen. I can't move in with you now. He will never look at me the same way."

"So ... you're more concerned about the way he looks at you than you are about the way I love you?"

"That's not fair. Our living together shouldn't change how you feel about me."

"It changes my proximity to be able to *feel* you."

Again, I suppress my giggles. I need him to be serious. "I am a sacred cow. I think we should wait."

"Wait to move in? You can't be serious."

"And I think we should wait to have sex."

He laughs. "Newsflash. We've had sex. And how would he know?"

"He'll see it on my face. I'm glowing after we have sex."

"You're always glowing, Scottie."

I blush. "You're just saying that so I'll have sex with you."

"No. I'm saying it because it's true. But if it makes you lose your inhibitions, who am I to object?"

"What about your mom?"

"I'd prefer she not lose her inhibitions."

I sit on the stool and spin in a circle. "But your grandpa—"

"Lives in la-la land. I humor him when I can. But this is too much. Listen, I gotta get back to work. We move forward as planned. We don't have to tell him we're living together."

"For the record, *you're* the one who told him."

"He asked me how things were going between us, and I told him you're moving in with me."

"And he took it that we're getting married."

"Well, that's on him. Love you. Gotta go. Bye."

"Bye."

CHAPTER

twenty-two

I was too nearsighted to see the bigger picture and too farsighted to see what was right before me.

Price

"DID Scottie tell you I asked her to move in with me?" Koen asks, jogging on the treadmill while I walk at an incline next to him for our warm-up before we lift weights.

"She might have mentioned it."

"Don't act like she doesn't tell you every fucking little thing."

Koen and I are over two months into our workout bromance, but he still has an angry tone when he references my relationship with Scottie. Maybe he needs a hug.

"Not acting. What's your point?"

"My grandpa found out, and today she called it off because he mentioned his disapproval of the idea because he's old-fashioned. Since when did Scottie give a shit what other people think?"

"She values family and relationships. If she's worried about what your grandpa thinks, it's because she thinks you two might be together for the foreseeable future, and she doesn't want unnecessary tension with your grandpa."

"Did she tell you that?"

"No. I haven't talked with her today."

"Then how do you know that?"

"Much to your chagrin, no doubt, I know Scottie. I know her better now than when we were together twelve years ago."

"How so?" Koen asks, sounding a little out of breath.

"I've had twelve years to ponder the memories of her. Time bestows clarity. Perhaps you should move away for twelve years and return when you see things more clearly."

He glances over at me. "You'd like that, wouldn't you?"

I chuckle. "I'm not your enemy. Not your competition."

"Doesn't feel like that."

"Why do you say that?"

"Because she talks about you like you're the exception to everything. The untouchable exception. The one who can do no wrong."

"I *am* pretty close to perfect."

Koen smacks the off button. "Fuck you."

I laugh, lowering the incline and the speed before shutting it off. When I get to the free weights, I hand him a clean towel that reeks of bleach. He's working much harder than I am.

"Listen, Koen. When she talks about you, it's like I'm witnessing a young girl in the front row of a boy band concert. She's high on whatever you're feeding her. And I support her happiness as long as you don't try to change her."

He wipes his face, eyeing me with his never-ending distrust.

"She's the goddamn fountain of youth, Koen. Eternal sunshine. The closest you'll ever come to feeling immortal. Don't fuck it up." I rest a firm hand on his shoulder and squeeze it harder than necessary.

"Why not you?" he asks as I lift weights onto the bar.

"Why not me what?"

"How can you say those things about her and not make a play for her? Why are you so willing to hand her to someone else?"

I pause for a second, staring at the bar. "Because I need her, but not in that way."

―――――

I'VE STOPPED TIMING my meditation. Time is not my friend. It's nobody's friend. I think time robs us of living. Time steals the moment. We don't exist in time because time doesn't exist. It can be that simple because it is that simple.

What if I stopped trying to understand life? What would happen? When I started this journey (a terrible time reference), I thought knowledge was my friend. The only thing I know now is I feel most at peace when I trust myself and honor my physical and emotional needs. The greatest thing I've ever done for myself is nothing. When my mind is quiet, the world is not filled with seven billion people. The world is one—a puzzle with seven billion pieces. When my mind is quiet, the lines between those pieces vanish. It's a oneness—a wholeness—I have never experienced.

My fear of suffering is gone.

Suffering is resisting. It's when the body won't listen to its inner voice. It's a byproduct of fear itself. I've stopped resisting, stopped fearing, and now the pain has no place to live. And I am at peace.

Without the pain, I can think of her and only feel love. The resentment has vanished. The days of missing her are gone because when I am at peace, when I am whole, we are one.

Do you feel that? If you let go of everything, you'll find that quiet place, and you'll find me. It's so beautiful. So simple. It's perfect. It's "now."

Now is not a moment. It's now. It's where we always have and always will exist.

I close my journal.

I cry my fucking eyes out.

I laugh.

I welcome all the feelings, and they make me whole.

Whatever happens from this moment forward, I will be like Scottie. I will be light in every way. I want to be the person others feel drawn to in their darkest hour.

Again, I laugh. Scottie is right. When you know what everyone else is trying to figure out, you can't help but laugh. I spent years chasing something, buying into the illusion of time, and collecting tangible things because I was too nearsighted to see the bigger picture and too farsighted to see what was right before me. Could it be that only the blind can truly see?

CHAPTER

twenty-three

Sometimes you find your dream, and sometimes it finds you.

Scottie

"WE'RE ABOUT TO CLOSE; hope you don't need much," I say to the customer who has the nerve to walk through the door two minutes before eight.

"I only need the girl behind the counter." He shuts off the *Open* sign.

I toss him the key to lock the door.

As soon as he steps behind the counter, I grab his shirt and pull him to me. "If you think I'm going to change my mind, you're—"

"What do you want, Scottie?" Koen asks.

I release him, eyes narrowed. It's not what he said; it's how he said it. "Sexually?"

He smirks. "No. Well, maybe we'll discuss that later. What do you want out of life? Do you want to get married? Do you want a family?"

"Are you proposing?" I ask with a laugh.

He twists his lips, sliding his hands into his back pockets. "I don't know yet."

My heart skips more than one beat. Is he serious?

Before I lose all composure, I clear my throat and find a good answer to his question. "I ..." I shrug as if he asked me about going for ice cream. "Yes. I mean, I'm not opposed to marriage or a family. We discussed this on Valentine's Day."

"What does that look like for you?" Koen keeps a serious face.

After another nervous laugh, I lean against the counter, hugging myself. "I don't know what you mean."

"Do you want to be home with your kids? Do you imagine working full-time and sending kids to daycare? Do you imagine your husband staying home?"

Jesus. This is a deep conversation.

"I'm not sure my income would support a family if my husband wanted to stay home. Are you looking for a sugar mama?"

His lips quirk into a tiny grin. "No."

"Koen, I ..." I shake my head. "I don't know how you want me to answer you."

"Honestly."

I frown. "I don't know the answer. I'm not a planner. I live in the moment. I figure things out when the time comes."

"Okay. Then marry me. And let's figure it out as we go."

Something between a laugh and a cough escapes my chest. "I don't know my timeline for accepting wedding proposals, but I'm pretty sure it's longer than two months."

He sighs. "At the risk of sounding like I'm making a case for you to be with Price, I have to say that it's possible he was pursuing you for that whole summer twelve years ago, but you were too caught up in your young mind to see it. Maybe you were too 'in the moment' to imagine a future. He probably wanted to love you the way I want to love you."

Rubbing my lips together, I sort through his words. Does he have a point?

"Marriage has nothing to do with love."

Koen narrows his eyes. "I'll concede that you don't have to love someone to marry them, and you don't have to marry someone to prove that you love them. But I'm not sure it's one hundred percent accurate to say marriage has nothing to do with love."

"So why do you want to marry me if you don't have to marry someone to prove that you love them?"

"I was raised to buy the cow before taking the milk."

"Stop it." I brush past him to the back room to hide my grin and retrieve the broom.

"Can I be honest with you?" he asks when I return.

I laugh. "When have you not been?"

"If I don't factor in my life going off the rails— sending me spiraling downward with addiction for a good year— I'm a traditionalist at heart. I'm a descendant of Herb Sikes. I'm not a purist, but I've spent many Sundays in church with my mom and grandfather. I want a wife who wants to have children. I want *us* to raise our children—to witness their first steps and words. And I'm willing to work as hard as necessary to provide for my family and to be a good husband and father. I want sleepless nights and a minivan with sticky seats and snacks littering the floor. I want handprints on the windows and markers on the walls. I want to bust my ass to get my kids into bed before my wife falls asleep so that we can have time alone every day. I want to have the family stickers on our minivan's window, the one with lots of kids. The one where the people in the vehicle behind us count the number of kid stickers and conclude that I need to stay the fuck off my wife for a while.

"And saying all of this to you scares the life out of me because I'm afraid it will suffocate every last ounce of your feminism. And that's not what I want to do at all. We wouldn't be equals. Nope. *You* would be the harder worker. You would be the one deserving the praise. Your part of this would be much harder than mine, but I want to believe it would be more rewarding, too. My mom stayed home with me and my brother until we were in school. And I can go weeks without thinking about my father, but I love my mom. I call her every day. And I want to be a great dad, unlike my father. But more than anything, I want my kids to love their mother to the ends of the earth."

Whoa ... just ... whoa ...

If he told me he lived on another planet and recently descended upon Earth, I would not be more shocked than I am right now. The look on his face is the epitome of honesty and raw vulnerability. He put it *all* out there.

"We're over. Aren't we?" He cringes.

It takes me a few more seconds to piece together my thoughts. Koen has dreamed of his future. I have not, at least not to this level of detail.

I slowly shake my head. "No. Uh ... we're not over. I'm just ..." I continue to shake my head. "I'm trying to imagine it. What if I can't have children?"

"Would you adopt?" he asks.

I don't know, even though I've considered the possibility that I can't have children. But I've never considered the part that comes after that. I've never had a reason to consider it.

"Scottie, say something."

My gaze flits to his. Do I want to marry Koen and have a family with him?

"You want me to be a stay-at-home mom?"

He presses his lips together for a beat before nodding.

"I see." I clear my throat. "I'm not sure what the definition of feminism is anymore. I think it's changed, or perhaps it's different for everyone. Mine is pretty basic. Women are equal to men; therefore, we should have equal rights and opportunities. Feminism should include all choices women make for their lives."

"But?" he says.

"But nothing. I appreciate your honesty. There's a long list of things I've come to love about you, but your honesty and transparency top the list. You're unapologetically yourself. You own your mistakes and don't hide what you want in life. There are no buts. What you said about your mother is so beautiful."

Koen slides his hands into the back pockets of his jeans and lifts his gaze to the ceiling for several seconds. "I'm sure that sounded like I want you to be barefoot and pregnant for the next twenty years while chasing kids and canning tomatoes. But that's not—"

"You didn't mention canning tomatoes." The harder I

try to hold in my laughter, the more it escapes as an unattractive snort despite my hand over my mouth.

He looks at me with heartbreaking vulnerability. "I love you, Scottie. And I don't care if it's been two decades, years, months, days, minutes, or seconds. This love I have for you is here to stay. And I don't want you to compromise who you are or your dreams, but if you can imagine sharing even a fraction of my dreams with me, then marry me, because I would be the luckiest man alive to be part of yours."

Crickets.

What does *the girl* say to *the boy* after he says all that?

"I need a minute." I hold up a finger.

My reply only intensifies his anguish. Koen's heart is out of his chest, in his hand, and he's offering it to me. He struggles to keep from deflating, but he returns a single nod.

"Take all the time you need. I'm going to head home and walk Scrot." He squeezes my hand while pressing a chaste kiss to my mouth. "Goodnight." When he reaches the door, he sighs. It's locked, and the key is on the counter.

"You're leaving before I'm done thinkin'?" I step around the counter as he turns back toward me. My lips twist. "I thought about it. And I don't know if anything in life goes as planned, but if making love, babies, and a life with you is even a potential plan, I'm in. Is there any better way to live in the moment than to experience life through the eyes of a child?" Tears well in my eyes like I'm seeing my dream for the first time. A flood of emotion fills my veins and takes my breath away. I think of the women who have come into the store holding their babies and how I've longingly looked at them without consciously allowing myself to desire that life because of fear.

Fear that I can't have it.

But what if I can?

"I want that life, Koen," I whisper, wiping my face. "I think you marrying me is the best idea in the history of all ideas."

Koen grins a knocked-it-out-of-the-park grin. He takes two long strides to reach me, lifts me off my feet in a big hug, and kisses the life out of me while twirling me in a circle.

I giggle as he sets me back on my feet. "Let's go to my trailer. I'll come back and mop the floor later." My hand slides beneath his shirt, teasing the waistband of his briefs.

He grabs my wrist. "Whoa. I thought we were waiting until marriage."

"It was just a suggestion. Herb doesn't have to know."

"Know what?" He narrows his eyes.

"That we've had sex." I tug at the button on his jeans. Maybe we can slide into the back room and get creative.

Koen steps away from me and buttons his jeans. "We haven't had sex."

I laugh.

He doesn't. Not even the hint of a grin.

"Is this how you're playing it?" I cross my arms.

He shrugs. "I don't know what you're talking about."

"When's the wedding? Tomorrow?"

"Of course not. I haven't met your parents and properly asked your father for your hand in marriage."

Again, we have a silent stare-off.

"Fine." I lift my chin, pulling my shoulders back. "It doesn't matter to me. I can take it or leave it."

"You're a thirty-one-year-old virgin. What's another six months to a year?"

Don't react!

He's baiting me. He's going to make it halfway to his truck, turn around, and ravage me with his naked body.

"I don't know if I'll even like sex. So, yeah. What's six months to a year?" I flash my teeth and bat my eyelashes.

Koen kisses me on my forehead. "Oh, you'll like it. Night." He exits through the back door.

I wait. Any minute now.

And I wait.

Then I see his truck drive past the front of the store.

"Oh, god." I cringe. He's not joking.

CHAPTER
twenty-four

If a woman lets you see her soul, it's your first glimpse of Heaven.

Price

"CAN YOU KEEP A SECRET?" Scottie asks while we unpack a new shipment of food.

You have no idea.

"I can try."

"I'm engaged," she says just shy of a squeal.

I feel her gaze on me and sense her trying hard to control her body, trembling with excitement. But I don't look at her. "Who's the lucky guy?"

"Stop." She wads up a piece of packing paper and throws it at me.

"That was quick." I toss the wadded paper back to her.

She stacks the bags of rice onto the counter with a content sigh. "When you know, you know."

"So he asked, and you right away knew?"

Her hesitation says everything. When she doesn't answer, I give her the hairy eyeball.

"Don't look at me like that."

"Like what?" I cut the tape and flatten the empty box.

"It wasn't your typical proposal."

"Have you been proposed to a lot?" I chuckle.

"Not as much as you might think, given my level of awesomeness." She flips her hair and smirks. "Koen's different." She scans the bags of rice into the register. "He's honest."

"If honesty is the bar, you need to set your standards a little higher."

As if I'm one to talk.

"It's different. Koen's honesty is all-revealing and all-consuming. Honesty can be as simple as the absence of lying. Koen doesn't hide who he is or what he wants. He owns his mistakes. And he's not afraid to tell me about his dreams, even when he doesn't know if I want to share them."

I open the next box. "I'm happy for you, but don't think for a second that he's not afraid to tell you those things. If he loves you, he's scared to death to tell you because he knows he could lose you if you don't feel the same. He's not fearless. He's brave. There's a difference."

"Mmm. I never thought of it like that. It makes me love him even more."

"So why did you say yes?"

"Because—"

"And don't say it's because you love him."

"Jesus, Dr. Phil, you're really in a mood today."

"The past few days, I've been seeing things clearly. It's ... freeing."

Again, I feel her gaze on me. "You're a miracle, Price Milloy. I hope you know that."

"You think?"

"Yes," she laughs, "I do. And for your information, I wasn't going to answer you with something as simplistic as 'I love him.' Although the simplest explanation is usually the correct one. What you really want to know is why I love him. Well, I've spent very little time dreaming about my future. I like the moment. So when Koen told me where he sees his future going, I paused momentarily. It's like someone asking what I want for dinner at one in the afternoon, and I haven't needed to think that far ahead. I might not know the answer right away, but that doesn't mean I don't want dinner."

"What does Koen want for dinner?"

Scottie blushes while shifting her gaze to me. She looks so innocent, so happy. "He wants a family and a wife who stays home with the kids. And maybe that would be offensive to some women, but not me. Not once did my mind go to my mom, who I love and admire, but she was never home. Steph and I had a nanny, and our dad was home with us on the weekends. We never felt neglected or abandoned. Our parents had big career dreams, and they followed those dreams *and* made a family life work."

I slowly nod. "There's no one size fits all."

"Exactly. So after Koen told me about his dreams, I started to imagine a life where I was holding a baby in my arms, and I imagined watching that life change a little every day. I thought about first smiles, trips to the park, nature walks on the trails, and teaching small hands to make jewelry with me. I thought of the sound of a child laughing. And the heartbreak of their cries. I thought of the times I wanted my mom, and she wasn't there."

Scottie holds up her hands. "And that was okay that she wasn't there. *Someone* was there. But what if I choose to be there, and I *can* be there?" She shrugs, giving me a teary-eyed smile. "I want that life. I want to be the mom who's there. I want it more than anything. And I want it with Koen."

I grin. "Then I think that's the perfect life for you."

Scottie narrows her eyes. "A-are you serious?" she fumbles her words.

"Scottie, you excel at life. You're gentle and patient with a soothing soul. I think you'll be a wonderful mother. I've always known that."

Tears fill her eyes—a lot of tears—more than mere happy emotions. This is not the reaction I expected after paying her such a high compliment. She covers her mouth and runs out the back door.

"What the hell?" I mumble.

I can't leave the store unattended, so I call her, but her cell phone rings from behind the counter.

Never mind.

Nobody's in the store, so I write on a sheet of paper and tape it to the front door before locking it.

Be back in 5 minutes

When I step out back, she's hunched over in a lawn chair under her trailer's retractable awning, head in her hands.

"What happened, Scottie?" I squat in front of her, resting my hands on her legs. "What happened to make you react like this?"

She sniffles, lifting her head and wiping her eyes. A sad smile bends her lips as she rests her hands on my cheeks. "You happened." She kisses my forehead and slides past me to stand. "Go back to work, Price. I need some space."

———

At eight, Scottie comes in the back door to close up shop, but she's not alone. Koen is right behind her, holding her hand.

"Everything go okay?" she asks without making eye contact. Instead, she leans past me for the front door key.

I silently plead for help from Koen. He presses his lips together, eyes wide, while he shrugs.

She didn't tell him what I did? Whatever that was.

"Everything went fine. You know, I've watched you clean, take out the register drawer, shut off lights, and set the alarm dozens of times. Don't you think it's time you let me actually close on the nights I'm closing?"

"I live ten feet away. It's no big deal." She breezes past Koen to the back room.

Again, I look to him for help.

He shakes his head. "I don't know, man," he murmurs.

Weeks earlier, I would have marched into the back room, pinned her in a corner, and demanded she tell me everything. That was when I lived under the illusion of control.

I go to the back room, but no marching is involved.

And I don't pin her in a corner, but I hug her when she tries to slide past me with the mop.

She stiffens, arms at her side while the mop falls from her hand.

"You have to hug me back," I whisper in her ear. "I have cancer."

"That's not fair," she replies, reluctantly sliding her hands around my waist.

"Life's not fair, but I don't make the rules." This time, it's me who presses my lips to her cheek. "I love you."

When I turn, she grabs my wrist. "And I you," she whispers so only I can hear her.

When I emerge from the back room, Koen glances over his shoulder at me. I don't say anything, but I hug him. He stiffens, and his reaction is a thousand times more intense than Scottie's.

"Red blood cells, man. Just building red blood cells."

He doesn't hug me back.

We'll work on that.

At least he's not on the verge of punching me. That's a good sign. His expression reads something like, "You weird, orange motherfucker."

I leave without another word, and as I drive past the front of the store, I slow down to witness Scottie in Koen's arms. He kisses her, but it's not a friendly peck on the cheek. It's passionate.

His hands in her hair, hers gripping his shirt.

I miss that feeling of euphoria—that shared all-consuming passion.

I miss *her*.

CHAPTER

twenty-five

Life is the dream that makes sense.

Scottie

I GASP OUT OF BREATH, jackknifing to sitting in the middle of the night. A sheen of sweat covers my skin, and I'm aroused. But Koen's at his place.

This is the third dream that I've had about Price in a matter of weeks. The third sex dream. These dreams don't feel like flashbacks to when we were together. They're present-day scenarios. He looks like he does now. And in the latest one, I cried while we had sex because I thought he was dying and we would never have sex again.

They're dreams. I don't control them. They don't matter.

Still, every time it happens, I feel shaken for days. I feel like Koen knows and that Price looks at me differently after these dreams. What if I'm with Koen some night and say Price's name?

I can't get back to sleep, so I opt for meditation to cleanse my mind and alleviate this anxiety. By six, I'm out for my walk. When I return, my favorite guy is playing fetch with his dog by my trailer.

"No work?" I walk straight into his arms and steal a kiss.

He hums, dragging his lips down my neck. "I don't work *every* weekend." His hands sliding to my butt send me back a few steps.

"You can't touch me like that until we're married."

Koen's blue eyes gleam with playfulness. I don't trust him.

"What if we just mess around?"

"You don't like messes." I pick up the ball that Scrot drops at my feet and throw it.

"I asked one to marry me."

"Did you just reduce me to an unflattering noun?" I park my fists on my hips.

"You're my mess." He reaches for me, but I hold up a stiff finger.

"Don't play with me, Koen. Are we haloed purists or filthy sinners? There's no middle ground."

His calloused hand encircles my wrist while he sucks my finger. "There's *only* middle ground."

Why? Why aren't my sex dreams about this man? I'm a mess of need just from him sucking my finger.

"I need to shower." I reclaim my finger and duck past him, straight into my trailer.

"Being good is only fun when it's sprinkled with a little naughtiness."

I ignore his theory while looking for a clean pair of pants. My dirty laundry clutters the floor around my bed.

I needed to wash it a week ago. Koen will divorce me after one kid.

When I find a "clean enough" pair of pants in the pile of clothes at the end of my bed, I turn, but Koen's blocking my way to the shower.

I square up to him, chin high, looking him straight in the eye. "Define naughty."

A devilish smirk hijacks his face. "Oral."

I shake my head. "Herb wouldn't approve of oral."

Koen's nose crinkles with his sour face. "Please don't say my grandfather's name in the same sentence as oral."

"Then make a better case for naughtiness."

"I'll watch you shower."

"My bathroom's the size of a shoebox. *I* can barely watch myself shower."

His lips twist to the side for a moment. I admire his determination.

"Touch yourself."

After a few slow blinks, I tap the tip of my finger to my nose, arm, and knee.

His mask slips, but just barely. He hides his amusement behind a clenched jaw, but his lips twitch.

My gaze slides down his torso as he unbuttons his jeans. "What are you doing?"

"I'm going to show you how it's done."

"I don't have a penis, and you don't have a vagina or clit. How can you possibly show me how it's done?"

"Scottie," he buttons his jeans and straightens his shirt. "You're the worst at being bad."

I eat up his frustration, one eye roll and tiny sigh at a time.

"Let's take your mom to dinner. I can see if Price will work tonight."

"My mom?"

"Yes. The woman who, I assume, gave birth to you. The one you call every day. My future mother-in-law."

Koen sits at my table, inspecting the current puzzle. He grins when one of the pieces fits.

"In my next life, I'm returning as a puzzle, so you'll give me your undivided attention." I pass him on my way to the shower.

He hooks an arm around my waist, pulling me onto his lap. "I think it's time you trust Price with the store so we can fly to Philly."

"Really?" I lean the side of my head against his.

"Really."

"And dinner with your mom?"

"I'll call her while you're in the shower."

"Okay." I sigh, melting into him a little more.

He hugs me for several seconds before clearing his throat. "Are you ready to talk about the other day?"

"I can't."

He stiffens. "Why?"

"Because it's too hard. It's too much."

"Scottie—"

"I'm begging you to let it go."

"Well, I'm begging you to let me in."

"If you love me—"

"No. Don't put conditions on my love for you. I can't do this. I *won't* do this." He lifts me off his lap and stands.

"Can't do what?"

"Any of this." He snaps his finger and points for Scrot to follow him to the door.

"What? Wait a minute." I shake my head. "Literally, two minutes ago, you were going to invite your mom to dinner with us. And now you can't do *any of this*? Any of what? Dinner? Meet my parents? Marry me?"

Koen holds out his hands in mock surrender. "You were visibly upset the other day. And when I asked you to tell me what was wrong, you begged me to drop it for that day. So I did. And when I went with you to close up the store, the tension between you and Price was palpable. But I didn't push you. I offered you my open arms and simply held the quiet space with you. But it's no longer that day."

I don't know what to say. And his shoulders sag a little more with my enduring silence.

"I need to talk to Price," I whisper.

With a grunted laugh, Koen opens the door. "I can't be the fucking third wheel in your relationship with him. I'm sorry."

"Koen—"

The door clicks shut, and he doesn't glance back. With tight fists and a determined stride, he leaves me to flounder in the mess I've made.

CHAPTER

twenty-six

Compassion is fearless ... and sometimes reckless.

I DON'T HEAR from Koen for the rest of the day. After closing the store, I head straight to Price's. No surprise, the lights are off. I contemplate waiting until tomorrow, but this can't wait.

It takes him forever to answer the door. He's no longer orange; he's pale with squinted, bloodshot eyes. Tonight, he looks unwell.

He doesn't greet me or wait for me to enter before he stumbles back to the bedroom.

"What can I do?" I ask, following him with my heart in my throat.

"Go home," he mumbles, collapsing onto the bed and rolling into a ball on his side.

I had a long spiel ready for him, but now I can barely breathe watching him suffer. Words aren't an option.

"Go ... home ..." he whispers.

I crawl in bed, resting one hand on his back while my other strokes his hair. After his breathing evens out, I find the courage to speak. "Why do you love me?" I whisper, but not to him. I think—I hope—he's asleep. "It's been twelve years. I know why I still love you, but I don't know why you still love me." I close my eyes.

An hour or so later, just as I drift off to sleep, Price's body jerks. He sits up with a grimace and flies out of bed, reaching for the wall and then the door as he stumbles into the bathroom and vomits.

I find a washcloth and wet it with cold water. When he collapses onto his butt, head tipped back to the wall, I blot his face and press the washcloth to his forehead.

"Have you thought about seeing someone? There are clinics that will supervise you. They can monitor you, make adjustments, and give you things for detox symptoms. And if you say you can't afford it, I won't believe you."

With his eyes shut, he rocks his head from side to side. "Nothing good around here."

"Again, I think you have the means to go anywhere. It makes no sense that you're here." I re-wet the washcloth with cold water and kneel beside him.

"It makes perfect sense," he mumbles, opening one eye.

"How can you say that?"

After a hard swallow, he wipes the back of his hand across his mouth. "When I got my diagnosis and the grim reality of standard treatment options set in, I started researching. I did *so* much research. Countless books. Stories of people with unconventional views of cancer, what causes it, and how to treat it." He swallows hard again.

"This one man's journey resonated with me so much; it felt like my whole world turned upside down. He believes what saved him from the six-month death sentence he'd been given was removing all stress from his life and welcoming every feeling, everything his body was telling him it needed. He said he thought long and hard about his life and tried to remember the last time he felt free of stress and living in the moment with no stress. Blissfully content. No worries. Just ... alive. And it was right before he started college twenty years earlier. A trip to Mexico with his best friend. So he called that friend, whom he hadn't seen in over fifteen years, and they went to Mexico and sat on a beach all day and watched funny movies at night. He slept in as long as he wanted and took naps. He listened to his body and reconnected to that feeling of bliss and contentment."

Price rolls his head to the side, looking at me with as much of a smile as he can muster. "Scottie Rucker, when I thought of a time in my life that I felt free of stress and nothing but sheer bliss and contentment ... I thought of you."

Emotion burns my eyes, and I bite my quivering lower lip.

"So yeah, I can afford to go anywhere in the world, get any treatment one has come up with for cancer. And you may not be approved by the FDA for treatment ..."

I laugh through my tears.

Price slides his knuckles along my wet cheek. "But I know being here, being in your world, is the best chance I have at living. So fuck the naysayers who think that I'm crazy, that there's no proof anything I'm doing will keep me alive. I'm still here. And maybe I did one too many coffee enemas today or put too much castor oil on my abdominal pack, but I haven't missed a single day of work yet."

Again, I laugh despite the tears.

His grin gains a little more strength. "And I haven't missed a workout with Koen. I've constructed six Lego sets, and not only can I touch my toes, but I can also do a wheel pose. I'm pretty much immortal."

Everything inside of me screams, *Tell him!*

But I can't because I don't want to be anything but his bliss. "I'm proud of you." I stand, setting the washcloth by the sink. "But being your bliss *and* your non-FDA approved cure for cancer is a lot of pressure."

"Don't..." his voice strains as he lumbers to standing "...sweat it. You're working really well." He rinses out his mouth and shuffles his bare feet back to bed. "Go home. Thank you for checking on me." He pulls the covers over him.

"Do you want me to stay?"

"I like Koen. Go."

"I'm not talking about him. I'm asking if you want me to stay."

"Scottie," he murmurs, almost slurring my name, "if I were marrying you and you offered to stay with another guy, I would be pissed off."

"You have cancer."

"But he doesn't know that. Does he?"

"No." I sit on the edge of the bed. "Because you didn't want me to tell him."

Price yawns, closing his eyes. "And you agreed it was

best not to tell him. But if it's causing issues between the two of you, then tell him."

I straighten his sheets. "How long were you living here before we 'accidentally' ran into each other at the store?"

"Truth?"

"That would be nice."

"Two days."

Jesus ...

"If I weren't engaged to Koen, would we be ... more?"

Again, he yawns, rolling onto his side with his back to me. "You couldn't possibly be more to me than you already are."

His words strangle my heart, making it impossible to walk away. So I slide into bed and wrap my arms around him until I can feel his heart beating.

"You're going to lose him," Price mumbles. "Don't say I didn't warn you."

CHAPTER

twenty-seven

Life is a journey, but love is an adventure.

I AWAKEN TO A BANGING SOUND. My head spins for a second as I orientate myself.

I'm at Price's.

The sun's not out yet.

And Price has his arms around me, the opposite of how we fell asleep.

"I'll get it." I untangle from his hold while he incoherently mumbles.

I run my fingers through my hair on the way to the door and yawn while opening it. And then ... my world implodes.

Koen stares at me. His gaze is lifeless, the kind that doesn't radiate any love or even an ounce of recognition. It's as if he's looking through me.

He removes his hat to scratch his head and then

replaces it. "Before you fuck another guy, you should turn off your location. I'm going to end him." He steps inside, forcing me to move out of his way. "It won't fix us, but I will end him."

"Koen, no!" I snag his arm.

He jerks out of my hold.

"Stop!" I grab at him again, this time getting a better grip. "We didn't do anything!"

Koen stops for a second when Price appears at the entrance to his bedroom, slowly threading his arms into his T-shirt.

"Couldn't keep your goddamn hands off her." Koen charges at him.

I lose leverage. "No!"

Price doesn't even flinch, but I do. It takes me a moment to react after Koen's fist connects with Price's face for the first time. And my scream sounds like a shallow echo in my head when he hits him a second time. Price stumbles backward a few steps, but he stays on his feet.

He doesn't speak.

He doesn't try to fight back.

I begin to rush toward him. His gaze cuts to mine while he rubs his jaw and gives me a sharp headshake.

Koen turns to leave, but I remain, blocking the doorway, keeping my attention on Price the whole time.

"Move or I will move you," Koen says.

My gaze slowly slides to Koen, his ridged body, clenched jaw, and the world of hurt in his eyes.

"He has cancer," I say in defeat. And I feel as though it's spreading and getting worse just from me saying those words aloud—spreading them to another person who can give them power.

I bat away a few tears, but I don't know why I'm trying to hide it. I love these two men. They own every single emotion I have left inside of me.

Koen glances over his shoulder. I can't see his expression, but Price bleeds remorse.

"I'm your Plan B," Koen says, turning back toward me. Then he laughs, shaking his head. "I'm your fucking Plan B."

This time, I move aside when he steps past me. How can I respond when I don't know what I'm feeling other than heartbroken in every way possible?

He slams the front door behind him, and I wince.

"No," Price says, still rubbing his jaw while brushing past me to the kitchen.

"No, what?" I follow him.

"I will not come between you and your happiness. I didn't come here for that reason." He wraps ice in a towel and presses it to his jaw.

"You came here for me."

He turns with a sigh, looking utterly drained. Did I do this?

"Yes, I came here for you. To be near you. To feel your light. But I didn't come here to be with you. And I'm sorry if I've confused you. I never meant to complicate your life."

"Well," I slowly shrug and shake my head. "I don't want ..."

What? What don't I want? What *do* I want?

"I don't want to be with you, either. And I don't want you to die. But I need ..." I can't do it, so I swallow the words, knowing they will eventually suffocate me and ruin my future.

"What do you need?"

Staring at the floor, I pinch the bridge of my nose. "I just need you to live," I whisper.

"I'm alive. And you're only responsible for the good things that happen to me."

He's unknowingly slaying me, a noose around my neck that gets a little tighter every day.

"The thought of you dying—"

"Scottie, don't. Go make things right, or you'll regret it for the rest of your life."

There's more to say. There will *always* be more to say. Does he need to know my truth if he leaves this world before me?

———

I FIND Koen's location on my phone. He's not too far south of here, so I follow him to a commercial building under construction, congested with workers everywhere.

"Excuse me." I stop an older gentleman in a hard hat. "Do you know Koen Sikes?"

He shakes his head.

"Uh, he's a welder."

The guy glances around and points to his right. "Probably there."

"Thanks." I turn.

"You can't be in here without proper protection. Sorry."

I frown.

"Sikes you said?"

I nod. "Koen Sikes."

"Wait outside. I'll see if I can find him."

"Thank you. I really appreciate it."

I wait by my truck for over ten minutes, and just when I start to give up on him coming out, he does.

Wearing navy coveralls and a scowl, Koen shakes his sweaty head, stopping at least ten feet from me. "I'm sorry he has cancer, but it changes nothing."

"You're not Plan B. He came back into my life before I met you. It was never a choice. I wanted—I want—to be with you." My eyes burn with tears. "Koen," I whisper, fighting the emotion clogging my throat.

He turns, heading back toward the building. "I can't."

I chase him, stepping in front of him so he's forced to stop walking. He glances over my shoulder, jaw clenched.

"I'm sorry. And I know that's not good enough. I messed up. I let my pain over Price's diagnosis drive a wedge between us. If I had it to do over, I would tell you about his diagnosis. I would choose us. Price let me walk away twelve years ago." I wipe my eyes. "It sucks when the person you love more than anyone else doesn't fight for you. It's something your heart never gets over. And you start to wonder if you're worth fighting for.

"Yes, I stayed with him last night because he was having a terrible night and didn't ask me to do anything. He didn't ask me to come to his house. And he told me over and over to go home. But he's my friend, and I do love him, so I did what he didn't do. I stayed."

I grab the collar of Koen's coveralls, gently shaking him until he looks at me. "I'm not letting you go without a fight. The woman who answered the door at Price's house is the woman who will give everything to the people she loves. To her husband. To her children. The only way I know how to love is with my whole heart. It's how I love my family. It's how I love my friends. It's how I love you. Does it have to be a flaw that I care so deeply for my friend who's battling cancer?"

He peels my hands from his collar, and I feel instant rejection. Then he sidesteps me and heads back toward the building.

"I've loved him," I holler, "for so long that I knew I would die alone if he never came back for me."

Koen stops.

"Before you came into the store the night we met, I planned on canceling our date. Twelve years. I'd wanted to be with Price for *twelve years,* and you changed everything in one night."

Again, Koen continues walking toward the building.

I swallow my nonexistent pride, drag myself back to my truck, and climb inside. Before I can dig my key from my purse, emotion wracks my body. Covering my face with my shaky hands, I cry.

Click.

My door opens.

I startle, quickly wiping my eyes and choking back my next sob.

Koen eyes me with deep lines trenched along his forehead. I can barely breathe past the strangled emotion clogging my throat.

"I needed a minute, baby." His hand cups my tear-stained face. "But it only took a second to realize I need to hold on to the girl, not my fucking ego."

The girl ...

"I'm sorry." His fingers tangle in my hair, and his lips press to mine.

I blink, releasing the last few tears with a shaky sigh of relief.

I'm not used to fighting this hard. My intuition has always been to let go, to let life unfold as it should. But I can't let go of this man—the boy.

CHAPTER
twenty-eight

Enemies are just misunderstood friends.

Price

IT'S BEEN a week since the incident. I've worked twice, but Scottie said less than five words to me both times. I don't think she's mad; I think she's scared. And maybe it's time for me to leave. She's found happiness. It's not fair of me to expect anything more from her.

As I meander barefoot in the backyard, contemplating my next move, the door to the gate squeaks open. I glance over my shoulder, expecting my neighbor.

It's Koen.

He adjusts his brown baseball hat and clears his throat. "I was an asshole."

I smirk, shaking my head while earthing through the thick, overgrown grass. "If the tables were turned, I would have put you in the hospital. Frankly, I'm disappointed in you."

"Why did you never marry? Have you pined for her all these years?"

Staring at my feet, I stop and curl my toes into the cool blades of grass that still have morning shade. "Have I thought about her? Yes. Pined for her? No. I've had a good life. Are there things I would change? Absolutely. But despite this ... predicament I'm in, I have very few regrets." I nod toward his feet. "Take off your boots and socks."

"I'm good."

I chuckle. "I was good too until they told me I had less than six months to live."

Koen frowns, but he unties his boots. "Do you regret letting Scottie walk away? Do you regret not fighting for her?"

"No." I glance over at him as he steps barefoot into the grass.

He narrows his eyes as if my immediate response isn't what he expected.

"I'm going to say something that you might not like hearing, but maybe you can at least grasp a better sense of understanding. While there's only a three-year age difference between me and Scottie, her innocence felt magnified twelve years ago. I didn't know she was a virgin until I was in the process of taking her virginity."

Koen frowns, brow tense.

"She was innocent in every way. Uninspired by money and status. Oblivious to big dreams and accolades of success. But take her out of the city to stare at the stars or sit in the grass at the park and listen to the birds, and then you see Scottie Rucker. A human unlike anyone I had met or will ever meet in my life. But even in those moments where I should have let myself be more like her, all I could think was ... how can I capture the stars and the sound of birds and sell it?" I laugh. "I wanted to make money. And I was good at it. She jokes about world domination, but she's not wrong. I've made a fuck-ton of money." I slowly shake my head and rub my lips together. "And the fruits of my labor are literally killing me. So I regret not learning more from Scottie, but I don't regret not fighting for her. She's exactly where she's meant to be."

Koen gives me a half grin. "She loves big."

I chuckle. "Being loved like that is ... indescribable." I close my eyes for a moment and think of *her*.

A buzzing noise in the distance pulls our attention toward the sky.

"Some rich fucker flying an ultralight along the river," Koen mumbles.

"Have you ever flown one?"

He grunts, giving me the hairy eyeball. "What do you think?"

I park my fists on my hips and stare at the plane in the distance. "I think we should go fly one today."

"You can fly one?"

I nod.

"I have to work. I'm already late."

I shrug. "Call in sick."

Koen eyes me with concentration. "You just happen to have a plane here?"

"No."

"Can you rent them?"

Again, I shrug. "Fuck if I know. If not, I'll buy one. Or I know a few people who have homes here along the river. One of them surely has a plane. We rich fuckers have all the toys." I wink at him while heading toward the porch door.

———

TWO HOURS LATER, we're in the air.

"God, I've missed this. I really should take more time to play," I say, surveying the winding river below.

Koen adjusts his headset and shoots me a quick grin. It's the biggest one I've seen from him. I would have done this weeks ago if I knew a little aircraft fun was all he needed to settle into our bromance.

"Have you taken Scottie flying?"

"Nope. I only took her virginity. I wanted to leave her with a few firsts for her husband to give her."

"Fuck you, Milloy." Koen laughs.

Like true bros, we go to lunch after we land to let our adrenaline rush subside. Koen says nothing about my salad or sixteen ounces of pressed juice until our empty plates and glasses are removed from the table.

"Do you think that's really curing you? Eating like a rabbit?"

"Curing me? Hell if I know." I dig cash out of my pocket and give him a headshake when he tries to pull money from his wallet. "But it's not killing me. It matters what fuel you put into your car or that plane. Changing the oil. Regular maintenance. Not pushing things past their limit. We respect the need to nurture gardens, house plants, and animals so they thrive instead of getting sick and dying. Yet, when it comes to humans and disease, we lose our minds and completely disregard common sense things such as good nutrition, mental and emotional nourishment, and reducing stress. So, sitting in a hospital with chemicals dripping into our veins becomes the norm because we've been led to believe it's the only option. And *it is* an option that sometimes works out.

"But listen, man, I have terminal cancer. Chemo and surgery don't have a good track record with my kind of cancer. So I have nothing to lose by eating like a rabbit. All this to say ... I've approached my diagnosis and grim prognosis with my eyes wide open. I've researched and questioned everything, as everyone should, because only then can you make an informed decision."

Koen nods slowly. "Had they told you the chemo would give you another five years, would you have made the same decision?"

I lift a shoulder. "Possibly. But I don't know. No matter how much you try to imagine what you would do in a situation, you don't know until you're in it. And I don't know how long I'll live. I'm taking it a day at a time. But I was told that without treatment, I had three months at best. Listen ... I'm living on borrowed time."

CHAPTER

twenty-nine

You know he's the one when he loves your greatest weakness like it's your greatest strength.

Scottie

IT'S Koen's first time in Philly, and he's meeting my family. It's my first time leaving Price in complete control of the store, and I don't know who's more nervous.

"They're going to love you." I turn toward him just as we reach the front door to their brownstone townhome in Society Hill.

He glances up. "Are all three levels theirs?"

"Yes."

"And you live in a trailer." He grins, shaking his head.

Before I reach for the door handle, he nuzzles my neck. "If your dad says no, I just want you to know I'll always remember you."

I giggle, squirming because his scruffy face tickles me.

"Maybe don't lead with how you want me to can tomatoes and pop out babies. Let him figure that out in real time."

"Noted."

I open the door.

"Sweetheart!" My mother saunters toward us in her wide-leg jeans and long-sleeved, ruffle-front blouse. Her chin-length silver hair is tucked behind one ear.

"Hey, Mom. So good to see you." I enjoy her warm embrace.

Koen's right. Good mothers should be treasured. Mine wasn't home with me, but I always felt her love, and she's always been nurturing. That's what makes her such an amazing doctor, too.

"Mom, this is Koen. Koen, this is my mom, Caitlyn."

"Dr. Rucker, it's a pleasure to meet you." Koen offers his hand.

She gives me an approving nod before returning her attention to him. "I'm only Dr. Rucker if you need a medical consult." She winks at Koen and bypasses his proffered hand in favor of a hug. "But if you're in love with my daughter, you should call me Caitlyn."

Koen doesn't give me a second glance when she releases him. With a confident smile, he nods. "Caitlyn, I love your daughter very much."

My mom's usually controlled with her emotions, but Koen has her fighting a few tears.

I hug his chest and kiss his jaw.

"Thought I heard the door open." Dad makes his way down the hardwood stairs that have an old runner rug down the middle of them. They added it after my sister took a tumble and had to get ten stitches in her head.

"Hey, Dad." I give him a quick hug. "This is Koen."

He offers Koen his hand. "Denny Rucker. Nice to meet you, young man." Dad tucks his hands into the pockets of his cargo shorts, which he's paired with a "Tree Hugger" green T-shirt. His signature white socks are pulled halfway up his knobby shins.

And much like Koen's usual attire, Dad's sporting a baseball hat. A red Phillies hat.

"Likewise, sir." Koen's comfortable. Too comfortable. It's not natural.

"Southern boy." Dad winks at me. "Well done, Scottie. But you should call me Denny. Come on in. Can I get you something to drink? Beer? Whisky? Wine?"

"I'm five years sober. Water works great. Thanks."

My heart squeezes until my whole chest aches. I'm in love with a man who is confident and honest. Owning his imperfections only makes him more perfect in my eyes.

Mom loops her arm around mine as we follow Dad and Koen to the kitchen. "He's cute, Scottie," she whispers with the giddiness of a girlfriend instead of my mom.

My grin swells. "Yes, he is."

Koen tosses me a curious glance over his shoulder, those blue eyes alight with curiosity.

"Mom and I were just discussing how homely-looking you are, babe."

"Oh, Scottie Ann Rucker. That is not true." Mom releases me and pats Koen on the back. "She's always been an ornery little thing. You've got your hands full with this one."

Deep satisfaction settles in his unwavering grin as I nod for him to sit in the horseshoe-shaped nook. Mom has three charcuterie trays on the table, enough for an army.

"So, what brings you two to Philly?" Mom asks. "I was surprised when Scottie announced your visit. We usually go to Austin." She eyes Koen, and he returns a smile.

For some reason, I don't trust that smile. What is going on?

Koen fills his plate with food. "I was hoping to speak to you, Denny, in private. But upon further consideration, I think tradition on this matter is a bit outdated. So I might as well take this moment to ask both of you." He eyes them with a stupid amount of confidence, and I realize it's happening.

Right here. Right now.

"Save the speech, son. You have our blessing. We've been waiting for this day." Dad doesn't skip a beat. "Take our daughter."

"Dad!" I cover my face while everyone laughs.

"Listen, my darling daughter," Dad grins at me when I drop my hands, "you have always walked your own path. I don't know why this young man thinks our opinions matter. And they shouldn't. One day, we won't be here, and I want to believe that you and Steph will be just fine without us and our opinions."

"But ..." Mom eggs him on as if they've carefully scripted this.

"But," Dad continues, "we knew if the day ever came that a man had the courtesy to ask for your hand in marriage, he would be *the one* just for having that good sense of kindness and respect."

My jaw hangs open, my eyes unblinking while stuttered thoughts struggle to line up into coherent sentences. "Y-you didn't even act surprised? I told Mom I had met someone special, but I didn't say more."

Mom hides her knowing grin behind her glass of red wine. "I knew because it's been forever since you've thought of a man in your life as 'special.' And I'm your mother. I could tell just from the tone of your voice. So I told your dad last week that you were coming home to introduce us to your future husband."

The room falls silent, all eyes on me. This makes no sense. My mother is a lot of things, but she's not one to read my tone on a phone call.

"Or ..." Koen angles his body toward me, and my mom squeezes my dad's arm, tears in her eyes. "I might have stolen your parents' number from your phone. I might have already had a long talk with both of them." He pulls a ring out of his pocket. "I might already have their blessing. Might you be interested in being my wife, Scottie Ann Rucker, the love of my life?"

Sneak-y Pete.

I shake my head. He knows the answer.

"Is that a no?" Koen feigns shock.

"I need to think about it."

Through the corner of my eye, my parents' faces are crestfallen.

Good. They can wallow in their deceitfulness for a few seconds.

"I'm done thinking. I'll marry you." I press my hands to Koen's cheeks and kiss him.

My mom claps her hands like a circus monkey.

"Sure you don't want to change your mind, Koen?" Dad asks. "If she's yanking your chain like that now, just imagine what you're in for twenty years down the road."

Koen slips the ring on my finger and grins at me. "I think I'm in for a pretty great life."

———

After a celebratory dinner at a nice restaurant, my parents head to bed, and Koen follows me to my bedroom, stopping at the door with his bag in one hand and his other hand scratching his head. "Which bedroom is mine?"

I toss my bag onto the floor and turn toward him. "Are you serious?"

"No premarital sex."

"What makes you think I'd have sex with you in my parents' house? Are you incapable of sleeping *next* to me instead of inside me?"

Koen steps into the bedroom and drops his bag next to mine. "My dick is like my other dog, well-trained. It is you who can't be trusted."

I roll my eyes before checking my phone.

"Call him," Koen says, closing the bedroom door.

"Who?"

"Price. Who else?" He hooks my waist and sits on the edge of the bed with me on his lap.

"I'm just ... checking my email."

"If you don't call him soon, he won't be at the store, which means you won't be able to reach him until tomorrow."

"Why do I need to call him?"

"Because he's watching my dog, and we need to know if he's taking good care of my Scrotum."

I grin, resting the side of my head against his. Koen

knows I'm concerned, but he knows I'm afraid to show my concern. And he's giving me an out.

God, I love this man.

"You're right. We can't let anything happen to your Scrotum."

"We really should start thinking of him as *our* Scrotum. Don't you think?"

Turning my head a fraction, I kiss his cheek. "I thought you'd never ask."

I call the store and put it on speaker.

"Drummond's General Store. Price speaking."

"Hi," I say in a fake voice. "I was wondering if you have anything for bad gas during sex?"

Koen snorts.

"As a matter of fact, I do. But the store is closed until tomorrow. However, if you have cayenne pepper and vapor rub at home, you can mix equal parts and rub it on your anus in a counterclockwise motion, and that should take care of it."

Koen presses his fist to his mouth and shakes with silent laughter.

"I'm worried about you," I say in my normal voice.

Price chuckles. "Me? I'm worried about you having gas during sex. Or are you calling for Koen?"

"Fuck you," Koen says.

"Oh, hey, buddy! How's your first time in Philly going?"

"My parents love him," I say, pinching Koen's cheek.

"I'm not surprised. He's spirited. And fiery. You know ... because he's a welder. Did you guys catch that pun?"

"Hilarious," Koen says.

"Did Scrot do okay at the store with you?" I ask.

"Other than the display of chocolate he ate, yes, he did just fine."

"I'm already regretting checking in on you, but Koen's been missing his BFF and copilot, so I said we could call before you left for home."

"Well, kids, I'm fine. Still kicking. I walked the mutt this morning, and I'll let him piss in my yard before bed. So take your time. No need to rush back to fragile old me. A little terminal cancer never hurt anyone."

I feel Koen's gaze on me as tears well in my eyes. "I ..." My voice cracks while attempting to clear the emotion from my throat, but it's lodged too deeply.

"Kiss my Scrotum for me, would ya?" Koen asks, saving me from drowning.

Price laughs.

"Welp, it's late." Koen squeezes my waist a little tighter as I struggle to keep a semblance of composure. "We love ya, buddy. Goodnight." He ends the call before Price can respond.

I cup a hand over my mouth and choke on a sob. Did Koen really just say that? Did my future husband feel my desperation and tell my first love, "We love ya?"

He's too good for me. I don't deserve Koen Sikes.

Sobs continue to wrack my body. Koen leans us back on the bed and strokes my hair while I make a teary mess of his shirt. And he does all this without knowing the true depths of my despair. I need to tell Price the truth. This is killing me.

As I catch my breath and the last of my tears release, the tide of my emotions shifts from grief to gratitude.

From gratitude to love.

From love to need.

I slide my hands along his chest and kiss his neck. "I never thought I could love someone..." my mouth brushes his ear "...more than I loved him." As my lips hover over his, and he gazes into my tired, swollen eyes, I whisper, "I was so very wrong."

Koen gives me the hint of a smile while his fingers brush hair away from my eyes. "He's a good person. And he's my friend, too."

A few more tears sneak out and down my face. "I need you."

"You have me."

I shake my head. "I *need* you."

His gaze searches mine. I don't want him to make me laugh or beg.

And he doesn't.

With tenderness and patience, he removes our clothes. His touch eases the pain.

His kiss stops time.

His whispered words give me hope.

And his naked body intertwined with mine is how I want to spend the rest of my life.

"I get to do this to you for eternity," he mumbles before sucking my nipple and teasing it with his teeth.

"Do what?" I whisper, slowly writhing beneath him, needing him inside of me.

"You know, baby ..." He deposits wet kisses down my body, inching himself lower until his hands grip my legs, spreading them wide. "This. I fucking get to do this to you forever."

My breath catches when his tongue teases me, wet and warm between my legs.

When his finger slides inside of me, I close my eyes,

squeezing my breasts, mouth opening to accommodate the growing intensity of each breath.

He adds a second finger.

"God ... YESSS ..."

There's no way I can chase my response and muzzle it before it reaches my parents' bedroom.

Euphoria wins.

Pleasure ripples through me, leaving my skin warm and flushed. He crawls up my body, dragging his lips along my skin.

Kissing.

Teasing.

"Koen." I sigh, feeling content and sleepy.

"More?" The head of his erection presses between my legs while he hovers above me, wet lips brushing mine.

He knows that answer.

And I know when he penetrates me with a firm thrust, it's going to be an awkward morning with my parents.

———

MY DAD's coffee grinder brings me out of my slumber.

"Scottie *Sikes*," Koen says, staring at the ceiling, hands laced behind his head.

"Not yet." I grin, rolling toward him, fingers teasing his bare chest.

"I'm just taking it for a test run."

"What do you think?"

"Koen, Scottie, and Scrotum Sikes. It has a nice ring to it."

I chuckle. "I will name our kids. Understood?"

"Come here."

"Where?"

He reaches for my waist, pulling me on top of him.

"Here?" I grin, straddling his chest and combing my fingers through my hair.

Koen's gaze affixes to my breasts. "Not quite." His hands grip my hips, scooting me lower until his erection slides between my legs.

I lift an eyebrow.

He grins. "Baby, can you be quiet this time?" His hips lift until he's inside of me.

I bite my bottom lip to suppress my moan before relinquishing a tiny nod. My hands rest on his chest as I move slowly with him. I have a beautiful ring on my finger, a future far beyond my simple dreams, and a man who has redefined love for me. This life is everything.

CHAPTER
thirty

Life is eternal, even if living is not.

I FIND my parents and Koen laughing and chatting in the kitchen after I shower. This guy ...

Who meets a woman's parents, proposes, makes her cry out in bed, and saunters downstairs for breakfast without a care in the world?

My future husband. That's who.

"Are you feeding my sausage-eating fiancé oatmeal and blueberries?" I grin, sliding into the nook next to him.

My parents, wrapped in matching white robes, laugh.

When I make eye contact with my mom, she smirks.

Oh god ... she heard.

"I just asked your mom and dad where they get their protein."

My dad winks at me while drinking what looks like a large glass of celery juice.

"Yeah. I'm sure you were." I rest my hand on his leg and lean in to kiss him.

Excitement radiates from my parents. I love that they're so happy for us and not upset that we were a bit loud last night.

"I think I'm going to show Koen around town today since I want to run a few errands," I announce, reaching for the cup of tea Mom made for me.

"Sorry. I already invited him to work with me. I have a new growing medium I want to show him." Dad eyes me like he's called dibs.

Koen shrugs. "Sorry, babe. Maybe tomorrow?"

"Fine," I fake grumble. "What about you, Mom?"

"Sorry, love. I have a consult in an hour. Maybe we can meet for lunch? In fact," she glances at her watch, "I need to get dressed and get going. Why don't you drop me off, and then you can use my car today."

"Sounds great." I give Koen one last kiss. "Don't have too much fun playing in the dirt with my dad."

He winks.

"If I can shift a few things in my schedule this afternoon, we can pop into a few bridal stores," Mom suggests, rinsing her glass at the sink.

Koen beams. There's no other word.

I return a smile that mirrors his. "I'd love that."

———

AFTER I DROP my mom off at work, curiosity leads me back to my favorite apothecary. I'm surprised it stayed open after so much economic uncertainty over the past ten years.

"Can I help you with anything?" a woman with brown skin, blonde dreads, and gold ear gauges asks while she waters the plants.

"I'm just checking things out. I used to work here."

"Oh, really? How long ago was that? I've been managing it for seven years."

"Twelve years ago. Do the Kettlemans still own it? Margaret gave me my first job here. I was sixteen." I twist the cap off one of the tester bottles and wave it under my nose.

"No. They sold it. The new owner hired me to manage it. I pretty much do everything."

I chuckle. "I know how you feel."

"I don't mind. I make twice as much as I did at my last job." She slides the stepladder a few feet to the right. "Do you still live around here?"

"No. I live in Austin." I admire the propagation wall. "Do you go to tradeshows with the new owner? I got to go to one with Margaret. It was so much fun."

She laughs. "Mr. Milloy doesn't go to tradeshows. I see him in person once or twice a year, is all."

I slowly turn toward her. "Mr. Milloy?"

She climbs down and sets the watering can behind the counter. "Yes."

With a hard swallow, I offer a nervous smile. "Price Milloy?"

"Yeah. You know him?"

Why does everything about that man make my heart ache? A good ache. A bad ache. And everything in between.

"I uh ... yeah. I know him. Knew him."

"I don't know him that well, but he's been very generous to me. Edward Goff, who owns the coffee shop across the street, said he's a successful banker or some sort of investment guy. And his wife's with a big advertising firm. But you probably know that."

I narrow my eyes. "Edward's wife?"

"No. Mr. Milloy's."

———

BY THE TIME I make it to my mom's car, I can barely catch my breath. Did I even say goodbye to the woman at the store?

Price is married.

No. *Was* married.

There's no way he's married now. A married man doesn't receive a cancer diagnosis and leave his wife to find his first love.

Why?

Why would he not tell me about her? It's been twelve years. I never expected him to remain single, even though I did.

Finding an address for Price Milloy in Rittenhouse Square doesn't take long. I check the time. I have an hour and a half before picking up my mom for lunch—plenty of time to drive by his place.

When I get there, I can't resist parking down the street and walking to the entrance. He's living in Austin. Surely, he sold this residence. Yet, I can't walk away until I know for sure.

I press the security buzzer to the high-class condo. Seconds later, a woman answers softly, "Yes?"

"Uh, hi. I'm looking for Price Milloy."

Nothing.

Maybe the speaker's broken.

"I'm sorry. He's unavailable."

"Oh. I'm an ... I'm an old friend visiting my family here for the next day or two, and I thought I'd surprise him. Are you his wife?"

"Yes."

"Do you know when he'll be home?"

Another long pause.

Then I hear what sounds like a sniffle.

"Can I come in?" I ask.

Again, she sniffles. "I'm sorry. He's not here. And I have to go get our daughter and take her to an appointment soon."

Our daughter ...

This isn't real.

I take a step away from the building.

Our daughter ...

I shake my head.

Our daughter ...

Somehow, I manage to return to my car where I sit staring at his place for the next hour. My thoughts die as tiny, muffled echoes before they reach my true consciousness. It's been twelve years since the pain has been so severe that my whole body surrenders until I feel numb. When I can no longer feel anything, and the well of tears runs dry, I put the car in drive to pick up my mom for lunch.

"Hey! How was your morning?" She hops in and

shuts the door. But the second she sees my face, her smile vanishes. "Scottie, have you been crying?"

I narrow my eyes as if I don't understand her question.

"Scottie?"

"He has a child," I whisper.

"Who has a child?"

"A daughter."

"Scottie." Mom rests her hand on my leg. "Who? What are you talking about?"

Three people know—my mom, dad, and sister.

And I don't want to see the look on her face when I tell her, but it's unavoidable now. So many things are unavoidable now. Life is eternal even if living is not. The past can never be erased or forgotten.

"Price."

Deep lines trench across my mom's forehead. "Sweetie, you saw Price today?"

I slowly shake my head, feeling eerily calm and resigned. "Price is in Austin. He works part-time at Drummond's."

"What?" Her confusion intensifies.

"He showed up, seemingly out of nowhere. He was diagnosed with terminal cancer. And he moved to Austin ... for me."

"Scottie, you're not making any sense. Price Milloy is in Austin?"

"He left Philly. He left his doctors and their advice. And he searched for me."

"He has ... cancer?"

I nod once.

"And what does he expect you to do for him?"

I meet her gaze, and the pain begins to dissolve the numbness. With a shrug, I murmur, "I don't know. Be his friend. Love him. Accept him and his decision not to do chemo."

"His decision to die?"

My brow furrows. "His decision to live."

"Did he get a second opinion?"

"I don't know."

"Did you tell him—"

I shake my head. "He's healing."

"Is he seeing doctors there?"

"No."

"Then you know he's not healing. Tell me you know that."

I give her a sad smile. "I don't know that. What if he is? He believes he is."

She frowns.

"But I ... I didn't know. He has a wife and a daughter."

"What kind of man leaves his family like that? Do they know about his cancer?"

Again, I slowly shake my head. "Mom, I didn't know until today that he has a wife and child."

She squeezes my hand. "Does Koen know about Price?"

With a nod, I gaze into the rearview mirror at the car behind me. "I have to go home."

"What about dress shopping?"

"I can't think about the future until I fix the past."

———

SEVERAL HOURS LATER, Koen and my dad return home. While my mom makes dinner, I take a hot bath. After two soft knocks on the bathroom door, Koen cracks it open.

"There's my beautiful bride. Do you think it's bad form for me to join you when your parents are just a flight of stairs away?"

My gaze lifts to his.

"Why the sad face?" He sits on the edge of the tub.

"Price has a wife ... and a daughter."

Koen's eyebrows draw together. "He what?"

I'm back to feeling numb. I've been in and out of this state all afternoon.

"Did you call him?"

"No." Even my voice is numb and lifeless. "What would I say? Hey, did you know you have a wife and child?"

"More like, what the fuck are you doing?"

I grunt a painful laugh. "I'll let you have that conversation with him."

"What will your conversation with him be? Don't pretend you're not going to say anything."

Here it comes, that wave of emotion that's been out to sea for the past few hours. It's ready to crash onto the shore, and I can do nothing to stop it because I can no longer keep this from Koen.

The tears come fast and hard before I get the first word out of my mouth. "I'm going to tell him about the baby."

CHAPTER

thirty-one

Because of you, I have her.

Price

I MIGHT GET A DOG. Or steal this one.

Before I can formulate possible ways to keep another man's Scrotum, there's a knock at the door.

Scrot jumps off the sofa when I get up to answer. "They're taking you back. Don't tell them how many apples I've fed you."

When I open the door, Scrot runs straight to Koen, standing several feet behind Scottie. She stares at my chest with a somber expression.

I glance at my shirt. Is there something on it?

"Call me when you're ready," Koen says, adjusting his baseball hat.

She doesn't respond.

"Thanks for watching him." Koen doesn't make eye contact with me either before leading Scrot to the truck.

As soon as he begins to back out of my driveway, Scottie asks, "Can I come in?"

"He's leaving you, so I'm inclined to say yes. It's just good manners." I laugh.

She does not.

What's happening?

"Who died? It wasn't me. Not yet anyway." When I turn back toward her, Scottie slowly lifts her gaze.

In a blink, tears fill her eyes.

I step toward her, and she shakes her head, holding up a flat palm. "Don't."

"Scottie, what is it?"

"I almost died."

"What?"

She looks fine. No cuts or visible bruises. Her gray off-the-shoulder blouse looks okay, but she does have a hole in the knee of her baggy jeans. I'd let my mind make pointless observations about her all day if I thought it might keep her from delivering the awful news she's prepared for me.

"We broke up. You went back to school. And I was heartbroken. I thought you'd come for me. I thought you'd tell me how stupid I was to let us end, but you didn't."

"Scottie—"

Again, she cuts me off with a headshake. "I missed my period, but I thought it was stress, and my periods were often irregular. After all, we were careful. Eventually, I started bleeding. At first, I thought it was finally my period, but things weren't right. I felt so sick. I stayed in bed for two days before I called my mom. She wasn't too far from my apartment, but I lost consciousness before she got there. I almost died." She wipes her face.

The last time I felt like this was when a second doctor confirmed my cancer diagnosis.

My need to hold her is unbearable.

"It was an ectopic pregnancy." Her lower lip quivers while she sniffles. "I was pregnant with your baby. And I thought losing it was fate because you didn't fight for me. You didn't come back for me. Losing the baby was confirmation that what we had wasn't meant to be. Everything we had together ... died."

"Scottie," I whisper. This fucking hurts. "Why didn't you tell me?"

"I would have." She laughs through her tears. "Trust me; I would have if I wouldn't have lost the baby. I would have knocked on your door and told you it was our sign to be together. Do you know how many times I've thought about us over the past twelve years? How many times I've imagined what it would have been like to be with you? To have a family with you? And then you showed up out of nowhere. And I was elated to see you, and you seemed happy to see me too, but not in the same way. So, once again, I felt rejected. Then Koen came along and took my heart so completely it no longer longed for you."

She shrugs. "And I thought you'd have this spark of jealousy, but you didn't. Then, I concluded you simply never loved me the way I loved you. And for once, it no longer mattered because I'd met Koen. When you meet *the one*, every other star in the sky fades."

I rub my face, leaving my hand over my mouth while slowly shaking my head. "I've thought about you—"

"No." She balls her fists. "You thought about me when you thought you were dying. And I can't tell you," she presses her fisted hand to her chest, "how that makes me feel." When she starts to speak, her words catch, and she releases more tears. "I f-felt ... I f-feel so honored t-to be that person. I left Philly t-to get away f-from everything that reminded me of y-you. But distance d-didn't matter."

"Scottie, we made a baby," I whisper because I need to say the words aloud for myself. And I need her to know how deeply I feel her confession. "I would have wanted that life with you."

She casts her gaze to the floor between us, eyes narrowed. "You have that life ... just not with me."

In the next breath, her eyes are on me. "You *did* love me. But ..." Her face wrinkles in pain. "You have a wife and daughter."

My lungs deflate. And I feel *everything*.

A painful longing.

A hollowed heart.

Regret.

And shame.

"Yes," I manage to say past my constricted throat.

"Do you love them?"

"Unequivocally." Emotion blurs my vision.

Scottie runs her hands through her hair, cheeks stained red and covered in tears. Then she averts her gaze to the side, wiping her eyes with her sleeve. When she looks at me again, I know she sees everything.

And then ... her arms wrap around me.

At first, I don't move.

Then, I don't breathe, trying to ward off the pain.

I lose.

My body shakes while I hug Scottie like I want to squeeze us into one person. And then ... I cry.

CHAPTER

thirty-two

Paris will have to wait.

Five Months Earlier ...

"HAPPY ANNIVERSARY." Amelia wakes me with breakfast in bed. The sun's not up. Astrid's still asleep. And my five o'clock alarm hasn't gone off yet.

Who am I kidding? It's the middle of the night.

Our bedroom smells like bacon and eggs, and my beautiful wife of ten years is wearing the sexiest pink lingerie I have ever seen. I rub my eyes and sit up in our bed while she places the wood tray of food over my lap, covered in white sheets and a soft blue linen blanket. She gathers her slightly tangled blonde hair and pulls it over one shoulder while giving me a giddy, wide-eyed look.

I love that look—usually.

I stare at the food. The eggs over-easy. The bacon from a turkey. The toast on the dark side. A small bowl of blueberries. And coffee black.

223

My favorites—usually.

"Not hungry?" She pouts at the prospect of me not feeling hungry in the middle of the night. I glance at my phone on the nightstand, reaching over to tap the screen —three a.m.

I haven't had much of an appetite in weeks. My five a.m. alarm calls have been snoozed every nine minutes until nearly seven in the morning. That's when I fly out of bed, grab coffee, and break all the speed limits on my way to work.

"If you want me to eat, move the tray and take that pink thing off." I'm not a hundred percent sure I can get it up or give her that kind of orgasm. But I feel like those odds are better than bacon and eggs.

Amelia smirks, taking a bite of the bacon before bringing it to my lips. The smell makes my stomach roil, but I take a tiny bite and manage to keep it down with a stiff smile.

"As much as it would be my pleasure to feed you this morning, I want to be the giver. We'll renegotiate later when we go to bed." She sets the tray aside.

Trapping her lower lip between her teeth, she works my underwear down my legs and situates herself between them, hands on my thighs as her tongue makes its first stroke. I close my eyes and focus on what feels good since that hasn't been much lately.

The good news? My dick hasn't gotten the memo that the rest of my body has gone on strike.

Twenty minutes, a partial blowjob, and a helluva bull ride later, she's naked, satiated, draped across my chest, and drifting off to sleep.

However, I can't sleep. It's taking everything I have not

to push her off me because I am not well. Eventually, my alarm saves me, and she automatically rolls to the side, freeing me to get out of bed.

If it were any other day, I'd stay home. But Amelia loves celebrations, and I don't want to disappoint her. So, I pop a few over-the-counter pain pills and go to work.

By noon, I'm past my breaking point and making a poor decision to drive myself to the hospital.

"Can I call someone for you?" the nurse asks while I restlessly wait for the doctor.

"No." There's no need to worry my wife on our anniversary if I'm just passing a kidney stone or something benignly delightful like that.

Hours later, after poking, prodding, scanning, and administering stronger pain medication, I head home with less discomfort but no answers.

Amelia makes her way down the stairs in a stunning emerald gown, blonde hair in loose curls, and nude lips perfectly glossed. "Don't tell me where you made dinner reservations; I want to be surprised. Just tell me if we're staying in town tonight or jetting off to another destination so I can let Hillary know when she gets here to stay with Astrid. And ..." When she reaches the bottom of the stairs, she holds out a black box with a white satin ribbon. "I know we don't usually exchange gifts until after dinner, but I couldn't wait to give you yours."

Dinner.

Gift.

I smile, praying to God that she doesn't see through my silent agony for having fucked everything up. In the box is a new gold watch.

"Since you lost the one your mom gave you."

My gaze lifts from the watch to her glimmering, soft blue eyes. She's so beautiful.

"Thank you."

She gives me a peck on the lips and wipes her gloss from my mouth with the pad of her thumb. "So, will we be back here tonight? I'll call Hillary while you're in the shower."

"We're staying in town. I hope that's okay."

"Of course. I know whatever you have planned will be spectacular." Her heels click along the white marble floor toward the kitchen while I drag myself up the curved staircase for a shower.

After closing the bedroom door, I call my assistant. "Megan, I need a huge favor. It's my anniversary, and I have nothing planned and no gift for my wife."

"Oh, uh ..."

Of course, she's caught off guard because I've used her for a million things. Still, I've never been the guy who asks his assistant to remember birthdays or anniversaries, buy gifts, or make reservations at the last possible minute.

"I'm sorry, but—"

"Nope," she chirps. "I've got it all handled. Are you staying in Philly?"

"Yes." I remove my already loose tie.

"Great. Can you give me ten minutes?"

I love her. She's getting a raise first thing in the morning. "Yes. I need to shower and dress."

"Keep your phone close; I'll send you all the details."

"Thank you, Megan. You are truly the best."

"Of course, Mr. Milloy."

I PULL IT OFF. Well, Megan pulls it off. A chef's table dinner at a new French restaurant and tickets to George Frideric Handel's *Julius Caesar*.

"Oh my god, Price! I can't believe you're taking me to an opera," she covers her mouth, "in Paris."

That makes two of us. I'm not a fan of the opera or Paris. And I now have mixed feelings about Megan. I thought she liked me better than this. Now, I'm forced to rethink her raise.

"I love you so much." Amelia stands to lean over the table and kiss me.

I smile when she sits back in her chair and adjusts her dress. "I love you, too, sweetheart."

She sips her champagne, eyes narrowing a bit before she sets it back on the table. "I've noticed you haven't been yourself lately. I know you say it's stress at work, but you've been sluggish, and your skin is pasty."

"I'm sure it's the lighting."

"No." She shakes her head. "I've noticed it at home too. When's the last time you had a physical?"

I watch the chef carefully place a sprig of rosemary beside two lamb chops. "I don't know." I lie.

When I know more, I'll tell her about my trip to the ER earlier today. But until I know something concrete, there's no need to worry her.

"Well, I think you should schedule something. It might just be a virus. That would explain your fatigue."

I nod several times while shifting my attention back to her. "I'm sure that's it. But I'll have it checked out if I don't feel better soon."

CHAPTER
thirty-three

Does "okay" have a real definition?

A WEEK LATER, I get the call.

The test results are back, and none too soon. I have no energy. Dragging my ass out of bed every morning has felt like running back-to-back marathons for a whole week. I'm basing this off the three that I've run in a span of five years. Honestly, I'd rather run the damn marathon than deal with whatever this is.

"Can we talk?" I ask when Amelia opens the door after dropping Astrid off at school.

She jumps. "You scared me!"

"Sorry."

After slipping off her cream wool coat, revealing her pink jogging suit, she folds it over the back of the white sage upholstered dining room chair. Rays of morning sun cut through the snow-flocked trees, searching for places to rest, like the empty Knotty Alder hardwood table and the matte black built-in buffet filled with dishes we never use.

Things ...

This thirteen-million-dollar home is filled with so many things that don't mean a thing.

"Why are you still home?" She sits beside me.

I stare at the half-filled glass of water in front of me, the one I used to take down a few pain pills minutes earlier.

"I didn't want to worry you." I reach for her hand. "And I still don't. But last week, I wasn't feeling well..." I laugh. "Let me rephrase, I was feeling fucking awful."

Her brow furrows as she squeezes my hand.

"So I went to the ER—"

"Price—"

"No. Please, let me finish. It was on our anniversary, and I didn't want to ruin it, so I got checked out. They gave me something for the pain. And I've been waiting to hear back on the test results. They're in now. I have an appointment this afternoon. I don't know what they're going to say. Perhaps nothing. Maybe it's a virus. Or something related to stress. But I want you to come with me."

She nods over and over. "Of course. It's fine. You're fine." But the look on her face conveys anything but fine.

I try a little harder, finding something more believable when I smile. "I know. It's ridiculous that they can't just tell me over the phone. We'll pick up Astrid after the appointment and go out to dinner to celebrate it being something very minor."

Amelia's eyes fill with tears, but she continues to nod.

Just as I start to speak, my phone rings. "It's Megan." I hold it up for her to see before heading toward my study.

"Sorry to bother you."

"It's fine. What's up?"

"Malcolm Herring wasn't happy about rescheduling his appointment with you. He flew in last night from LA. He said he's taking his business somewhere else. I wasn't going to call you, but Alex said to—"

"No. It's fine." I rub my temples, collapsing into my desk chair. "I'll deal with him."

"What do you want me to tell Alex?"

"Nothing. I'll deal with him too."

"Okay. I hope you feel better."

Me too.

"Thanks, Megan."

I toss my phone on the desk. This room has no window, just floor-to-ceiling shelves stuffed with books I have never read. The wood is too dark, and the paint is a godawful shade of dark green. This is my least favorite room in our home, but I can't bring myself to leave it because the woman I love is on the other side of that door. And the look in her eyes is the same look she had when we put her cat down a year after we married.

So I do what any mortal man in my shoes would do: I hide in here until it's time to go to my appointment. The fact that Amelia never comes in here to check on me says a lot.

She's just as fucking terrified as I am.

———

ON THE WAY to the appointment, my wife keeps a tight grip on my hand, only letting go long enough to get out of the car when we arrive at the doctor's office in the hospital's north wing.

By the time we're seated in his office, Amelia has picked off every last speck of her red nail polish. She balls her hands into fists and gives me a sad, guilty smile when I glance at them.

I angle my body to hers, uncurling her tight fingers so I can hold both hands. "It's going to be okay."

Holding her breath and a painful well of emotions captive in her red-rimmed eyes, she nods.

"I mean it. No matter what news we're given, our family will be okay. You and Astrid will be okay. *I* will be okay."

Her nodding turns into head shaking. "How can you say that? What if you're not okay?" She barely gets the words out.

"Because every single second of every single day is a gift. And I know this. I will be okay, no matter what we find out."

A tear makes its way down her cheek, and she wipes it just as the doctor enters the room—a balding man with a halo of gray hair, a clean-shaven face, and a polite smile.

"I'm Doctor Wills. Dr. Faber will be joining us in a bit. She's still on a call." He offers his hand.

"Price. And this is my wife, Amelia." We both shake his hand just before he pulls his desk chair closer to us.

Although I know he's not here to deliver good news, I'm still unprepared.

Unprepared to wrap my head around the word "cancer" as he says it.

My brain slows, capturing only the bad stuff.

Amelia's hand trembles as she reaches for me.

Dr. Wills's lips move, but I no longer want to hear him.

Cancer.

Biopsy.

Metastatic.

I go completely numb when Dr. Faber, the oncologist, joins us.

Stage four.

Chemotherapy.

Control symptoms.

Palliative.

"What questions can we answer for you?" Dr. Faber asks, brushing her thin brown hair away from her eyes. She looks about our age and can surely put herself in our shoes.

Questions? I've got nothing.

"How long?" Amelia asks.

"Until we confirm with a biopsy—"

"HOW LONG?"

"Sweetheart," I say, squeezing her leg gently.

Dr. Faber doesn't flinch. With a practiced expression that shows just the right amount of compassion and professionalism, she says, "There's a one percent five-year survival rate."

Amelia clears her throat, teeth clenched. "That's not what I'm asking."

Dr. Faber folds her delicate hands in her lap. "Maybe

six months to a year with treatment. Three months without."

Amelia's face wrinkles in disgust before a new round of tears escapes. I wrap my arm around her while she shakes with sobs, hiding her face in my chest.

"I can do the biopsy tomorrow," Dr. Faber says, looking at me. "We'll schedule it before you leave."

After a few seconds, I return a slight nod.

CHAPTER
thirty-four

Least likely to ... live.

IS THERE A PROTOCOL FOR THIS?

I've never thought about receiving a cancer diagnosis.

The key to the city? Sure.

Getting hit by a bus? Absolutely.

But not cancer.

If someone had asked me what I thought my chances were of cancer in my thirties, I would have said close to zero for plenty of naive reasons.

I'm too young.

I don't smoke.

I'm not diabetic.

None of my grandparents or parents have had cancer.

I exercise.

I eat a healthy diet.

Yet here I am with somewhere between three months to a year to live and a wife who's fading before my eyes. Is it normal for people with cancer to spend their time consoling those around them? Sometimes, I feel like I'm not her husband. I'm not the one with the cancer diagnosis. I'm just a friend—a shoulder to cry on.

"It's been four days. They said two to three," Amelia says over a mouthful of suds, brushing the hell out of her teeth.

I finish towel drying my hair from my shower and pick at the thin strips of paper tape over my biopsy site. "I'll call them in the morning."

"We're getting a second opinion."

She's mentioned this at least fifty times. I miss my even-keeled wife, who balanced my hyper-work drive with grace and patience. The woman who rocked our fussy daughter all night long for months, refusing to let me take a shift because she knew I had to work, and who swore Astrid was exactly where she needed to be—in her mother's arms.

Who was I to argue? Inside Amelia's embrace *is* the most incredible place on earth.

Now, she's either prematurely grieving my death or mad as hell at the whole world.

"A second opinion," I repeat with a submissive nod.

After she spits and places her toothbrush in its holder, she turns, leaning against the double vanity, hands on the edge of the counter, hair brushed into silky straight strands down her chest over her black nightie. "How are you feeling?" She asks me that almost as often as she brings up the second opinion.

I step into our spacious closet, which has black suits and white shirts on one side, colorful dresses, rows upon rows of shoes and handbags on the other, and an island of drawers in the center.

"I'm tired. But it's eleven at night." I pull on a pair of black briefs.

"That's not what I mean."

"Sweetheart, I honestly don't know what you mean."

"Are you in pain?"

I make my way to her, sliding my arms around her waist. "It pains me that you have to deal with any of this. It pains me that we have to put on a show around Astrid until we know with certainty. Then it will pain me to tell her. Life cannot be lived without pain."

Her blue eyes remain unblinking while she swallows hard. "It's a misdiagnosis. I know it. And we're going to be so glad we got a second opinion. You hear about it all the time. Someone gets diagnosed with cancer. They spend all of their money ticking things off their bucket list, only to find out they never had cancer."

I smile, pressing my lips to her forehead, and hum just the right way so she thinks I agree with her.

I don't.

It's a rare case that someone's misdiagnosed with stage four metastatic pancreatic cancer. Early-stage breast cancer? Maybe. Early-stage lung cancer? Perhaps.

Hope soothes her.

That hope will eventually run out. But for now, I let her have it.

"Let's go to bed." She wraps an arm around me as we head into the bedroom.

As soon as she's asleep, which has been taking a lot longer since my diagnosis, I slide out of bed and spend most of the night in my study researching cancer online.

There's no "cure" for what I have unless I buy into the stories of miraculous natural cures. Cancer is an insidious plague that we've come to accept as almost a "normal" part of life.

Tragic. But all too common.

Truth? I *am* looking for a miracle in the truest sense of the word. So, I go back to the basics.

What is cancer?

Why does it grow?

What do these "miraculous" cures have in common?

This is a rabbit hole deeper than the journey to the center of the earth. But time only matters to those who don't have much time left. So, I have to take this journey because I love my life.

My wife.

My daughter.

And I don't want to live a life where I know my time. If that bus hits me tomorrow, so be it. But I don't want to know today that tomorrow is my time.

———

By noon the next day, the biopsy results confirm the initial diagnosis. An hour later, Amelia has me scheduled for a second opinion.

I bite my tongue. Smile. And nod.

As much as I want to tell her we must be prepared to hear the same scenario, I don't. If I spend my nights researching miracles, it's okay for her to cling to any little scrap of hope she can find.

"*If* we don't get a better prognosis," she rolls toward me in bed while I read a book that arrived in the mail today, "then I say we start chemo as soon as possible."

I turn my head, eyeing her twisted lips and narrowed gaze. "I certainly hope 'we' are not starting chemo."

"You know what I mean." Her face relaxes while her hand slides along my chest. "And we have to discuss how we're going to tell Astrid. If you're sick or losing your hair, she'll know something's wrong."

While I'm glad that she's keeping an open mind to the nearly one-hundred-percent chance that the second opinion won't be any better than the first, I'm not sure why she thinks it's a foregone conclusion that I'm having chemo.

"I agree. We need to decide how we're going to approach this with Astrid. But I'm not having chemo."

Her face sours. "What are you talking about?"

"Why would I go through chemo?"

"Uh ... to live longer and maybe lessen your symptoms."

"But palliative chemo has side effects. Why would I totally give up on my body and accept a slow drip of chemicals in my veins for six months to a year? And not good months. Name one person you know who had an 'easy' time with chemo."

She lifts onto her elbow. "But what if it's more than a year? That's just a guess. Everyone is different. There is a one percent five-year survival rate. And I know ... honey, I *know* that feels like zero. But we have to believe in miracles."

I turn my book so she can see the cover. "You're right. This guy survived stage four colon cancer without chemo."

Amelia frowns. "You have pancreatic cancer that's in your liver too."

"I don't think it matters. His story isn't about the type of cancer. It's about his approach to cancer."

"Approach? What does that mean? How does one approach cancer?"

I slip the sticky note onto my page and close the book. "I think stress has caused my cancer, or at least has played a role in its growth."

"Then take some time off work."

I slide my book onto the nightstand and sit on the edge of the bed with my feet dangling off the side. "Amelia, I'm not *taking time off*. I've been given three months to a year to live. I'm simply not going back to work."

"It's *just a guess*."

I laugh, shaking my head. "Listen to yourself, baby. Either I'm going to die before our daughter learns how to drive and gets her first kiss, or something really fucking life-changing has to happen for me to have a prayer of beating the odds."

The mattress dips behind me, and I glance back at her sitting cross-legged in the middle of the bed, tears painting her cheeks.

"You h-have to f-fight."

I stand slowly, grabbing my aching back for a second before running my fingers through my hair. "What if I live instead of fight? What if I let go of everything? Sleep when I want to sleep. Only put things into my body that are good for it. Meditate. Spend time walking barefoot in the grass? Get rid of my phone, my computer, and the television. What if I took away everything that cancer loves? Starve it."

"Then the chemo would have a better chance." She wipes her tears and nods.

I deflate. "No. Not chemo."

"Price—" She shakes her head, pointing to the book. "That's bullshit. Maybe he didn't even have cancer. Or if he did, maybe it wasn't really stage four. If sleep and walking in the grass cured cancer, don't you think it would be all over the news?"

"No." I laugh, resting a hand on my hip. "I don't. But it doesn't matter, Amelia. This is what I want. I want this headache to go away. I want my back not to feel like a goddamn truck is sitting on it. I don't want to add more pain. And I don't want to die."

"Dr. Faber said it could help with the symptoms."

I blow out a long breath. I'm eternally tired. "If I do the chemo, I will die. If I don't do the chemo and keep doing my routine, I will die. My body is screaming for me to listen to it. Maybe *nothing* is the greatest *something* I can do right now. And it's what I want. Don't I get a say in what happens to my body?"

"How can you let Astrid watch you die without a fight?" She wipes more tears.

"What if I don't have to die?"

"Price, it's a year. A year might not seem like much, but I want every single second. A year is a lifetime to my heart, and it will be to Astrid's, too. If you don't do this for me, at least do it for her."

"Amelia, I am doing this for her *and* you! What if I don't have to die?"

Before she can speak through her soft sobs, our bedroom door cracks open.

"Mom?" Astrid shuffles her bare feet into our bedroom, rubbing her eyes behind the blonde hair hanging in her face. She's a miniature version of her mom.

Amelia quickly turns away to hide her emotions.

"Hey, sunshine. Sorry. Did I wake you?" I scoop her up, ignoring the searing pain in my back.

"Are you fighting?"

"No. We're not fighting. I'll tuck you back into bed."

"Can we read more of *Moon Over Manifest*?"

"We can read whatever you want." I kiss her head and carry her to her white canopy bed with a pink polka dot quilt and so many stuffed animals that I don't know where she finds room to sleep.

As soon as I toss her into the pile of animals, she giggles and hops out of bed, retrieving the book from her white and turquoise flowered bookshelf.

We manage to wedge ourselves into the tiny space, her tucked under my arm, one of my legs hanging off the side. By the time I get four pages past her marked spot in chapter seven, she's asleep.

I've wiped a lot of Amelia's tears since my diagnosis, but I haven't shed one of my own until now.

One tear.

Two tears.

Three, four, five tears.

They slowly descend my face, and I let the book drop

from my hand to the rug beneath her bed. Where did the time go?

"I'm pregnant!" Amelia squealed, leaping into my arms when I opened the door to our first apartment. It was a one-bedroom main-floor apartment with an old gray carpet and a few mice. "I know it's not the best timing, but—"

I kissed her to shut her up. The woman I loved more than any other human was pregnant with my baby. Fuck the timing.

"Are you sure?" I set her on her feet and kissed her again, unbuttoning her blouse.

She giggled.

"Because," I kissed down her neck, walking her backward toward the bedroom, "we should make sure you stay good and pregnant."

Her giggles multiplied as we lost all our clothes.

As we fell into bed.

As I filled her.

Then they stopped, replaced with soft moans. Her fingers curled into the muscles along my back. I ducked my head and sucked her breast, bringing her nipple into a hard pebble between my teeth.

She hissed. "Shit ... my nipples are sensitive."

"Sorry, baby." I softly kissed it.

She pushed at my chest, nudging me to roll onto my back. Amelia enjoyed being on top. And I fucking loved the view. I couldn't wait to see her riding me with a little baby belly.

I licked the pad of my thumb before pressing it between her legs right where she liked it. Her fingers tangled in her hair, eyelids heavy and intoxicated. I could come just looking at her.

"God, I love how deep you fill me." She hugged herself.

Played with her breasts.

Sucked her fingers and smeared saliva over her nipples. Taunting me. Reminding me I could no longer touch them.

My wife had no inhibitions. She was sexy as fuck and knew it.

I gripped her hips, thumbs caressing her belly. We were having a baby.

———

I MET *Amelia Havana Armstrong a month before I graduated from college. She was turning right in her red Mini Cooper; I was zooming through the intersection on a bike.*

Thunk!

I dented her Mini. She broke my arm and clavicle.

She always hated how I told the story, but it's how I remember the moment. As I stared at the partly cloudy sky, she and her golden blonde hair appeared above me like an angel. I heard harps and birds singing a heavenly tune.

I was dead. And that was good because the bike was my roommate's—a ten-thousand-dollar Cervélo.

She unfastened my helmet, throwing spinal injury caution to the wind.

Pinched my nose.

And covered my mouth with hers, blowing entirely too much air into my lungs while I tried to exhale.

I coughed. She coughed.

"Oh, thank god you're alive! Someone call 9-1-1," she yelled, not leaving my side. "I'm so sorry. Reeeally sorry. You came out of nowhere. And the sun was bright, and ... oh god ... what if you don't make it? I'm so sorry."

Jesus, I thought. How bad was it?

I could wiggle my toes and most of my fingers. My left digits were a little more of a challenge.

"My ... arm ..." I gritted past the pain.

"This one?" She lifted it off the ground.

"FUCK!" I cried.

"Oh, god! Sorry." She wrinkled her nose, resting my arm on the ground as I began to pant and moan like the injured wildebeest taken down by an African wild dog I'd watched on a National Geographic documentary.

"If you live, please don't sue me," she whispered an inch from my face, her hair tickling my cheeks. "My dad said he'd cut me off if I got one more moving violation. And I don't know where hitting a biker falls, but I was moving in my car, so ..."

"Miss, can you give us some room?" the police officer said as more sirens sounded in the distance.

"Listen, I work at a big PR firm. I can get you the best tickets to the Eagles, the 76ers, or the Phillies. I'm talking VIP seating. How does that sound?"

She smelled like a flower. Not a rose, more like my favorite fabric softener scent. Maybe honeysuckle?

"Miss, please step aside."

"I'll meet you at the hospital. We'll get this all figured out." Her smile reached her blue eyes, one with a tiny brown mole just below her lashes on her cheek.

Amelia remained at the hospital for both nights of my stay despite discovering my father was an attorney. She brought me food, flowers, balloons, and tickets to all the best games. During my recovery, she dropped food off at my parents' house and offered to help me across the stage if I needed assistance receiving my diploma.

My dad quickly determined we weren't suing her because my mom was already planning our wedding. "Nicest young lady we have ever met," they concluded. "And she's one hell of a cook."

A week into physical therapy, I asked her out on a date—I drove.

Three months later, I proposed.

CHAPTER

thirty-five

Dying to laugh.

"You saved my life, only to watch me die," I say.

Amelia doesn't turn. She continues cutting up the pineapple on the cutting board. It's nine on a Saturday. I'm still exhausted, stiff, and sore from sleeping with Astrid all night, but it was worth it to have her in my arms for so long.

"She still asleep?"

"Yes." I wrap my arms around her, resting my chin on her shoulder.

She pauses her cutting for a second before resuming. "How did I save your life?"

"The day we met, you performed CPR."

"Stop," she says. "I'm not doing this. You're not going to make me laugh—not this time. It's no longer funny."

"It will always be funny, baby. All those years of watching *Grey's Anatomy* paid off."

"Except you were breathing."

I release her, but I don't miss her tiny smile.

"It was the thought that counts. And our first kiss."

"It was not our first kiss." She eyes me (her expression at war with her emotions) as I ease onto the kitchen stool opposite her.

I try to hide my grimace, but I can't. And that sucks because I want—I *need*—her to smile.

"When are you going to tell your parents?"

I shake my head. "I don't know. After the second opinion, I suppose. And after we talk to Astrid."

She slides the chunks of pineapple into a glass bowl. I pluck one out and pop it into my mouth.

"What about work? Can you quit an investment firm when you're one of the co-owners?"

"I'll take a sabbatical."

"A sabbatical until when?"

"Until I'm ready to return to work, or until I'm ..."

Her crestfallen expression digs into my chest like the tip of a sharp knife.

"Ready to retire." I give her a toothy grin.

"Don't joke."

"Laughter is the best medicine. In fact, I think we should wake Astrid and spend all day watching funny movies."

"I don't feel like laughing." She snaps the lid onto the glass bowl.

"Fine. Then, let's watch movies with people who die of cancer and see how Astrid reacts so we can gauge the best approach to tell her. *The Fault in Our Stars. Sweet November. The Bucket List.* What else?" I scratch my chin.

"STOP!" She hurls the bowl of pineapple across the kitchen. It hits the edge of the counter and shatters. "Stop..." her words fight through labored breaths "... joking about your goddamn awful prognosis."

"Mom?" For the second time in less than ten hours, Astrid walks in on Amelia losing control of her emotions.

Amelia presses her palms to the side of her head and blows out a shaky breath. "Astrid. You might need to spend the weekend with Grandma and Grandpa Milloy."

Astrid shakes her head. "What's wrong?"

"Come here." I hold out my arms and lift her onto the counter. "Sweetie, I'm sick."

"I'm sorry." She frowns.

"Yeah, me too."

She touches her neck. "My throat's sore."

"Oh, well, I bet mom can make you some tea with honey. I'm sick in a different way. Do you remember Kelsey's mom being sick last year?"

Astrid nods. "Yes. She had cancer, but she's better. Do you have cancer?" She narrows her eyes.

"I do. Mine is a different kind of cancer."

"Are you going to lose your hair too?"

"No."

"We don't know yet, baby," Amelia adds.

I glance over Astrid's shoulder at my wife. Her arms are crossed, and she quickly averts her gaze.

"There's a lot we don't know yet." I rest my hands on Astrid's legs.

"Are you going to die?"

"I hope not, but cancer is a serious illness. And sometimes people die from cancer. All I know is that I'm going to do everything in my power not to die. And that means I'm going to take time off from work to take better care of myself and spend more time with you and Mom. But while my body works to feel better, I might have some rough days where I'm not doing as well. And that's okay. You and Mom have each other. I want you to go out to dinner with Mom, go Christmas shopping, and do all the fun stuff so you can come home and tell me all about it. Can you do that?"

She rests her warm hands on mine. "What if you don't get better?"

Amelia sniffles, but I don't look at her. It's taking everything I have to find the best way to answer Astrid. "My lovely girl, you are so smart. So I don't want to tell you anything but the truth because I know you are brave enough for me to tell you this. Nobody knows how long they have to live. Every day is a gift. And when someone we love dies, it's sad. It doesn't matter if they are nine like you, thirty-four like me, or one hundred. But that sadness slowly disappears, and you find a new kind of happiness in your memories of them."

"Like Gumbo?"

I chuckle at her reference to her dead goldfish. "Yes. Remember how sad you were when Gumbo died? But now you see fish and smile because they make you think of Gumbo. Well, if I die, whenever you see a handsome man with a little gray in his hair who eats an entire jar of black olives in one sitting, you'll smile and think of me. And a little part of you will still miss me, but you'll also be happy to know that I'm taking care of Gumbo."

Astrid slays me with her brave face.

"Why don't you go upstairs while I clean up the mess? I don't want you getting any glass in your feet." I run my fingers along the bottom of her bare feet.

"Stop!" She giggles and squirms.

I lift her off the counter and carry her to the steps. When she's halfway to the top, she turns. "Daddy?"

"Yeah?"

"Do you think when people die, they can miss other people? If you die, will you miss me and Mom?"

The lump in my throat nearly suffocates me. I can't fucking speak, so I find a believable smile and nod.

CHAPTER
thirty-six

Just surrender with me.

THE SECOND OPINION confirms the first.

My wife pleads her chemo case again.

I can't do it.

The pain gets worse. I get worse.

But I keep reading. And if I can't keep my eyes open to follow words on a page, I listen to the audiobook.

While Astrid's at school, I try to meditate, but it's hard to do it when Amelia refuses to leave my side. Her fear and worry feel as debilitating as the cancer.

I try to eat foods that help fight cancer.

Amelia makes my "favorites," so I try to eat them to make her feel better.

I turn into a robot, a sick robot, trying to please my wife and daughter. The two people I love most have become my biggest obstacle to getting better. And I believe I can beat this.

Fuck the odds.

Modern medicine can't predict or control the most important component of life.

One's mind.

The spirit within.

Thoughts are powerful.

I believe they are the most powerful force in the world. They control actions and reactions on every level of human existence.

Mind over matter isn't a mere cliché. It's the secret to life, but it shouldn't be a secret. Humans have a knack for overcomplicating everything. The simple answer is usually the right one.

"Seeing you like this is killing me," Amelia whispers, sitting on the edge of the bed a couple of weeks before Thanksgiving.

I peel open my eyes. The pain comes and goes in unpredictable waves.

"I'm just tired. I didn't sleep well," I mumble. "Just let me sleep, and I'll be fine when she gets home from school."

"Your mom said there's a doctor in Boston who's seen some success with a new drug for pancreatic cancer."

"Stage four?"

"I don't know, but I think it's worth looking into, don't you?"

"No." I roll in the opposite direction because my back is as stiff as can be.

She climbs into bed, lying on her side to face me.

"You are the love of my life," she whispers.

I find a smile. "And you are mine."

"I feel helpless."

"Then surrender," I murmur.

"What does that mean?"

"Stop trying to control this outcome."

"I can't." Her forehead wrinkles.

I know she can't. I'd feel the same way if she were the one with cancer. Our love is big. All-consuming. And it's bright—a blinding kind of love that makes it impossible to see what needs to be done. And it's literally killing me.

"You're the quirkiest, funniest, and kindest person I have ever known." I rest my hand on her cheek. "Nothing we've ever done has been anything less than earth-shattering."

She grins. "I hit you with my car."

"You did."

"The tire on our getaway car after the wedding blew out, and we landed in the ditch." She giggles. It's been too long since she's laughed.

"Astrid was born in the car a mile from the hospital," I say.

She slowly nods.

"Baby, just don't let me get in a car, and I'll live forever."

"Done," she whispers, leaning toward me and kissing my forehead.

"You can go do something. Just let me rest," I mumble.

"I can't leave you."

I know you can't, sweetheart. So I'll do it for you. I'll do it for us.

CHAPTER
thirty-seven

The perfect tragedy.

Scottie

"How do you do it?" I murmur, ghosting my finger over the lid to Price's record player after he pauses and takes a long breath.

A woman named Amelia has his child and his heart.

It's perfect. And tragic.

"Do what?"

"How do you show up in my life after no word from you for twelve years and look at me like you never stopped loving me? Yet you fell in love with a woman who ran you over, and you have a child ... a whole life with her."

"I guess I'm lucky in love but not in life."

I sit on the opposite end of the sofa, and a spiral-bound notebook catches my attention. "Are you journaling?"

"Sort of. Among other things."

"Other things?" I hug my knees to my chest.

A wry grin settles on his lips. "Have a look." He nods to the notebook.

"You want me to read your journal?"

"I don't care if you read it. It's basically a hard-to-follow story of my marriage interwoven with my mental shift since my diagnosis. But that's not what I want you to see."

I lower my feet to the ground and slowly reach for the journal.

"I can draw," he says when I open it to the first page.

It's a cat in a window. And it's incredibly detailed. "Price, this is ..." I flip through more pages, not stopping on the ones with writing. They're too personal and not for my eyes. "How did you not know you could draw?" I chuckle, admiring his detailed drawings.

"I never took the time to listen."

"To listen to what?" I glance over at him.

A victorious smile graces his face. "Ah ... the student has become the teacher."

I surrender with a slight nod and a knowing grin.

"I've never taken the time to listen to my body. I don't mean just acknowledging the pain. Imagine all the gifts people have but don't take the time to listen. I never sat with a pencil in my hand and no purpose—I never doodled. It's tragic."

Again, I thumb through the drawings. "Is this your wife?" It's a woman with an open book in her hands, but she's looking up from it with her lower lip trapped between her teeth.

Price smiles. It's the kind of expression one has when they think of someone they love—a beautiful smile.

"Yes." He laughs. "After she hit me with her car, she wouldn't leave my side at the hospital. Whenever I glanced at her, she looked at me with a cringe. I don't think she read a single page of that book. And I knew ..." He breathes a content sigh. "I knew she would leave a mark on me that had nothing to do with the accident. It's as if she knew the accident was meant to be, but she didn't want to suggest it while I still had broken bones."

I love this story, except for the part where he's here with me and not with her.

"Does Amelia think you're dead? Does your daughter?"

His smile fades. "No. I left her with a note." He rubs his hand over his face. "A fucking note. I said, 'I can't do it. Please forgive me.' Then, I went to New York to stay with a trusted friend. I told him death was knocking at my door and that I needed a safe place to escape. For two months, he gave me space. He didn't question the foods I ate, the pain I endured, or my need to be alone. I told him I'd let him know if the time came to call Amelia, if I felt I was losing the fight. But I didn't get weaker; I got stronger. And I knew seeing *you* would reset my life because you are peace and gratitude. You are serenity. You embody the essence of what it means to live without the fear of ..."

"Of what?" I whisper.

He narrows his eyes, gaze cast downward. "Death."

My heart skips. This man sees something greater than I've ever seen in myself.

"Scottie, do you remember on our first date, we discussed the mayor's passing? He was only thirty-seven.

I said it was scary to think of life ending so soon. And you said you didn't fear death because—"

"Nothing is easier than not existing," I whisper with a smile.

Price smiles, too. "Yes. What you fear, you draw near. I stopped fearing death, and I focused on life. The tiny details. Every single thing I put into my body. Every emotion. Every twinge of pain. Every memory that brought me joy. I dove headfirst into gratitude and focused on living instead of dying."

Words fail me. I'm honored and heartbroken. I'm hopeful but scared. He's living my life better than I am. "Price, I don't know what to say, but I can't shake the uneasy feeling I have about you being here and your wife and daughter living with uncertainty about your where-abouts or if they'll ever see you again. Doesn't that bother you?"

He slowly nods, eyes narrowed. "This is such a selfish journey. I believe it when people say you can't take care of others if you don't take care of yourself. Amelia loved me too much to see that her fear was killing me along with the cancer. She couldn't bear the thought of me not doing the chemo. She couldn't give me space, mental or emotional.

"Most days, I feel normal. Scottie, I'm living. I know it. I'm winning. So I don't let my mind linger on how they're feeling. Every time it tries to go there, I redirect my thoughts to all the times we were happy before my diag-nosis. I pretend I'm on a long business trip, and they're missing me but excited for the day when I return."

I understand him, but I also know what it's like to love him. I know what it's like to miss him. "You're amazing." I pause to let that sink in. He needs to understand that he is *so* amazing and brave. I've never been more proud of anyone in my life. Yet, he's still human. And as much as he wants to keep his feelings at bay, I know he can't. Not entirely. "I'm sure it's hard to fight the pain of missing them. Because you must miss them. Right?"

He rubs the back of his neck. "Do I miss them? So much that thinking about it feels as debilitating as the cancer. Do I regret leaving when I did and the way I did? No. I'm going to go home and be with them again, and I have to hope that they will be so relieved that I'm alive *and well* that they will forgive me for what I felt I had to do to stay alive."

"And me?"

Price lifts his gaze.

"Will you tell your wife about me? Does she know I exist? Does she know you bought the store where we met?"

Realization ghosts along his face. "You went to the store."

I nod. "Why did you do that?"

He slowly shakes his head. "It was a business decision. They were going out of business. Real estate is a good investment. And that was the only place in town that carried those specific crystal butt plugs."

I snort. "Stop."

Price scoots closer to me, pressing my hand between both of his. "You were my first love. You showed me what it felt like to fall in love. And it's how I knew Amelia would be my wife. You are a good person—a truly compassionate, positive, shining soul. And you loved that store. And I loved our love story, albeit short. So I bought it to keep it open, to keep that summer alive forever, and to keep a tiny piece of your light in my life forever because I think some of the best parts of Price Milloy come from the summer he met Scottie Rucker."

I thought the tears were done. I was wrong.

He smiles while I wipe my face. "No. Amelia doesn't know about you. She doesn't even know I own that building."

I sniffle. "That's not right, Price."

He nods. "Honesty is virtuous. You have me beat in that department. I won't try to pretend otherwise. But compassion often lies somewhere between the truth and the omission of truth. I didn't tell you the truth when I entered the store months back, but you knew something wasn't right. *Yet,* you didn't push me on it because, deep down, you weren't sure you were ready for the truth."

I pull my hand from his and dig through my purse for a tissue. "It's been twelve years. She deserves full disclosure."

With an easy, thoughtful nod, he hums. "She deserves a lot. And I believe I will live to give her everything. Are you marrying a man who will give you everything?"

I can't speak past the emotion thick in my throat, so I nod.

Price waits, unafraid of the silence.

I've never sat this long in silence with another person.

Eventually, my composure returns, and the words come to me. "I'm marrying the man who feels secure enough to let me be a little in love with another man."

The tiniest smile touches his lips.

"I'm marrying the man who I trust with the most vulnerable pieces of myself. I never thought I'd tell

259

another soul outside of my family about the baby I lost before telling you first. But I had to tell Koen because I've given him my heart, which means I trust him with everything in it."

He's the one who will carefully glue those vulnerable pieces together, gently wrap them in tape, and always see me as whole.

Just the mention of his name makes me miss him. So I slide my phone from my purse and text him to come pick me up. Then I stand, slinging my bag over my shoulder as Price stares at the open journal with his wife staring back at him. "It's time for me to go home."

CHAPTER

thirty-eight

It's been too long, but maybe not long enough.

Price

"Sir, do you need help with something?" the driver asks as I stare at my condo from the back seat of her black sedan.

Spring is in full bloom. The cherry blossoms have passed their peak, but the showy white magnolias are stunning.

"I'm good. Thank you," I say, opening the door.

After I retrieve my suitcase from the trunk, I push past the fear and make my way to the front door of my gray stone condo.

It's quiet when I step inside the entry. Astrid should still be in school. I didn't check the garage for Amelia's car. As I set my suitcase on the marble floor, I sense movement above me. Glancing up, my wife grips the railing at the top of the stairs with one hand while her other cups her mouth.

In a blink, tears pour down her face. And I'm left feeling just as vulnerable because I love this woman beyond all reason.

Long waves of blonde hair flow down her shoulders, a little unruly, like she let it air dry after a shower. Her dark jeans fit looser than the last time I saw her, and she's wearing one of my white dress shirts, tied at the waist.

"Hi," I say with my heart in my throat. Every emotion I avoided feeling about her so I could heal is bursting to the surface tenfold.

I thought if things went south, I could die alone. But I'm no longer dying (I truly believe it), and I don't want to live alone. I can't live without her. Without our little girl.

Amelia takes the first step, but her shaky legs falter, and she lowers to her bottom, one hand still holding the railing.

As much as I want to run up the stairs and wrap her in my arms, I can't hurry this moment. I don't want to hurry another moment for the rest of my life. A life I hope is long and filled with meaningful moments. When I reach her, I kneel on the step below her feet.

She covers her face with both hands and sobs. I surrender to the moment and let my tears free while I pull her into my arms. She hugs me so tightly I swear she might shatter my heart and every bit of strength I mustered to come home.

"Y-you're alive."

"I'm alive."

I bury my face in her neck.

"I h-hate you s-so much." She sobs. "But I love you more."

My fingers thread through her hair, and I kiss her neck, wet cheeks, and trembling lips. It started the day we met, and I hope I feel it until the day I die—this woman knocking me on my ass two seconds before pressing her lips to mine.

Framing her face, I pull back just enough to look into her red-rimmed eyes.

"Why did you leave us?" she whispers. "Where did you go? Why would you do something so awful to us?"

I rest my forehead against hers. "I felt like it was my only chance at living. And I wanted to live for you and Astrid. But I knew I couldn't make you understand what I needed."

She blows out a slow, shaky breath. "I have so many questions."

"Can they wait?" I stand with her wrapped around my torso, carrying her toward the bedroom.

Her eyes search mine; concern bleeds from them.

I lay her on the bed, her back to my chest, and I just hold her. "I'm not the same man who left. I can never be him again."

"Who are you?" She strokes my arm.

"I'm the man you ran over on his bike. Vulnerable but strong."

Amelia turns in my arms to face me, hands on my cheeks. "I told Astrid you went—" She chokes, releasing more tears with a blink. "I told her you went to a special hospital far away. I told her you might have to leave us to be with God," she whispers. "What am I supposed to tell her now?"

I turn my head just enough to kiss her wrist. "We'll tell her God wasn't ready for me."

Her gaze holds a million unasked questions and disbelief, like she's looking at a ghost. "Where have you been? And how are you still ..." She swallows hard.

Alive.

She wants to know how I'm still alive.

"I couldn't breathe. I couldn't think. And I knew you needed answers that I didn't have yet. I needed space that I knew you couldn't give me. And I didn't blame you because had it been you, I would have wanted to hold you in my arms and never let you go. So I went to New York to stay with Rob. I knew he'd give me space. I also knew he'd contact you if things got too dire."

She sniffles. "Did you see a new doctor?"

I shake my head.

Her brow wrinkles. "It doesn't make sense."

"Does everything in life have to make sense?"

She frowns. "I'm so sorry. I didn't give you enough. I was just *so* scared."

"No, baby. You gave me too much. You loved me too much. And I needed to be alone. Then I needed to be with people who weren't afraid to let me die so I could have a real chance to live." I slide my leg between hers, needing to be as close to her as possible. "Promise you'll never stop loving me like that."

"Promise you'll never leave us again."

Ouch.

Can I promise that? Can I live (or die) with the consequences of that kind of promise?

She's not looking at the man who left with nothing

more than a note. I've changed, so I can do this. I will do this.

"I promise," I whisper.

Her fingers unbutton my jeans. "Can we do *this*?" Her gaze slides up my body.

I grin. "Let's find out."

She returns a shaky smile. Face red. Eyes swollen. My wife has never been more beautiful.

———

"WHO ELSE THINKS I'M DEAD?" I ask while we wait in the pick-up line outside of Astrid's school.

Amelia taps the steering wheel. "Nobody thinks you're dead. They think you're at an expensive hospital getting treatment, and I'm a terrible wife who's not there with you because we agreed not to interrupt Astrid's life." She glances over at me and frowns. "You should call your parents. They know you ran away."

"Is that what you told them?"

She stares out the front of her Mercedes. "What did you want me to tell them? That's all I knew. Our friends. Family. Neighbors. What was I supposed to say?" Her tone has an edge.

I don't blame her for being upset.

"I hate that I left you to deal with everything. But if I would have stayed—"

She doesn't look at me while reaching for my hand, squeezing it. "I know. You don't have to explain. What's happened is awful. And there's no easy way through it. There's no easy way to explain it. Even now ... what will we tell people? That you've been miraculously cured of terminal cancer? And is that even true? Is your cancer gone? That can't be true. Can it?"

Lifting her hand to my lips, I kiss it. "Well, I don't feel like I have cancer. So we tell them I'm alive. That's it. We don't owe anyone anything. I can't let myself worry about it. I can't let you worry about it. Sometimes selfishness is self-preservation."

Amelia turns her head, eyes slightly narrowed. After a few seconds, she gives me a single nod.

"There she is." I open my door as Astrid exits the building, chatting with a group of friends. When she sees me, she freezes. The next ten seconds feel like one of those videos where a parent—serving in the military for a long time—finally returns home. I tell myself I'm not going to get all emotional.

Such a lie.

"Dad!" She drops her bag on the ground and sprints toward me.

I'm not going to die of cancer; I'm going to die of happy heartbreak.

I lift her off her feet and turn in a slow circle while she cries.

"Are you better?"

"I'm better, baby."

Please, God. Let it be true.

"Astrid, you left your bag." Her friend holds out the bag as I set Astrid on her feet.

"Thanks." She wipes her tears and takes the bag.

"Are you okay?" her friend asks.

Astrid glances up at me and smiles. "I'm great."

CHAPTER
thirty-nine

It's the bigger picture.

THE HERO'S homecoming doesn't last. I guess beating death (yes, yes ... knock on wood) isn't as heroic as risking one's life for one's country.

Astrid's life goes on as it should.

Dance.

Flute.

Swimming.

Golf.

Amelia volunteers at the school and works twenty hours a week with the advertising agency, mostly from home.

And I exist.

"Have you thought about visiting the oncologist?" Amelia asks from the bathroom, curling her hair after school drop-off while I read a book in bed.

"I have not." I keep my eyes on the page.

"Don't you want to know if you're really better?"

"According to the doctors, I should be dead by now. But I'm not. I think it's fair to say I'm better or at least going in the right direction. Maybe it's borrowed time, but I'll take it."

She sighs. Lately, I've been the lucky recipient of so many heavy sighs. "I'm going to call Rob. Since he was your refuge, maybe he can convince you to see your doctor."

"I was with Rob until January. He's not convincing me of anything. I went to stay with him because I knew he'd let me live *or die* in peace."

She cranes her neck past the doorway to give me a narrow-eyed look before unplugging the curling iron. "Then where were you the rest of the time?"

I mark my page and close the book, setting it on my outstretched legs. "Austin."

"Texas?"

"Yes."

"Why?" She adjusts her belt and leans her shoulder against the doorway between the bedroom and bathroom.

Can I phone a friend? Maybe Koen can reassure my wife that my relationship with Scottie is nothing to worry about. I've been avoiding this conversation because I don't know how to explain it in a way that will make sense to my wife, who doesn't understand how I'm still alive.

"Do you have work to do?"

She nods. "I have a call at ten."

I glance at the alarm clock.

"That's not for a half hour," she adds. "We have time to talk."

"No. I don't think thirty minutes is enough time to explain this."

"Explain what?"

I chuckle. "I'll explain it later."

She frowns. "Tell me."

"Later." I open my book again.

"Did you have a hot affair?" Her eyebrows lift.

I don't look at her. That's my first mistake. No, that's my second mistake. Telling her I was in Austin when she has a call in thirty minutes was my first mistake.

"Jesus, Price, look at me."

I do. And I have no idea what my face looks like, but I fear it's bleeding guilt when I have no reason to feel guilty.

"*What* were you doing in Austin?" She curls her hair behind her ear, her voice a little shaky.

"Amelia, who makes you feel like you don't have a care in the world? Do you have someone who inspires you to live in the moment?"

"You."

I shake my head. "No. That's not true, not even a little. I'm not asking you who you love. I'm asking if you've ever known someone who has an *energy* about them that's calming. Someone who makes you feel like you're over-thinking life, working too hard, and focused on things that don't matter in the big picture."

With a downcast gaze, she squints, lips twisted. "I don't think so." Her eyes find mine. "Do you?"

I pause for a second before slowly nodding.

She swallows hard. "Please don't tell me it's a woman."

Setting the book on the nightstand, I slide to the side, letting my legs dangle off the side of the bed, hands folded. "Let's talk after your call."

She snags her phone from the bathroom vanity. "I'm canceling the call." Setting her phone back on the vanity, she pads her bare feet toward the gray chair by the window. It's where she likes to read, listen to music, or watch the birds build their nests.

"Can we take a moment to acknowledge a few things?" I ask.

After a few seconds, she relinquishes a nod, tucks her feet under her, and hugs the yellow floral pillow to her chest.

"If I would have stayed here, I would be dead or very close to it. Or I would have done the chemo, and maybe that would have given me a few extra months, albeit miserable months. But either way, I think we can agree that by this Thanksgiving, I would be dead."

She flinches.

"And I'm not saying this to make you feel guilty for wanting me to stay or wanting me to do the chemo. I'm saying this for perspective. There is a bigger picture than why I went to Austin or who I saw there, which brings me to something else we need to establish. When we started dating, you told me you had been in a three-year relationship with a guy you met in college. That's it. I know nothing else about him because you didn't elaborate, and I didn't ask—because it didn't matter."

Pressing her lips together, she holds my gaze.

"And I told you I'd been in a relationship with

someone over the summer between my junior and senior years of college. Like you, I didn't elaborate. And, like me, you didn't ask for more information. But now I'm going to tell you."

Again, she swallows.

"Her name is Scottie."

Amelia blinks, releasing tears just from hearing Scottie's name. She knows I'm on the verge of telling her things that will hurt. It's hard to hear that the person you love has given away pieces of themselves to someone else. And it doesn't matter how tiny the pieces are; Amelia and I share an all-consuming love. I selfishly want her whole heart as she wants the same of mine.

Over the next hour, I tell her everything from falling in love with Scottie to the last conversation I had with her before I returned home. With as much tenderness and consideration as I can offer, I tell her why Scottie's part of the reason I should live to see another Thanksgiving. I tell her about the apothecary I bought, the lost child I never knew about, the job I took at the general store, and my new friend who's marrying Scottie.

I hate that it's heartbreaking for my wife, but I must live in the light of my truth.

She sets the pillow aside and stands, combing her hands through her hair while gazing out the window. "Do you still love her?"

"I love my parents. I love your parents. I love my sister—"

"That's not what I'm asking."

"Then ask it differently."

"Are you *in love* with her?"

"No."

"How can I believe you?"

"Because I'm here."

She turns, hugging herself. "She's engaged. But what if she weren't?"

"She wasn't engaged when I got to Austin. She hadn't even met Koen."

"And what if she wouldn't have met him?"

I stand, holding out my arms. "I would still be here."

"Because of Astrid."

"Because of you."

She shakes her head.

"No." I close in on her, holding her tear-stained face. "We can't do this. I didn't leave you and Astrid for anyone but *you and Astrid*. I didn't go to Austin to get Scottie back. I went to Austin so I could get better *for you and Astrid*. I didn't go see Scottie to remember why I loved her. I knew she'd let me—"

"Die?"

"No. I needed to remember what it felt like to live in the moment, not fear death, honor my body's intuition, and nurture my spirit. And Scottie's the epitome of those things. I didn't need her. I needed her light."

Amelia closes her eyes, more tears breaking free. "I w-want to be h-her. I want to b-be the person w-who helps you live."

"No, sweetheart." I kiss her head. "You don't want to be Scottie. She tragically lost a baby, and she nearly died. You gave us Astrid. And you are the reason I want to live. That. Is. Everything."

She takes a step back, wiping her face. "I need time."

After a sigh of surrender, I retrieve my notebook from the closet and hand it to her. "This is what I did every day in Austin. I figured out I could draw. And all I wanted to sketch were things that made me think of you. And the words I wanted to write ... well, they were all about you too." I slide my hands in my pockets. "I'll give you whatever you need. Time. Space. Anything."

With a blank expression, she flips through the pages. It hurts that she won't look at me. Love does that. It hurts. I'm unsure why humans are so obsessed with it, but we are.

CHAPTER

forty

Every end has a beginning.

Scottie

I MISS MY EMPLOYEE, the one who never cashed a single paycheck.

Koen leaves early in the mornings. And mornings are when I have a little extra time since the store doesn't open until nine. By the time I close the shop in the evenings, he's walking Scrot and ready to turn in for the night.

I'm missing my two favorite men for different reasons.

The door chimes as I refill the bulk jars with the recent candy order and figure out how to find another employee who will work for free.

"Mr. Drummond." I smile. "Good to see you."

The store's owner gives me a sad smile while slicking back what little gray hair he has left on his head. His eyes are dark and weary, skin wrinkled and dotted with age spots and moles.

"I'm afraid I don't come with good news. Clara is receiving hospice care. All of my money's gone out to pay medical bills. I can no longer pay rent for this building."

"Oh," I wad up the empty candy bag, "I had no idea she wasn't doing well."

He glances around the store as if already appraising what he might liquidate. It's jarring. This store has felt like my home for the past ten years.

"Her heart is failing."

"I'm sorry to hear that. Is there anything I can do?"

He shifts his gaze to me, adjusting his giant belt buckle. "You can sell as much of this stuff as possible by the end of the month."

That's in two weeks.

"I'll need to sell the trailer too."

I nod. Clara has been so kind to me. I've loved working here. And I know so many customers will be disappointed too.

"I'd love to visit Clara if that's okay."

"Of course. She's at Wellings."

"I can be out of the trailer this weekend."

"I'm sorry, Scottie. I know Clara wanted to keep the store for you. But I just—"

"Don't." I shake my head. "I understand."

"Well," he says with a sigh. "I'll check back with you next week and see where we are on inventory. If you have anything on order," he frowns at the full jars of candy, "please see if you can cancel it."

"I will."

THERE'S a knock on the store's door just after nine-thirty. Perched on one of the swivel stools, sipping a soda, I glance over my shoulder.

Koen frowns. Baseball cap backward. Finger pointed at his watch.

Grabbing the key, I unlock the door.

"You're not answering your phone? What's going on?" He steps inside with Scrot and takes the keys to lock the door behind him.

Making a lazy inspection of the checkout area, I shrug. "My phone's ... somewhere."

He tosses the keys on the counter and pulls me into his arms. "Tell me what's going on."

"Today, I got fired and evicted."

Koen's eyes narrow.

"Clara, the owner's wife, is dying, and he needs to sell this place and the trailer."

"I'm sorry. I know you love this place. My grandpa will be disappointed, too."

I nod several times.

He gathers my hair, pulling it off my neck. I love it when he messes with my hair. It's easy to imagine him doing the same to our daughter if we have one.

"I can't do much about the store." Koen ducks his head to kiss my neck. "But I can let you sleep on my sofa until you find a new place." A smirk steals his lips when he stands tall.

My gaze lifts to his.

And I wait. I'll wait all night.

He wrinkles his nose. "Not in a joking mood, huh?"

I don't blink.

His head bobs a few times. "Maybe you should move

in with me. Sleep in my bed. Make a mess. Spoil my dog. Get me in trouble with my grandpa. Plan a wedding. Have sex with me on the kitchen table. Or maybe Scrot's bed. Yeah, that's it. Let's fuck on his bed. He's humped the hell out of my pillow, so I feel like that would be good payback."

He wins.

I snort, rolling my eyes. "I'm not going to make a mess."

His eyebrows peak. "That's what your objection is? Not the sex on the kitchen table or the dog bed?"

Lifting onto my toes, I trap his lower lip between my teeth and grin while he draws his head back to release my hold on it. "I will have sex with you anytime ... anywhere."

"Don't tease me. I know there's a back room." He bites my bottom lip like I did to his.

I laugh when he palms the back of my legs to carry me to the back room. "I was hoping I'd get to have sex back here one more time before the store closed."

Koen slows his pace, scowling while releasing me to my feet. "One more time?"

With a shrug, I nod. "Do you really think Herb comes in every day just for produce?"

"Fuck no ..." His face wrinkles, but he can't hide his grin. "You cannot say that shit and expect me to get an erection."

Hugging his torso, my hands dip into his back pockets. "Herb never has a problem."

"Scottie Ann Rucker, you are one sick chick."

"But I'm your sick chick, right?" I bite his pec muscle.

"Turn around and pull down your pants; I can't look at you when we do this."

A fit of giggles robs all of my composure. "Doggie style must run in the family."

"Woman, stop!" Koen grabs my face and kisses me so hard I could suffocate. When he releases me, his hands slide down my arms, and he lowers to his knees, hugging my legs, forehead resting on my stomach.

"What are you doing," I murmur, removing his backward baseball hat to run my fingers through his hair.

"Getting used to this feeling."

"What feeling is that?"

"You bringing me to my knees."

I grin. "In the best way, right?"

"The very best." His hands ghost along my curves. "God took so much time with you," he whispers. "I must remember to thank him one day."

My heart leaves my chest every time he whispers words like that. The irony of the perfect man thinking I'm the one God spent a little extra time on is upside-down logic.

This impatient heart of mine wants more, and it wants it now.

I realize I haven't had sex dreams about Price since I told him about the baby. All of the emotions for Price Milloy that I held on to for twelve years and the mixed and misplaced feelings that shook my heart when he came to Austin, were all tied to our baby. I don't hold on to things that don't matter. That's why I've lived a simple life. But *that* moment mattered.

And so does this one.

Until this very moment, I never allowed myself to see

how desperately I needed to tell Price about the baby so I could let go of the pain ... let go of him.

"Let's call my parents and sister and tell them to come to Austin when the store closes. I want to marry you now, in your backyard, with just our families."

Koen pauses his motions for a breath before grabbing his hat and standing tall to inspect my sincerity.

I shrug. "This summer's tomatoes aren't going to can themselves."

I see my future in his eyes, and it's bigger than any dream.

"You're moving in tonight." He slides his hat on the right way.

I laugh. "It's late."

"Nope. You don't have that much stuff. Let's throw it all into the back of our trucks and go home."

"Sounds messy."

He takes my hand, leading me toward the front of the store. "Baby, you're going to be a fucking tornado in my life. But I'm here for every single disastrous second."

CHAPTER

forty-one

Are humans meant to fall in and out of love?

Scottie

IT'S HAPPENING.

We have a date, but it's not for two months due to everyone's schedules.

I'm still heartbroken over the store closing in five days, but I've cleared out a ton of inventory with huge close-out sales.

I visited Clara for an emotional goodbye.

And I've called the owner of the apothecary store in Philly to get a contact number for Mr. Price I Don't Have A Cell Phone Milloy. But I can't bring myself to call him despite Koen telling me Price is considered family now and, therefore, he should be at our wedding.

He has my number, so if he wanted to keep in touch, he would have called by now, right?

I lock the back door after closing and take a moment

to stare at the empty trailer. I'm okay with this chapter ending because the next one will be even more amazing.

"Excuse me?"

I jump, pressing a hand to my heart.

"Sorry," the lady says, stepping toward me. She adjusts her purse strap with one hand while the other slides into the front pocket of her white capris.

Her perfectly pressed yellow button-down shirt looks nicer than anything I've ever owned. And her long blonde hair is almost as smooth as her blouse. I can't place her, but her face is familiar.

"Are you Scottie?"

"Yes."

A tiny line forms along her forehead as if she's thinking about my response. "I'm Amelia Milloy."

My lips part, but I don't know what to say. I glance over her shoulder.

"Price isn't here."

My gaze returns to her.

"I had to meet you."

My throat begins to constrict. Something happened to him. That's why she's here alone. "Is he—"

"He's fine," she smiles.

I relax.

"I uh..." she shifts her weight from one foot to the other "...I don't know what you know about me, but I feel like I know everything about you. And that's why I had to meet you."

I take a step closer. "I know a little about you." I smile. "I know you're loved by an extraordinary man. I know you have a daughter together. And I know he spent his time here trying to get better for you and your daughter."

She blinks back her emotions and takes a deep breath while holding out her hand. "It's lovely to meet you."

I stare at it for a few seconds before taking another step and wrapping my arms around her. She stiffens for a second, then slowly wraps her arms around me.

"Want to take a walk?" I ask, releasing her.

Her head swivels, inspecting the area. "Sure."

We stroll toward the park, where I fell into the pond with Koen and Scrot.

"What can I do for you?" I ask.

"Do for me?" She gives me a quick, sidelong glance.

"You didn't fly to Austin to shake my hand. And I gather Price has told you everything there is to tell about me. So there must be something on your mind that you're afraid to ask him."

"Perhaps you're right." She chuckles, but the laughter quickly dies. "He told me about your summer together, the breakup, his time in Austin, and how he knew it was time to come home. He even told me about the baby you lost, and I'm very sorry that happened to you."

Keeping my gaze on the sidewalk before us, I nod and murmur, "Thank you."

"But out of everything he told me, the part that hurt the most was the apothecary he purchased after we were married. I knew nothing about it."

I consider telling her that I knew nothing about it either. But I don't think she's looking for me to sound relatable. Without knowing what she needs from me, I simply listen.

"I just can't ignore the possibility that his feelings for you never died, not even after we married. Why would he not tell me? The only explanation is that he knew I wouldn't understand."

We reach an empty playground, and I nod to the left.

Amelia sits on the swing next to me, two girls with our feet dangling beneath us, hands gripping the chains, hearts sharing memories of the same boy.

"I don't know if humans are meant to fall in and out of love," I say. "Perhaps by trying to make these hard lines where something ends so another thing can begin, we stifle our heart's true potential. If a doctor retires, is he or she still a doctor? I believe so. We try to apply the rules of the physical world to the emotional world. I don't think we must let go of everything to move on emotionally. I'm in love with my fiancé and want to be his wife and have a family with him. We share a strong desire for each other. But I didn't fall out of love with Price to love Koen. I love your husband, and I will always love him. Our time together has a special place in my heart. Relationships end for many reasons, but the love doesn't have to. Let your heart be big. Let it hold on to everything beautiful. If Price bought the store where he met me, just imagine what he would do for you and Astrid. The two people he loves most in this world."

Amelia sniffles and I reach for her hand. She takes it, squeezing hard while letting go of what I hope is the fear keeping her from feeling the true depths of Price's love.

We make our way back to the store, and Amelia tells me all about Astrid and how she looks like her but has Price's drive to conquer the world.

"I'm glad I came." She hugs me one last time. "Looks like a great store."

I glance at the sign. "It is, but it's closing in five days. The owner can't afford to keep it open."

"I could write a check and buy the building," she says.

When I glance at her, she grins. I think she's serious.

"Price would be proud of me." She winks.

I laugh, shaking my head. "The new manager of the apothecary is very nice. She's thrilled that it's still open. But I'm the sole employee here. And I have a new path I'm excited to take, so ..." I shrug. "It's time."

"Well, then, I guess we'll see you at the wedding."

I narrow my eyes. "The wedding?"

"Yes. Your fiancé called Price and invited us. That's another reason I had to come. I didn't want to meet you on your special day and seem like the jealous wife."

Koen.

I smile. "I'm glad you came. Have a safe trip home, and give that husband of yours a big hug from me and Koen."

"I will." She squeezes my hand before heading toward her Tesla rental.

———

BY THE TIME I get home, Koen's in bed. I shower and brush my teeth. When I crawl under the covers, he hooks an arm around my naked body and pulls me toward him.

"You're late. Still having trouble leaving the store?"

I bury my face in his neck. "Amelia Milloy flew to Austin just to meet me before our wedding. I can't believe you broke into my phone again and called Price."

"I had to. We're honeymooning at one of his *five* homes."

My head rears back. "What?"

He doesn't open his eyes, but he grins. "Baby, I know more about him than you do."

I deposit kisses all over his chest. "Do you think it's a good idea?"

"Knowing so much about your ex-lover?"

I giggle at his ex-lover comment. "No. Staying at his place."

"He's not going to be there."

I love this guy. He's the whole package.

"Do you work this weekend?" I ask.

"No."

"Want to put together a puzzle with me?"

His hand slides along the curve of my butt. "You're pressing your naked body to mine and suggesting a puzzle?"

I giggle and then squeal when he rolls on top of me, pinning my arms above my head. My laughter simmers into something more intimate. "Love me always," I whisper.

He grins and echoes, "Always," before kissing me.

CHAPTER

forty-two

This is the beginning of the end.

Price

SHE LEFT ME WITH A NOTE. I guess that's fair since I started the whole note-writing thing.

> *Be back in a few days. x*
> *—A*

It's been a few days, and true to her promise, she's back. The door clicks shut just after one in the afternoon. Astrid's in school, and I've gone through my morning journaling, sauna, meditation, juice, and yoga ritual.

"Hey," she says softly as I come down the stairs. "Are you leaving?"

I shake my head. "I'm going outside to walk in the grass."

She hesitates for a second before nodding.

"I'll carry your suitcase up first." I kiss her before bending down to take the suitcase.

"You're not going to ask me where I've been?" She follows me up the stairs.

"Do you want me to ask you?"

"I want you to care."

"Sweetheart, I'm here for you. I'm always ready to listen or talk or ... whatever you need. Giving someone space is sometimes the best way to show you care." I set her suitcase in the closet. As soon as I turn, she's a foot away from me.

"You left because I didn't give you space."

I shake my head. "What? No. I mean, yes, but—" I pinch the bridge of my nose. "Baby, what more can I possibly say to make you understand? And if the answer is nothing, what can I say or do to get us past this? I can't undo the past. I've promised never to leave again. I don't blame you for anything that's happened to me. I've told you that our life together with our beautiful daughter is the reason I did what I did to keep from dying so quickly." I rub my hands over my face. "I'm ... I'm so lost right now. Just tell me what I'm missing. What can I do to make things right again?"

"I went to Austin."

My hands flop to my sides.

"Are you surprised?"

I shake my head.

"No?" She crosses her arms. "Why not?"

"Because I know you."

Her head jerks backward. "I'm predictable?"

287

I step back, shaking my head. "Jesus Christ ... what is going on? Who are you? What happened to my wife?"

"You abandoned her and your child!" She bites her lips together and shakes her head a half dozen times, regret pooling in her eyes.

"Say it, Amelia. We'll never get past it if you don't say it."

She crosses her arms, fingernails digging into her skin. "I can't," she whispers. "I don't mean it."

Taking a step backward, I lean against the closet island. "You wouldn't think it if you didn't mean it a little." I sigh, dropping my chin. "We don't have to get through this with any sort of grace or pride. It's okay to let go of the ugly. I can take it."

When her gaze meets mine, I see resignation. "You left me to be with your first love. And yeah, I met her." She frowns, shoulders slumped. "Scottie seems very kind. And she loves you. She'll always love you. And that just ... what? Is okay? But I'm the woman who apparently loves you too much. And that doesn't feel as okay."

I can tell from the pain in her expression that the words aren't there, but she's finding the best ones she can. It's how I've felt since the day I was diagnosed.

"And now you're supposedly ... *miraculously* cured, but I don't know that for certain because you won't go to the doctor. You're too busy with your new full-time job of spending the whole day going through your rituals. And I get that it's important, but my life feels like it's on its head. I'm trying to keep some sense of normalcy for Astrid, but nothing about our life is normal. You're not at work. I'm tiptoeing around you because I don't know what I can ask of you. You're back, but it doesn't feel like you're really here."

I don't react. Not yet. There's too much to consider. What are we doing if I can't be her safe space and accept her raw emotions without judgment? What is the point of this marriage and our commitment to each other?

But I'm human too. The reaction I'm holding back is disbelief that she can't see that I'm alive. Maybe Astrid's dad doing whatever he can to stay alive is more important than anyone's feelings. I *so* badly want to let those words fly off my tongue.

But I don't.

"I'm an awful person," she whispers. "Because I want to go back to the life we had before your diagnosis, but we can't. I wish I could un-know that you bought that apothecary. But I can't. And I don't know how to deal with these stupid thoughts and insecurities that won't go away. I'm so sorry."

I take two long strides and pull her into my embrace. "I got the diagnosis, but you've felt just as much pain. I don't want you to apologize. Not ever. The 'sickness and health' part of marriage is hard to comprehend until we're in the trenches with no good way out."

When I step back to hold her at arm's length, I focus on her tired, sunken eyes and prominent cheekbones. What is this doing to her health?

The stress.

The worry.

The guilt.

"Maybe it's time for me to put on a suit and return to work for a few days a week. Give you some sense of normalcy again."

She glances around uneasily, eyebrows pulled together. "Are you sure that's a good idea?"

"I don't know. It's hard to judge an idea as good or bad until you try it."

After a few breaths of hesitation, she nods. "Promise to let me know if you're feeling too much stress or unwell in any way?"

So many promises. It will be hard to keep them if anything goes wrong. Still, I smile and offer several tiny nods.

Relief washes over her face, and she hugs me. "Let's go out to dinner tonight. Astrid's been asking for pizza and ice cream."

"That's ..."

The beginning of the end.

"Great. Sounds great."

"Can you do me one more tiny favor?" She leans back, holding up her thumb and forefinger an inch apart.

"Anything."

"Will you go to the doctor?"

———

I'M the only one in the room who is not surprised by the results of the scans.

Not surprised that they don't detect cancer in my liver.

Not surprised that there's only one tumor left in my pancreas, and it's tiny.

"It's rare, but sometimes we see situations like this that we can't explain," Dr. Faber says.

Situations.

Can't explain.

I gave my body exactly what it needed, and it's been healing. Why does that only make sense to me? Oh, that's right ... it didn't make sense to me before I experienced it —before I became the miracle.

So, I don't need Dr. Faber to bend a knee and admit that there might be more than one way to fight cancer. Even if I'm living proof, it doesn't make me an expert.

Maybe it is nothing more than something rare and unexplainable.

I'm alive. My cancer is nearly gone—no more symptoms.

Do the details matter anymore?

If Amelia and the doctors want to call it a miracle from God, go for it. Really, I don't care. I'm not looking to preach on the matter or write a book.

My wife wipes her happy tears.

"We can treat the remaining tumor," Dr. Faber says.

I give her a look like she's lost her fucking mind.

With a tight smile, she nods slowly. "Or we can recheck things in a few months."

Or I can walk out of here and be done with this. No more poking, prodding, and scanning my body.

Amelia squeezes my hand as if prompting me to speak.

"Thank you for your time." I stand. "If we have any more questions, we know how to reach you."

"We'll schedule a follow-up," Amelia says while hiking her purse onto her shoulder.

"Or you can send me a reminder card like my dentist." I give the doctor a toothy grin.

As soon as we exit the building, Amelia screams and jumps up and down.

Okay, this right here makes the follow-up appointment totally worth it. I haven't seen her this excited since she discovered she was pregnant with Astrid.

"Baby! You're going to live!" She throws herself into my arms.

I chuckle. "One day at a time."

Truth? I don't know how long this will last.

She kisses me over and over again, giggling like our daughter. "I know. Thank you. I wanted to believe that you were better, but knowing it for sure is exactly what I needed. We have to celebrate. I'm going to invite everyone." She takes my hand and pulls me toward the car.

I hope that my body can feed off of her happiness because it feels like we're slipping back into the same life that allowed me to get sick in the first place.

CHAPTER

forty-three

I thought it would be you.

Scottie

"I'M NERVOUS. I can't believe I'm nervous. Why am I so nervous?"

Mom steps behind me, resting her hands on my bare shoulders while I stare out the window at the small gathering seated in white chairs behind the house.

Koen built a beautiful arch, and his mom and brother wrapped it in pink garden roses and lavender peonies beneath the boughs of his majestic Encino Oak tree. The front yard has a rented tent with tables for a small reception.

"You have a guest." Steph pokes her head into the bedroom.

"Koen can't see me." I turn toward the door.

Steph adjusts the waist of her light-blue chiffon

sleeveless V-neck dress that matches all three of her girls. My three flower girls. "It's Price."

My mom smiles. "I'll give you a few minutes."

As soon she disappears, my first love steps into the room looking dapper in his heathered, light-gray suit, tailored to perfection.

White shirt. Royal blue tie.

"Nervous?"

I shake my head, and his gaze lands on my hands as I pick at my fingernails, which have been professionally manicured for the first time in my life.

"A little. I don't like being the center of attention. And I'm worried that I won't remember my vows. Maybe I should run. What do you think? Will you drive me? I'll leave Koen. You'll leave Amelia. And we'll ..." I scrape my teeth along my bottom lip several times. "I don't know. Maybe we can go to an island. I bet you could buy an island for us, huh?"

A slow smile swells on his handsome face while he casually slides a hand into his front pocket. "I could probably swing a small island." He glances at his gold watch. "But if we're going to do it, we should probably go before it's too late to get a flight out."

"There's no way you don't have a private jet." I run the pad of my finger below my eye. Why did I let my sister talk me into makeup? It feels weird, even though she says it's light.

"I might. Do you want to think about it before we make a rash decision?"

He's so calm. That used to be my role.

"You're stunning, Scottie."

"Don't." I fan my face. "I'm wearing mascara. If you make me cry—"

"Shh ... stop interrupting the universe." He pulls something from his pocket and saunters toward me.

"Stop stealing my line." I grin.

"I'm sure Koen would rather I steal your line than steal the bride. Here." He opens his hand. "Don't worry. It's for your ankle, not your wrist. No one has to see it. It's white gold and—"

"Blue sodalite," I whisper, picking up the delicate anklet.

"For tranquility and emotional balance." He takes it from me and hunches at my feet.

I lift the tulle skirt of my vintage boho A-line dress. It has a lace bodice with a low back, and I feel like a princess. Price fastens it around my ankle.

"I thought it would be you," I say softly.

He lifts his gaze. It's surprisingly sad. "What if I said okay? What if we could be on the island before sunrise tomorrow? What if everyone else has just been part of a complicated and emotional path back to each other?"

I start to smile because it's funny. We're being silly. Right? But my smile dies when I see something in his eyes that I haven't seen in twelve years.

This isn't the man who left Austin two months ago. That man had found peace with his body and mind and yearned to be reunited with his wife and daughter.

I can't speak. The mind keeps emotions alive long after the moment has died. We spent a summer in love, and when everything died, including our baby, my mind kept Price alive. It fed my imagination just enough to keep one tiny ember burning in my heart.

My lips part to speak.

"Time's up." Steph and the girls breeze into the bedroom, bringing a fresh floral scent from the bouquets in their hands.

Price stands, straightening his jacket and tie.

My heart flutters out of control, and the words on the tip of my tongue vanish like waking from a dream.

He smiles, sliding my wispy bangs away from my eyes. "In our next life," he whispers.

"Do you have the rings?" Steph asks Price while she fixes Winnie's barrette.

He turns. "I do."

The second he disappears, I silently gasp.

"Are you okay?" Steph snaps her fingers at the girls. "All three of you, on the bed. Hands to yourselves. And stop picking at the flowers." She turns back toward me. "You look like you saw a ghost."

I shake my head. "It's all the powder you put on my face."

She rolls her eyes. "Don't be ridiculous. Here, let's gloss your lips one last time. And stop picking at your nails."

I fist my hands at my side and give her a guilty smile while she swipes the lip gloss wand over my lips.

"I still can't believe Koen asked Price to attend your wedding. I don't know what kind of witchery you use on men to make them fall in love with you *and* each other, but it's impressive." She recaps the lip gloss. "It's time. Are you ready to say 'I do'?" Avery jumps off the bed and hands me my bouquet.

I smile at her and nod to my sister. "Take me to my prince."

"Follow me, girls," she says. "Do it just like we practiced yesterday. Avery, hold Winnie's hand the whole time."

"I will."

Steph and the girls take a left to head to the backyard when we step out the front door.

My dad greets me with a smile and offers his arm in his black suit. "Cold feet?"

I walk several steps and turn the corner, immediately making eye contact with Koen, and the rest of the world fades away.

Those blue eyes alight just for me.

The black three-piece suit and gold tie.

Sexy, wavy hair.

And that smile ...

"No cold feet," I say, gently squeezing my dad's arm as he walks me toward my groom while a friend of his mom's plays Paul Hankinson's wedding version of Taylor Swift's "Lover" on a keyboard.

It's just our family and a few close friends, but I don't see anyone but Koen.

Six months ago, I didn't know he existed. Now, I feel like we only exist for each other.

"Love you." Dad kisses my cheek. Then he sets my hand in Koen's and says, "Take care of my girl."

Koen nods. "Always."

Price is right over my shoulder, but I can't spare a single glance. And that's how I know there will be no island for us. My heart knows it.

Taking me and everyone by surprise, Koen leans forward and kisses me.

The minister clears his throat.

Koen returns to his space, rubbing the lip gloss from his mouth. "Sorry, I couldn't wait."

Our family laughs.

It's a short and sweet ceremony. I remember my vows. And Price gets Scrot to bring us the rings on cue in a velvet box attached to his collar.

I fight the tears as Koen slides the ring onto my hand. And I lose the fight when I slide the ring onto his finger, and the minister pronounces us husband and wife.

"*Now* ... you may kiss your bride."

"Forever, I will kiss my bride," Koen whispers before we kiss.

His hands gently cup my face, and mine grab his jacket, making a lifelong claim.

He's mine.

There's clapping. Kaleb whistles. Both moms wipe their tears. And Scrot barks.

It's perfect.

Koen interlaces our fingers and walks me to the house and up the stairs to the bedroom.

"We have guests." I giggle before he kisses me.

"I think there's something," he kisses his way down my neck, "in Texas law," he kisses my shoulder, "that says for a marriage to be legal, it must be consummated within thirty minutes of vows being exchanged." He drags his mouth back up my neck, grinning the whole way.

I laugh, fingers playing with his wavy hair. "My nieces will be looking for us in a matter of minutes because they know we have to cut the cake before they can have any."

"Let's wait several years before having kids." He laughs. "I want you to myself for a while."

I ... well, I try to laugh, but I can't.

"Why the look?" He narrows his eyes, fingers teasing the back of my neck.

Pressing my lips together, I shake my head.

His eyes narrow a little more. "Scottie Sikes."

I fight my grin, loving the sound of my new name. My nose scrunches. "I stopped my birth control the day you proposed to me."

Koen's eyebrows climb up his forehead.

"And it's been a while since I've had my period. So, I bought a test and planned on taking it tonight. But now you want to wait, and—"

"Where's the test?"

"In the bathroom."

He pulls me into the bathroom, opening drawers until he finds the box of pregnancy tests. Ripping open the package to one of the sticks, he hands it to me. "Pee."

I laugh. "Later."

"Now." He lifts the toilet lid.

"My dress."

"I'll hold it up for you."

Suddenly, after being excited about it all day, I'm scared to take the test. If it's positive, will he be happy? Or did I make a flawed assumption and a terrible mistake?

"I have one ovary. I might not be able to get pregnant."

"You only need one."

I frown, taking the test from him and lifting my dress. He holds it while I pee on the stick. We have family and friends waiting for us. This isn't how I imagined this happening.

He takes the stick from me while I wipe and flush the toilet. I can't stop staring at it while I wash my hands.

"The best time to take the test is in the morning. I might have diluted hCG levels from—"

"Scottie, it's positive." He holds it up for me to see as I dry my hands.

The two lines stare at me. I know how I feel. And it's killing me to hold back my excitement. I have another chance at this. "Are you ... disappointed? I didn't know you wanted to wait."

"Scottie," he runs his fingers through his hair. "We're going to have a baby!" His grin reaches his ears before he kisses me.

And if I wasn't pregnant two seconds ago, I am after this kiss.

He squats and lifts my dress, hiding under it like a fort. "Hi, baby. I can't wait to see you." His hands grip my hips while he deposits kisses below my belly button.

I giggle. "Stop. She's the size of a raspberry. I don't think she can hear you yet."

Koen paws at my dress, digging his way out, hair all mussed as he eyes me. "*She*?"

I shrug. "My sister has all girls."

"Yes, but my sperm decide the sex of the baby."

"Are you saying you don't want a girl?"

"No." He stands, backing me into the counter, hands on either side of me. "I'm saying he could be a boy. That's all." That grin of his is so contagious.

"We're having a baby," I whisper. "But I don't want to tell anyone. Can we keep it a secret?"

"Yes, Mrs. Sikes, we can keep it a secret. After all, my

grandpa will be told it's a honeymoon baby, and we haven't left for our honeymoon, so mum's the word, Mommy."

My arms wrap around his neck. "Let's go celebrate. This dress was made for dancing."

CHAPTER
forty-four

There are never enough miracles.

Price

AMELIA WORE her mother's bridal gown. An ivory dress with a high lace neck. By all accounts, it was the ugliest thing either one of us had ever seen. The back of the dress had twenty-seven tiny buttons. Needless to say, we fucked like maniacs with the dress still on because we were both a little drunk, and I wasn't allowed to tear off the buttons that seemed too big to fit through the tight holes.

Her mom died of colon cancer three weeks after our wedding.

The dress resides in a white box on a top shelf in our closet. Amelia hasn't decided if she will pressure Astrid to wear it one day.

I vote no. Fuck sentimentality. Let the girl wear her

own beautiful dress. I'd say with fewer buttons if I weren't her father.

Not once since my diagnosis have we discussed her mother's death. But I've thought about it. I've thought my wife doesn't deserve to lose another person in her life to cancer.

"You're awfully quiet," she says while we watch the happy couple cut their small, two-tiered cake adorned with pink roses that look real.

I reach under the table and take her hand. "I was thinking about our wedding and all those damn buttons."

She snorts. "*So* many buttons. You unbuttoned half. We fell asleep. Then you finished unbuttoning them in the morning. How many brides can say they slept in their wedding gown?"

"It was a rough night. All pussy, no tits."

"Shh ... stop!" Her other hand reaches for my mouth to silence me. "You are terrible." She laughs.

"I should have been given something ... like a Purple Heart. My fingers were nearly bleeding after all those buttons. Talk about wounded in the line of duty."

She slides over to my lap, and I push back in my chair to make room. "I love our life." Her hand presses to my face before she kisses me.

I love this soft kiss. And I love her and Astrid. But something about our life or lifestyle led to my cancer. We've been inching our way back to how things were because it comforts my wife and daughter. It doesn't feel sustainable.

If Scottie had said yes to getting on a plane with me and jetting off to an island, I might have done it.

Not because I don't love Amelia more.

Not because I want to abandon my daughter.

Not because I regret my life.

I would have done it to live.

I'm not ready to die. Why does living have to feel so selfish?

Scottie would live in the moment with me. Our life would be simple and beautiful in its own way. And I would love her. My love for her would grow. Had she not lost the baby, I would have married her, and we would have had a good life.

How can I love my wife *and* love another woman?

I wouldn't have had the answer to that question a year ago. But when you let your mind step outside social boundaries, the rules lose meaning, and love feels limitless.

"Let's sell the house and leave Philly," I say while we watch the bride and groom eat cake and laugh with Scottie's nieces, who can't decide if they want to lick the frosting from their fingers or twirl in circles to the music.

Amelia leans to the side to look me in the eye. "What?" She laughs.

"We can live anywhere in the world. Let's pick someplace that feels new. Someplace with lots of sunshine and fresh air. Far away from the city. Astrid can learn from books and life experiences. Her social network won't involve likes and follows. She'll make real friends and communicate real emotions and words instead of abbreviations and emojis. Maybe we'll give her a brother or sister."

The confusion on my wife's face softens with that last part. "Astrid loves her life in Philly. She loves her friends and her activities. My dad lives two hours from us. And your parents are a ten-minute drive away. My brother just started working for you, and he's engaged. Also, I love my job. We ... we're already living the dream." She runs her hand along my tie. "And you've been given a second chance. Are you unhappy?"

"I *have* been given a second chance, which means it would be foolish not to make a change so that I don't waste it by repeating the same thing."

"You're not doing the same thing. You're eating better. And you're only working three days a week."

"I'm eating worse than I was eating to get better. And last week, all three of my days were ten-hour days because I have the kind of job that relentlessly takes until I have nothing left to give."

"You're your own boss. Delegate. Or quit. You don't have to work. And if you want to move, let's look for a place in Chesterbrook or Ardmore so Astrid can still see her friends."

I frown. "Amelia ... it's more than that. I don't want to live in the burbs. And I don't want to live in a polluted city where we endure months of cold weather. I don't want Wi-Fi in my house, and I don't want to carry a cell phone. I don't want my daughter glued to an iPad and complaining that her friends have a phone, but she doesn't. It's not just about me. I've changed. And this isn't the life I want for you or Astrid, either."

She chuckles. "You want to leave our families and live in the middle of nowhere?"

"That's a simplified, lackluster version of what I'm suggesting, but ... yes."

She gazes around the tent, slowly shaking her head. "You can't ask this of a nine-year-old."

"What happens when the cancer comes back?"

"We're not going to let that happen. Even though you didn't want to make a follow-up appointment, I did it for you. We'll monitor you and catch anything before it gets too advanced again. But it won't. You're better. I feel it."

This is the woman who tried to perform CPR on me while I was still breathing. God, I'm madly in love with her, but she's not good under stress. And her heart won't let her see reality when it's not filled with rainbows and roses. It's an endearing quality that's also dangerous.

I start to speak just as Koen and Scottie approach our table. The blushing bride doesn't look me in the eye, and I can't blame her. I tried to steal her for purely selfish reasons.

"I haven't had a chance to meet your wife," Koen says.

"That's right." I smile. "Koen, this is Amelia."

She slides from my lap back to her chair and offers her hand to him. "It's very nice to meet you. Thank you for inviting us. We needed an excuse to get away by ourselves for a little while."

"Thank *you* for coming." He releases her hand.

"I heard you built your house," Amelia says. "That's impressive."

Koen goes into a long spiel about the inspiration and the process while Scottie's gaze floats around the tent with her hand resting flat against her stomach.

I can't take my eyes off her hand as she occasionally moves it in a slow circle. Either she's hungry or pregnant. Her hand stills, and she abruptly drops it to her side. My gaze lifts to meet hers.

After a few slow blinks, I offer her a tiny grin. A beautiful blush paints her cheeks.

"Excuse me," I interrupt. "I'll be right back."

Amelia ignores me, and Koen gives me a quick nod while talking. As I emerge from the tent, I loosen my tie and stroll toward the backyard, where the chairs have been picked up. Then, I follow a flagstone path behind the detached garage to a firepit, stacks of wood, and open barrels stuffed with pieces of scrap metal.

"Amelia is perfect for you."

I turn.

Scottie steps closer, the skirt of her dress gathered in one hand.

"Is this where I say Koen is perfect for you?"

"Is he not?"

I lift a shoulder. "He's fine."

"Fine?" Her eyes widen.

"You'll have babies and most likely grow old and die together surrounded by grandkids and great-grandkids."

She laughs. "Sounds like a horrible life."

My hands slide into my pockets. "The first night we had dinner in Austin, had I kissed you, had I shown interest beyond friendship, would you be standing here today in that wedding gown with that ring on your finger?"

"Price—"

"Humor me."

She sighs. "No."

I nod several times.

"Had I kissed you and told you about the baby, would you have left your wife and daughter to be with me?"

I grunt a tiny laugh with my lips pressed together.

"Humor me," she says.

"No. I would not have."

"Why?" She cocks her head.

"For the same reason we're standing here instead of sitting on a private jet. Things like love and lust aren't always choices. They're emotions. But commitment is one hundred percent a choice."

Scottie does her headshake to brush her bangs away from her eyes. "Yet, when we were standing in the bedroom minutes before I committed myself to Koen, you offered me something." Her eyes narrow. "And I don't think it was a joke. Why now?"

I rub the back of my neck, staring at my brown leather dress shoes, perfectly polished for the occasion. "I don't know if I can make my wife happy *and* beat this cancer. She thinks I'm a miracle. And maybe I am. But I think it will take a lot more miracles for me to keep living." Blowing out a long breath, I lift my gaze to Scottie. "I'm struggling with it. And I hate that it was easier to *live,* in the most literal sense, when we weren't together, but it was. She can't see how desperate and vulnerable I feel. And I'm afraid to show her because I feel guilty for ..."

"Having cancer? Doing what you felt you needed to survive?"

I nod slowly. "I feel so weak and ... lost."

Scottie fiddles with her wedding band. "If I would have said yes, would we be on that plane right now?"

It takes a few seconds for my thoughts to shift back to my "proposal." I know the answer, but I don't know if she's ready for it. As soon as I doubt her ability to handle the truth, my conscience nudges me to wake up. She's not Amelia. Scottie can handle the truth.

"Yes," I whisper.

Tears well in her eyes despite her soft smile and shaky inhale. Lifting her dress again, she takes two steps toward me, and her free hand reaches for mine. "You don't need me anymore. You don't *need* anyone to live. You said it yourself: commitment is a choice. If you must choose between your life and a life with Amelia, even if it's shortened, there is no wrong choice." She releases my hand, ghosting her fingers along my palm, gazing at our hands. "Whatever you decide, it will be the bravest decision you've ever made."

No man has ever been luckier in love. The women I've loved—and will always love—have bestowed upon me everything beautiful and worthwhile in my life.

"We'd better get back," I whisper.

"You go ahead. I need a minute."

As I step past her, I press my hand to her stomach.

Her breath hitches.

"If it's a boy, Price and Henry are great names."

I take the next step before she can cover my hand with hers.

And the next.

And I keep going even if I don't know where this will lead or how long I'll be there.

CHAPTER
forty-five

A sacred intimacy.

Scottie

MY HEART HAS NEVER FELT this full.

Filled with love and hope—and a little bit of sadness.

Just before midnight, the last few guests (our parents) pull out of the driveway, leaving us alone for the first time in two days.

"Thank you," Koen says.

After a final wave, I turn toward him, his suit jacket draped over my shoulders. "For what?"

"Marrying me."

I take his hand and place it on my stomach. "Thank you for this life. Even if I'm a little terrified of losing it."

"Or you could just be elated that by this time next year, we'll be sleep-deprived and obsessed with our tiny human."

My arms snake around his neck. "I like your idea the best."

He scoops me up, stealing my breath. "Time to carry you over the threshold, Mrs. Scottie Sikes."

I giggle while he hauls me into the house; my sandals fall off my feet before we reach the bedroom. His gaze snags on my ankle as he sets me on the bed.

"Is that your something blue?"

I pull my knee to my chest and unhook the anklet. "I suppose it is. Price gave it to me. It's blue sodalite for tranquility and emotional balance. He bought a blue sodalite from the apothecary the summer we met. I told him it was a butt plug; then he told me it was a gift for his parents' anniversary. Also, a lie."

Koen chuckles, taking the anklet from me and inspecting it before setting it on the nightstand. "I'm glad he and Amelia made it." He offers me his hand, pulling me to my feet. "He's a miracle." With gentle hands, he reaches behind me and slowly unzips my dress. "Not as miraculous as my wife." With a grin, he ducks his head and kisses my jaw to my ear and down my neck while my dress pools at my feet, leaving me in white lace underwear and a sea of goosebumps.

"I couldn't breathe, Scottie," he murmurs, fingers whispering over my skin, one hand sliding into the back of my underwear. "Seeing you for the first time today, I couldn't breathe."

My eyes drift shut from his intoxicating touch.

"You looked at me—only me—the whole way. And I felt so scared. I thought of all the ways I could mess this up. You're all I think about." He kisses me slowly for a few seconds. "I just want to give you the world."

I slowly remove his tie and work the buttons to his shirt while he pulls the hairpins from my hair. "Koen, you've already given me the world, and we haven't even consummated the marriage." Biting my bottom lip, I grin and lift my gaze to his as my fingers finish with the last three buttons.

After the last one, he shrugs off his shirt, and I unfasten his pants.

Nothing is hurried.

Time is irrelevant.

We kiss.

Our hands explore.

My breasts feel a little heavier in his hands, my nipples a little more sensitive when he teases them with his teeth and tongue. Everything just *feels* more tonight.

A sacred intimacy.

A true belonging.

And a life that lives inside me, part of Koen inside me.

He guides me to my stomach, peppering kisses along my back, fingers curling into the lace to drag my underwear down my legs.

I glance back at him while he loses his briefs. Every muscle shifting and flexing, mesmerizing as he crawls over me.

He kisses my shoulder, and his hand slides between the bed and my stomach, lifting my pelvis and driving into me.

A soft groan vibrates his chest, and my lips part to accommodate my breaths that he's stirring into a frenzy of need.

"You're the most stunning creation on this earth," he

whispers in my ear, driving deep inside me. My back arches, fingers curling into the bedding.

He kisses the back of my neck while his hand on my stomach slides lower, hand on my inner thigh, thumb circling my clit.

The tension builds until I can barely keep my eyes open, and the tiny grunts we share fade into nothing because all I can hear is my own heart hammering against the mattress.

He pulls out, turns me over, and reenters me. Our fingers interlace while we kiss, chests flush and rubbing together with each desperate thrust.

My legs lock around his waist, thighs burning as I grind into the tension that's ... it's ... oh god ...

Every nerve in my body pulses with blinding pleasure —one wave after another.

"I love..." he lifts onto his hands for leverage "you ... so..." his face tenses, and it's vulnerable like a beautiful pain "...fucking much." He stills, pelvis jerking several times before he collapses on top of me.

Before I can free my arms from his to hug him, he rolls us to the side and pulls me into his chest, face buried in my hair.

"Consummated."

I laugh, my body vibrating with pure joy. "I want to soak in a big bathtub with you, but you don't have one. What are we going to do about that?"

He hums, kissing my head. "I think your husband should build a house for his wife and children."

"That's so sexy."

He pulls his head back. "Are you being serious?"

"You building me a house? Uh ... yeah." I can't hide my grin.

"Hmm ..." His lips corkscrew. "What else do you find sexy about your husband?"

Husband ...

This life with Koen is going to be the best.

CHAPTER

forty-six

I think this year I will put a big bow on my head and hope my family gets the significance of it.

Price

I STAY.

Three work days turn into four—ten-plus hour work days. I could quit and stay home, but it wouldn't matter. My home is not my refuge. It's a fortress of the excess that no longer serves me.

Amelia and Astrid settle back into the pre-cancer routine.

Eight hours of sleep turns into six, sometimes less, because my wife is a night owl who likes to binge TV shows, and sex takes place after those shows. And if sex doesn't happen, then she assumes something is wrong with me.

Reassuring her I'm fine is a full-time job, much like doing things to actually be fine was a full-time job. And if

I hint that I'm not fine, her answer involves a trip to the doctor. I could leave again ... but I need my wife and daughter. So, I'm letting this play out, trying to stay positive and not feel burdened by the stress.

By Thanksgiving, we're celebrating the holidays and one-year post-diagnosis. By all accounts, I should be dead.

"They're gone." Amelia dramatically wipes her forehead and leans against the front door after my parents, her dad, and my sister leave. "What's that look?" Her smile dies when I sit on the stairs.

I fold my hands between my spread legs. "I haven't been feeling well."

She frowns. "Haven't been feeling well as in—"

"I think the cancer's back."

Slowly, she shakes her head. "You shouldn't have skipped your last appointment. I'll call first thing in the morning."

"Babe, if it's back, it's not because I skipped an appointment."

She kneels on the floor before me, pulling her hair over one shoulder before resting her hands on my knees. "I'll go grocery shopping and get you everything you need. It's the holidays; I think you can take time off work. Whatever you need."

I cover her hands with mine. "We need to leave Philly. I can't do this here."

The lines along her forehead intensify. "You want to move," she murmurs, eyes glazing over like they did at Scottie's wedding when I suggested it.

"Move where?" Astrid says.

I glance over my shoulder while she descends the stairs.

"Nowhere. Dad and I were talking about something else," Amelia stands, brushing off the knees to her gray slacks.

"I don't want to move." Astrid wraps her arms around me. "Casey moved last year, and now I only have two friends left."

Amelia presses her lips together, eyeing me like I'm the bad guy.

"Sometimes people move, and they make new friends, maybe even more friends." I kiss her hand before pulling her down to sit on my lap. "Life is an adventure. Don't you think a new adventure would be fun?"

Her lips corkscrew to the side while her nose wrinkles. "I like it here."

"We're not going anywhere anytime soon, sweetie." Amelia rests her hand on Astrid's head while passing us to climb the stairs. "Let's get you ready for bed."

———

OVER THE NEXT FEW DAYS, Amelia hovers, picks at her nails, and suggests I call the doctor. I feel her internal struggle but don't know how to ease her mind. And I know the doctor will not give her the news she wants.

Despite my efforts to take care of myself, I can't meditate. My mind won't settle. Six inches of snow make it impossible to walk in the grass. And Astrid's activities are in overdrive instead of slowing down for the holidays. The hustle and bustle of life isn't ideal for healing cancer.

Three weeks before Christmas, I get a video call from Koen while we eat dinner.

"Christmas came early," he says, giving me a toothy grin before flipping the camera to Scottie sitting in a rocking chair with a baby pressed to her chest sleeping.

"Did she have the baby?" Amelia stands bent over behind me. "Oh my goodness," she draws out the words in a half squeal. "How precious."

"Congratulations," I smile because I couldn't be happier for her. "Did you name him Price or Henry?"

Scottie kisses the baby's head and grins. "We named *her* Penelope Ann Sikes."

Amelia squeezes my arm, a silent reminder that I suggested we have another baby; that was also when I suggested we move as far away from modern civilization as possible.

"How's the house coming along?" I ask, noticing a plastic wall in the background.

Scottie eyes Koen, and he quickly flips the camera around to himself again. "Let's not talk about that. My brother met someone and knocked her up, so—"

"Got her pregnant," Scottie corrects.

"That's what I said, darling. I'm going to give Price a tour. You just keep being amazing." He blows her a kiss while walking toward the plastic. "She got a little high maintenance," he whispers, sliding through a slit in the plastic wall, "during the last month. I thought she was going to kill me. I'm talking about a version of Scottie I never knew existed. I haven't picked up a hammer in the past month."

"Hormones. Settle into that, buddy."

Amelia sits back in her chair, giving me the stink eye while taking a bite of salmon.

Koen nods slowly. "For sure. But I'm close to finishing. If my brother can give me a hand with the rest of the cabinets in the closets, I bet I can have everything done by February. How are your holidays going? Are you feeling good? Scottie's been dying for an update, but she knows you're probably sick of people asking you that." He moves the camera around to show me the turquoise tile shower and marbled vanity, before moving into the closet that needs cabinets and has a temporary closet rod with clothes against one wall.

Amelia squeezes my shoulder before slinking back into her chair at Koen's request for a health update.

I shrug. "I'm alive."

Koen chuckles. "That's good to hear." He backtracks, bringing Scottie into the picture again. "Price is alive."

Scottie eyes me, but she doesn't smile. And I draw in a deep breath to keep my fake smile inflated.

She clears her throat and rubs Penelope's back. "You're looking a little thin."

Is she saying that for my benefit or Amelia's?

When I don't respond, Scottie follows up with a pleasant smile. "What does Astrid want for Christmas?"

"An electric scooter," Astrid says over a mouthful of green beans.

"And by electric scooter, she means Legos." I wink at Astrid.

"Noooo ..." Astrid giggles. "Not Legos."

"Well, there you have it. Legos. What does Penelope want for Christmas?"

Scottie chuckles. "Nothing. That's just a sign of good

parenting—raising kids who want for nothing. I don't know what you're doing wrong, Milloy, but you should try a little harder."

Both Astrid and Amelia giggle.

I want to crawl through the phone and hug my friend. I want to tell her how happy I am for her. Everyone deserves that level of happiness, especially my friend, who encompasses so much positivity and hope.

"I think this year I will put a big bow on my head and hope my family gets the significance of it." I laugh.

Scottie smiles, but it's a sad one.

Astrid ignores me.

And Amelia's eyes fill with tears.

Shit.

I've lost my touch with the ladies.

"I don't want to keep you from that bundle of joy. Merry Christmas, friends. I'm incredibly happy for you," I say.

"Merry Christmas," they chime together.

And I hate that Scottie knows my life isn't perfect at the moment, but I'm alive, and that's all that matters today.

After setting my phone on the table, I pick up my fork.

"I'm done," Astrid says. "Can I play on my iPad?"

I nod.

When she skips out of the dining room, I reach for Amelia's hand. She stills, staring at her plate of half-eaten food.

"I'm sorry. It was a joke. A bad joke."

She doesn't respond. The hum of the furnace seems to get louder the longer we sit here without speaking.

Silence magnifies everything. When I left home a year ago, silence wasn't my friend.

Now, I crave it.

"Are you still feeling bad?" she whispers.

"Does it matter?" I'm too tired to lie to her. She knows that answer.

Her gaze stretches to mine. "Don't say that. Of course, it matters."

I release her hand. "I feel like ..." Shaking my head, I weigh my words. "I feel like I worked really hard to remove the weeds from an overgrown garden. And there was this moment, a sigh of relief that I did it—a hard-earned accomplishment. But if I blink and I'm not vigilant, the weeds will get out of control again."

"But how are you feel—"

"Tired," I cut her off because I know she needs the simple truth, even if she doesn't know what to do with it. And she doesn't. She's so lost in her emotions that she can't feel me. Maybe I'm so lost in mine that I can't feel hers. "I'm tired, and sometimes my back hurts. This morning, I felt nauseous."

Her eyes redden. "And you *are* thinner."

Planting my elbows on the table, I rest my face in my hands, rubbing away the tension and building exhaustion.

"You shouldn't have skipped your follow-up visit."

"Jesus ... we've been over this."

Her lips part, taking a breath to speak, but she releases it without a word.

"I'm going to ask my mom to come get Astrid."

"Why?" She squints.

"Because it's going to get ugly."

CHAPTER

forty-seven

Let's hurt tonight.

"THANK YOU," I say to my mom while waiting for Astrid to climb into the backseat. "We'll get her in the morning. Goodnight, sweetie." I kiss Astrid's head.

My mom glances back at me, concern lining every inch of her face.

"Hope you and Mommy enjoy the movie," Astrid says with an innocent smile.

"We will." I shut the door, chalking this up to one more lie I've been forced to tell so that the people I love don't suffer as much.

But my wife is not ten. She's not my child. She is my partner. And I can no longer protect her from the truth. This is our sickness and health. This is where we decide what those vows mean. And I hate how angry I feel returning to our condo.

322

After I lock the door, I find her in the kitchen with a glass of white wine in one hand and her other resting on the edge of the counter. "I don't know how to do this."

I grunt, glancing up at the intricate details of the custom-molded ceiling. "Do *this*. What is *this*?" I meet her gaze. "Marriage? Cancer? A difference of opinions? Solving a problem? Pivoting when life puts up a really fucking huge roadblock?"

She sips her wine, hand a little shaky, emotions raw in her eyes.

This, whatever it is, will hurt. I can't avoid it any longer.

"I don't know how to let you go," she whispers with the first few tears.

"You don't know how to hold on to me. I feel like all you're doing *is* letting me go. Escorting me to my grave." I hate my words, but I can't hide them any longer.

"That is not fair." Her reply cuts through the air, making a chilling transformation in the mood. "How can you say that?" She wipes her cheek with the back of her hand.

"Because I work forty hours a week, and we don't need the money. And I know I could quit and stay home, but I don't want to be here either. I can't focus here. I can't journal or meditate because I spend all day thinking about this life that's killing me. It's cold as fuck outside, and I haven't seen the sun in weeks. You have Astrid, a ten-year-old, in every goddamn activity she can possibly be in, which means we are constantly on the go. And people who are on the go rarely eat at home or eat anything that's good for them. So, I'm back to putting shit in my diseased body. Tonight was the first time since

Thanksgiving that we've eaten at home. I don't have grass to walk on. I've given up on juicing because ... what's the point if everything else is in chaos? I get six hours of restless sleep, and that's on a good night. So, you tell me ... if your refusal to pack up and move to 'the middle of nowhere' is not escorting me to my grave, then what are you doing?"

Wiping more tears, she mumbles, "It's all about you."

Pressing my hands to the side of my head, my fingers dig into my scalp. "Jesus Christ, I'm *so* sorry I'm the one who has cancer. It should have been you. Then, you could have gotten all of the special attention. I love this. I love the pain. I love that not dying takes literally everything I have. You should be jealous. Cancer is ah-fucking-mazing!"

She sobs, shaking her head. "You're an asshole. A c-cruel asshole."

I nod. "Yep. I sure am. That's a good start to my eulogy. Should we write that down, or—"

"STOP IT!" She hurls the wine glass at me but misses by a mile. "You want me to hate you? Is that it?"

"Hate me?" I laugh, shaking my head. "No. I'm waiting for you to love me. To. Fucking. Love. Me! You hit me with your car and tried to perform CPR while I was breathing, staring you straight in the eye. You instinctually tried to save me when I wasn't dying. And I swear that's when I fel—" Pinching the bridge of my nose, I try to keep my composure, but this hurts.

My nose burns first, then my eyes. And my throat thickens. I can't stop it. "That's when I fell in love with you." I swallow hard, dropping my hand, voice shaky. "And now, eleven years and one child later, when I *know* I love you to the depths of my soul, and I need ... I fucking *need* you to save my life, you won't even look at me."

She drags her gaze from the floor to meet mine, making no attempt to keep up with her tears. And as much as I want to look away and not blink to keep my tears in check, I don't. I bleed every emotion. I lay it all at her feet because this is the only moment we have. There is no guarantee of another one. And if I continue to protect her from my truth, we are already over. I'm already dead.

"Astrid—"

"No, Amelia. This isn't about Astrid."

"How can you say that?"

"Because she's ten. And she's resilient. When she's old enough to process this properly, she'll be brokenhearted that she's had to grow up without her father. And it won't matter how many friends she has, how accomplished a dancer she becomes, or what worldly possessions she's accumulated. Nothing will make this right.

"Or ... she will experience a new way of living that truly values life. And maybe, by some miracle, we'll look back *together* on this moment and laugh at how ridiculous it was that we gave the decision a second thought. So this has nothing to do with Astrid and everything to do with you and your fear of change. Your fear of losing control. Your fear of losing me. But if I stay, this is the beginning of the end because I'm not going to let them cut me open or dump toxic chemicals into my body so that you can feel good about the choice a doctor thinks I should make. I can either live *with* you or die *for* you. It's your decision."

She returns a blank stare. No more tears. Barely any

detectable emotion. "Price, everything you do is for us. You're the sacrificial one. The martyr. And I'm being truthful when I say that. I've never taken for granted how hard you've worked for our family. But in that process, I've been raising our daughter. I'm the one who comforts her when she's sick. I'm the one who listens to her when she's had a bad day at school. When you left, I was the one left to explain your absence without breaking her heart. I'm the one who's done everything possible to keep her from feeling this pain that's been residing in our house for over a year. And if you die, I'll be the one to pick up the tiny pieces of her heart and put them back together. So you say this isn't about Astrid, but that's just convenient for you. If you die on my watch, Astrid will blame me. If you die on your doctor's watch, she'll chalk it up to life. But at least she'll always believe we did our best to fight it."

I rub my eyes and then my temples. "You have me dying in both scenarios." I turn. "There's nothing left to say."

CHAPTER

forty-eight

I'm dying. Go ahead and talk dirty to me.

> Scottie: Hi. Can we talk about my
> boobs? They're leaking uncontrollably.
> And my little girl won't stay awake long
> enough to help her mommy out. But we
> have our Christmas tree up. Look!

IT'S BEEN three days since I've talked to my wife.

Three days since I've gone to work.

I spend all day in my miserably gloomy office. When Astrid comes home from school, we play the part of happy parents. We interact with her without saying a word to each other.

Amelia sleeps in the guest room at night after Astrid's in bed.

I lean back in my desk chair and inspect the Christmas tree on my phone screen. It makes me smile.

> Price: This isn't the torrid love affair I imagined us having. Don't start with your boobs and then send me a photo of a tree.

She replies with a photo of Penelope in a wrap carrier on her chest.

> Price: Still not boobs. But arguably more precious.

Scottie: Whatcha doing?

Planning my funeral.

> Price: Trying to convince yet another woman to escape this life with me. It's earned me the silent treatment. We're on day 3.

She doesn't respond immediately, so I put my phone on the desk and lace my fingers behind my head.

Scottie: Give her time. She's making decisions for her and your daughter. She's trying to understand this journey you've had to take without her.

> Price: Time might not be on my side.

Again, there's a long pause.

Scottie: Whatever you decide to do, it will be the right decision.

> Price: How can you say that?

> Scottie: Because I had a decision to make on my wedding day. And I knew either decision would be right. Make the decision. Then, make it right.

> Price: Nothing is easier than not existing

> Scottie: That's my line

> Price: I might need to borrow it

> Scottie: Don't leave without saying goodbye

I nod slowly to myself. "Define leaving," I whisper.

> Price: Merry Christmas

> Scottie: Merry Christmas x

Swiveling in my chair, I gaze at the photos in matte black and gold frames. Amelia and I attended so many professional sporting events because she got tickets through work. And we took pictures at all of them.

So in love.

Best friends.

A perfect match.

There was never a time in our marriage that I thought we wouldn't last, never a time where I imagined myself with anyone else. Not even Scottie.

Everyone who knows my wife knows she's filled with life. Feisty. The life of the party. She knows no enemies. She loves *so* hard. But unlike Scottie, Amelia has many fears. With her, there's no living in the moment. Her mind is always three steps ahead, anticipating everyone's needs, or three steps behind, figuring out what went wrong with a proposal at work or why Astrid didn't have fun at a friend's birthday party. She's a fixer.

But she can't fix me the way she thinks I need to be fixed. She's carrying enough fear over losing me for both her and Astrid.

"Dad! Guess what?" Astrid runs into my office with her backpack falling off her shoulders.

"What?" I turn in my chair.

"Emma's sick. So, I get to be Clara instead of a fairy." She hugs me.

God, I love this girl.

"My daughter's the star of The Nutcracker. I'll need your autograph."

"My autograph?" She pulls away from me, wrinkling her nose.

"Yes. Right here." I uncap a Sharpie and point to the top of my desk. "Write your name."

"I can't write on your desk."

"It's my desk. If I say you can write on it, then you can write on it."

She giggles while writing her name in big letters. "Can we get pizza tonight?"

"No, honey," Amelia says, stepping into my office, arms crossed. "I'm making dinner. Lots of veggies and cabbage soup."

Astrid's nose wrinkles. "Cabbage soup? Can we have blueberry muffins in case I don't like the soup?"

"No."

"We can have pizza," I say, lifting Astrid off my lap and standing.

"Yay!" Astrid runs out of my office.

My wife opens her mouth but closes it just as quickly, turns, and leaves me alone in my office.

There's nothing easier than not existing.

I head up the stairs and peek in on Astrid, who ignores me while playing with her iPad.

When I get to our bedroom, Amelia's hanging the clean clothes in the closet.

"I'll go back to the doctor. And we'll see where I'm at on this. If they suggest chemo, then I'll do chemo. We'll let Astrid be part of this so she understands what's happening every step of the way."

She turns to face me. "Don't do this for me," she whispers.

"I'm doing it for her."

After a few seconds, she nods.

———

FOUR DAYS BEFORE CHRISTMAS, we get the news. The cancer is spreading again. It's no surprise to me, and this time, I can see from Amelia's composure that it's no surprise to her either.

"I have the same options for you as before," Dr. Faber says, folding her hands in her lap.

"Let's do the chemo," I say with a firm nod and fake smile.

"Do you want to discuss it?" Amelia rests her hand on my arm.

I shrug. "What's there to discuss?"

Her forehead wrinkles while her teeth dig into her lower lip.

"We can start right after Christmas or wait until after New Year's."

"The sooner, the better," I say.

Dr. Faber nods. "I'll walk you out and get everything scheduled."

I stand, and so does the doctor, but Amelia doesn't. She stares at her lap, hands gripped to the edge of the chair.

"Coming?" I hold out a hand.

She's expressionless. When she glances up, her vacant eyes find mine. Without taking my hand, she stands, and we follow the doctor.

We schedule future appointments.

We drive home in silence.

My mom greets us as soon as we open the door. "How did it go?" she asks, wringing her hands together.

I can only imagine what she must be feeling. No parent wants to lose a child.

"Well, the cancer has spread again, but I'm lined up to start chemo after Christmas. So, all we can do is take it one day at a time."

Lips pressed together, she nods several times, tears building in her eyes.

I hug her. "It's not the end of the world," I whisper.

She sniffles. "M-my boy. You are my world."

Amelia wipes her eyes and jogs up the stairs.

As my mom pulls away, she digs out a tissue from her pocket and wipes her nose. "Why don't you go away again? Whatever you did before worked, right?"

"It's not sustainable. It's not fair to leave Amelia and Astrid again. And for how long? This is my life here. I'll do what I can here."

"I hate this." She blots the corners of her eyes.

"I don't exactly love it, but it's part of life, and I'm at peace with whatever happens. I will enjoy Christmas with my family and deal with everything else as it comes. One day at a time."

She gives me another hug. "I love you. I love you more than anyone. And I can't have you leave this world before me. Do you hear me?"

I can't fucking speak, so I nod.

When she drags herself away and the door closes behind her, I take a deep breath and climb the stairs.

"Hey, sunshine. Can we talk?"

Astrid sets her book aside and sits up straight on the edge of her bed. "About what?"

Amelia's hand rests on my back for a second, and then her fingers interlace with mine.

"My cancer is back. And this time, I'm going to have a special treatment called chemotherapy to slow its growth. And we don't know if it will work, but we're going to try."

She frowns. "Are you going to die?"

Amelia squeezes my hand just before I release hers to make my way to Astrid. I kneel in front of her, resting my hands on her legs. "I don't know, baby girl. And I know that's not what you want to hear. I wish I could promise you more, but I can't. But whatever you feel about my cancer is okay. If you're sad or angry, that's okay. If you feel confused or scared, that's okay, too. I don't want you to hide your feelings."

Crocodile tears slide down her cheeks in a blink, and her lips quiver. "I d-don't want y-you to die."

I wrap her in my arms, kissing her head over and over. "I know," I manage to squeak two words while I pray for time to slow down so I can just hold my little girl as long as possible.

Amelia sits next to Astrid and hugs both of us, her sobs leaking out despite how hard I know she's trying to be strong.

Some things in life just hurt, and there's no way to acknowledge them without the pain. Disease sucks. Dying sucks. And what hurts the most is knowing my part will be the easiest.

There's nothing easier than not existing.

CHAPTER

forty-nine

I forgot to dream this big.

Scottie

"TA-DA!" Koen opens the bathroom door.

The tiled shower has been done for a month, but my big soaker was on backorder.

"Merry Christmas." He takes Penelope from me.

She always looks extra small in his hands. And I love nothing more than seeing her nestled against his bare chest.

"Did you wake up early to finish this?" I step onto the tiled floor, my nightie soaked from leaky breasts. I know I smell of sour milk.

"I might have. So why don't you take a nice warm bath while Penelope and I make breakfast and see if Santa came last night. Oh, and I got a late-night text from Price wishing us an early Merry Christmas. Evidently, I'm not the only one who didn't sleep last night."

335

I plug the drain and turn on the water to fill the tub next to a window overlooking our new wooded lot just a few blocks from the shipping container house we're renting out as a vacation home per Price's suggestion.

"I think his cancer's back. I recently messaged him."

"Is that what he said?"

"He alluded to it." I peel off my nightie and hide in the toilet stall to remove my postpartum diaper, as I call it.

"Should we expect a guest soon who needs to walk in our grass and drink juice until he's orange?"

I flush the toilet and step into the bathtub. My eyes nearly roll back in my head; it feels so good. "I'm afraid not. I think he's staying for Amelia and Astrid."

"Staying as in doing all of his rituals at home or staying as in ..."

Dying. He won't say the word, and he doesn't have to.

I shrug. I can't talk about this. "I'm starving."

Koen gives me a comforting grin, getting my hint. "Okay, Mommy." He holds her tight, bending down to kiss my head. "Take your time. Breakfast will be waiting."

"Damn," I say just as he reaches the door.

He glances over his shoulder.

I grin. "My husband is *hot*. I think you should always be shirtless in the house."

He winks at me. "Careful, you'll end up pregnant again in no time if you keep saying things like that."

"Wasn't that the plan from the beginning?"

With a chuckle, he starts to slide the door shut, then stops. "Are you happy, Scottie?"

I adjust the water temperature. "Happy? Is that a real question?"

"Do you miss working at the shop? You said you never took the time to dream, so you weren't sure if this was your dream. But now that you're living whatever this is, are you happy? Content? Because if you're not—"

"Koen," I slide down until my shoulders are submerged, "I had this discussion with my mom last week when she called to give me their flight information. It's sad that we still devalue women and their choices. If a woman works full-time, it means she's not prioritizing her family. If a woman chooses to stay home and raise a family full-time, it means she's sacrificing some sort of goals that society thinks she should have. I'm exactly where I want to be, doing exactly what I want to do. And this life we have together has exceeded even my grandest expectations. If someday I desire more than what I'm doing now, you'll be the first to know. And I don't know if I'm old enough to declare my 'life's purpose,' but I knew when I held Penelope in my arms for the first time that she is unequivocally my heart's purpose."

His smile grows in tiny increments. "Thanks for choosing me."

After he shuts the door, I close my eyes. I could have argued with him that it wasn't a choice, that my heart always knew it was him. That would be a lie. It's okay that love is messy and complicated. If loving too much or too many people is my biggest offense, I'll die with no regrets.

I've thought about the baby I lost more than once since I gave birth to Penelope. During the twelve years Price and I spent apart, I thought about a life with him. And it was always a good one. It took me a while to accept the loss of our baby as nothing more than an unfortunate event. It didn't have to mean anything more or less than that. It wasn't a sign.

It was life.

After my luxurious bath, I dry my hair and slip into reindeer lounge pants and a matching tee. And my husband got the memo that I didn't officially send. He's wearing his reindeer lounge pants, and he dressed Penelope in her reindeer onesie with matching socks pulled up past her knees.

"I put my mom's cinnamon rolls in the oven five minutes ago," Koen says, dancing with Penelope to "Jingle Bell Rock."

I turn on the light and peek into the oven.

"How was your bath?"

"Oh my god, *so* perfect." I fill the tea kettle and plug it into the outlet. "When's your family coming?"

"Not until closer to five. They wanted to give us some alone time for our first Christmas." He continues to bounce and sway in the living room.

"You mean all day cuddling on the sectional? What if we open gifts?"

"Just one. Let's spread them out through the day."

"Then we have to open this one first." I pick up a box wrapped in red and gold stripes with a gold bow.

Koen sits on the sofa, laying Penelope beside him. She kicks and sucks at her fists.

"Shouldn't Penelope open a gift first?"

I smirk. "I think she'll be fine with you opening one first."

He grins, untying the bow while I pick up my little girl and give her the boob she wants more than her fists.

"Worst gift ever," he says.

I giggle. "I'm going to remind you of that when it's past midnight, and you're working on that two-thousand-piece puzzle instead of taking your diaper-changing shift."

He inspects the picture. "Is this …"

I nod. "It's the park where I fell in the pond. I took a picture and had it made into a puzzle."

"It would be better if you were in the pond."

"Har har." I roll my eyes.

"Let's go, Scrot." He stands. "Let's get your breakfast."

Scrot jumps up from his bed and follows Koen to the kitchen. Our precious Scrotum hasn't decided what he thinks of Penelope, but he whines when she cries, so we believe he's her advocate and protector.

"Have you checked the weather? Will your parents have good weather to fly down here tomorrow?"

"I think so. Mom will lose her mind if the flight is canceled. She's itching to hold my baby."

"Your baby?" He sets Scrot's food bowl on the tile and joins me on the sectional.

"Yes. She's mine. I grew her in my garden. I harvested her. I feed her. What do you have to offer, buddy?"

"Baby, I planted the seed." He slides off one of Penelope's socks because he's obsessed with kissing her baby toes.

"And for that, I let her carry your last name. But that's where it ends. You get your name in the credits."

He smirks, settling on his side so his mouth can reach her toes.

I love this life we're making. *This* moment trumps all others before it.

CHAPTER

fifty

She's worth the last breath.

Price

I THINK my cancer is pissed off that I tried and nearly succeeded at its eradication. The pain has reached a new level at warp speed. In a matter of weeks, it's dug its claws into me, bringing me to my knees just in time for chemo.

I'm grateful we had one last Christmas together.

I'm grateful I got to see the look on Astrid's face when she unwrapped her scooter.

I'm grateful that Amelia and the rest of my family didn't treat me like a lost cause, even if I knew they were thinking it.

My dad was the only one who let the words "it was too good to be true" slip out at dinner. My mom quickly corrected him with her declaration of gratitude for miracles.

As I slide on my T-shirt, my back protests. Everything

340

protests. I don't remember giving my body permission to give up, but my mind hasn't been where it was the first time I tried to fight this. Today feels like an official waving of the white flag. Cancer, you win.

And I hate that I can't trick my mind into believing I can beat this despite the highly toxic drugs that will be dripping into my veins by ten o'clock this morning.

"I packed several books, your headphones, water, and snacks," Amelia says as I descend the steps to the foyer. "Your mom's in the kitchen making breakfast for Astrid. I'm interviewing several personal chefs next week. I want you to have whatever you need. I should have suggested it a long time ago." Her gaze drops to her feet.

I nod slowly.

A brave smile touches her lips as she glances back up at me. When she digs her key fob from her purse, her shaky hand drops it on the floor.

We squat at the same time. I grab it, and my other hand takes hers as it shakes. When we stand, she eyes me with regret and unshed tears.

Cupping her hand, I bring it to my lips, closing my eyes while kissing her wrist, palm, and fingers. When I open my eyes, she blinks out her tears.

"Are you scared?" she whispers, her words trembling as much as the rest of her.

Keeping my lips pressed to the pulse point on her wrist, I shake my head. "No, my love."

I hope she finds love again when I'm gone. She has so much to share. Some lucky guy will find himself in her path, hopefully not on a bike at a busy intersection, and his life will forever be changed for the better.

"Listen to me. *You* are the greatest love of my life.

And I'm so very sorry for every unkind word I've said out of anger, frustration, and fear. Nothing that has happened or will happen to me in the future is your fault. I credit you with everything beautiful in my life. Being your husband and Astrid's father is an extraordinary gift. Whether I have five days, five years, or five decades left, I could not possibly feel more *whole* than I do right now."

My wife shakes in silent sobs.

"Let's go." I squeeze her hand before releasing it and picking up the bag she packed for me.

The entire way to the cancer center, I rest my hand on her leg. This is her grueling journey, not mine.

I will be fine.

We update labs, and a young brunette nurse named Rose walks us through the procedure and asks if we have any questions.

When Dr. Faber discussed placing a port, I declined. So we're doing an IV infusion in my arm.

As Rose places the IV, Amelia blinks back her tears.

"Baby, you don't need to stay. Why don't you take a walk or check in with Astrid?"

She shakes her head, eyes glued to the IV.

"There's a cafeteria," Rose says. "The coffee's pretty good. And it's early enough that the bagels might not be too hard." She softly chuckles.

Amelia doesn't even look like she's mentally in the same room. Tears continue to fill her unblinking eyes.

The nurse inserts the syringe into the line.

"No!" Amelia lunges for her. "No. No. No ..." She rips the needle out of her hand, tossing it aside before pulling the IV from my arm. "I'm sorry. I'm sorry. I'm *so* s-sorry."

She sobs, climbing onto my lap while the nurse presses a cotton ball to my arm.

Amelia cups my face, forehead against mine, while she falls to pieces. "We'll go. We can go anywhere y-you want in the whole w-world."

I close my eyes. My heart feels like it's been permitted to beat again.

"Not l-like this ..." Her trembling fingers caress my cheeks like I'm fragile. "I can't do th-this. I can't do life without you. Let's go." She lifts her head. "Let's take Astrid and leave everything and everyone else behind." The pad of her thumb brushes my lips. "I was trying to save myself." Again, she rests her head on mine.

The nurse tapes the cotton to my arm and leaves us alone.

"I'm sorry, baby," my wife whispers. "I can't save myself if you're gone. I'll d-die right beside you." She sniffles. "And Astrid needs us. Live for us. P-please."

I wrap my arms around her. "Let's go *live*."

———

IN LESS THAN TWENTY-FOUR HOURS, we say goodbye to our family and a few close friends. The goodbye to my mom is the hardest because as much as I want to promise her that we'll see each other again someday, I can't.

The cancer is more advanced. I feel it.

I don't know if having Amelia and Astrid with me will help or hinder my fight.

I'm in pain.

I'm weak.

And I'm just so exhausted.

Before we left for the cancer clinic, I'd made peace with dying. And I still feel that peace.

But if I'm going to die, I'm glad it will be someplace beautiful with my wife and daughter. It's really all anyone could hope for when their time comes.

And this might be my time.

CHAPTER

fifty-one

There's nothing easier than not existing.

Scottie

KOEN WHISTLES a tune while we remove the ornaments from the tree.

Penelope sleeps on the sofa while Scrot stands guard.

My phone vibrates.

I pick it up from the floor by the plastic tub we bought to store the decorations.

Crash!

The glass ornament falls from my hand as I stare at the screen.

"Scottie?" Koen says my name, but it's nothing but an echo.

Clank!

My phone hits the wood.

My knees give out as my gaze meets Koen's, and I fold to the floor.

Hand over my mouth.

Lump in my throat.

Tears burning my eyes.

I can't breathe ...

Koen pulls me away from the glass and picks up my phone, staring at the message on my screen.

Price: Goodbye <3

EPILOGUE

Eighteen Months Later...

Amelia

"Do you miss him?" Astrid asks from our lounge chairs on the balcony while we drink our fresh-pressed juice. The first time I saw our eye-popping view of lush rainforests, majestic mountains, and epic waterfalls, I knew we would never leave, no matter Price's fate.

"Of course, honey. But life goes on. We'll keep his memories alive."

It's been a life-changing eighteen months atop this high knoll in the middle of a 1,000-acre nature reserve in Costa Rica's Osa region. We have a breathtaking view of three valleys and Mount Chirripó. And because of its high elevation, there are no mosquitos. Nearly everything we eat is picked on the same day.

No TV.

No internet.

We had a private chef when we first arrived since I wasn't prepared to care for Price *and* Astrid physically and emotionally during the transition. Those were the worst days of my life as a wife and a mother. I'd never felt so helpless. And I still wonder if seeing Price's suffering has left a permanent mark on our daughter.

I hope not.

Astrid has friends in town whom she sees weekly. She's been unschooled, reading a book a day, learning about life by living it, and I believe she's thriving. It's what Price imagined for her.

"I think he's in Heaven. Or maybe he's already been reincarnated. Do you believe in reincarnation?"

I chuckle. "I don't know what to believe." I tip my head back and close my eyes. I blame Price. His diagnosis changed me on every level. It shook me to my core. It made me question my faith, my blind trust in modern medicine, my need for control, and it challenged my biggest fear—death and losing the love of my life.

Price taught me to let go of that fear. He said, "There's nothing easier than not existing."

I no longer live with regret; it doesn't serve me. But I struggled with my decisions for a long time. Why couldn't I see what he needed after his first diagnosis?

I wanted him to compromise; he just wanted to live.

Why did my love turn into fear?

Why didn't I trust his intuition to do what was best for him?

When he returned from Austin, why didn't I embrace a new life with him instead of mourning and longing for the old one?

Price was right; I was killing him under the guise of love.

It was fear. A soul-crushing fear of losing control, of losing him. I made it about me and how I felt as his wife and the mother of our child.

The day I told Price it was okay to die, okay to let go, was the day I, too, let go of my mistakes and the regret they carried. I had to be whole inside for Astrid.

"It was a great hike, but my lazy girls refused to get out of bed."

I smile, hearing his strong voice, yearning for the kiss I know he's about to press to the top of my head.

The day I told Price it was okay to die was also the day everything changed. It was the day his body and mind decided it was time to live. I think he was waiting for me to let go.

Price's favorite quote is from Lao Tzu: "The Master does nothing; yet he leaves nothing undone."

When he kisses the top of my head, my skin tingles. Then he steps closer to the balcony's edge, drinking a glass of water and gazing at our view of Heaven.

"We should take Astrid to town today to distract her from Samuel. She's missing him," I say.

Price glances over his bare shoulder. His shorts are low on his waist, and his skin is a delicious bronze. "He's not dead."

Astrid sits up, folding her legs beneath her. "You don't know that."

"He's camouflaged and high up in the trees."

"Dad, I saw him every day for a week. And now he's just gone. I bet it was a jaguar." Astrid easily gets worked up over animals, and Samuel was (is) her unofficial pet sloth.

"He's in the trees. He came down to mate; that's why you saw him, but now he's in the canopy again." Price is good at arguing with her. He calls it "challenging" her.

"Daaaad, they mate in the trees."

Price eyes me as if I'm the one who will confirm if she's correct. I shrug. We know Astrid is smarter than us, especially about wildlife.

"Just say he's dead, and you're happy he's in Heaven," Astrid says, tipping up her defiant little chin.

Price rubs his lips together, no doubt trying to hide his grin. "You're right. It probably was a jaguar."

Astrid stands. "Was that so hard?" She pivots with an extra dose of attitude and heads down the stairs.

Price chuckles, reclining in her empty chair. "We've got a spicy one."

I sip my juice before nodding. "That's what we get for teaching her to question everything. Now she's a know-it-all with an extra side of sass."

Again, he chuckles. It's a beautiful sound.

We have a beautiful life.

I don't know how long it will last. We live a day at a time, grateful for each miraculous moment. My heart still knows I could lose him—the odds may never be in his favor. We sometimes share a knowing glance like we're getting away with something, and it's only a matter of time before this blissful bubble pops.

"It's a good day to go to town. I think we should use that picture of us by the waterfall for postcards," he suggests as if it's not a big deal.

I don't cry, but I want to. It's a huge deal.

We have not contacted family or friends for eighteen months. When we departed, they knew it could be a long time before they'd hear from us, and they knew it could be the last time they saw Price. So I've left it up to him whether or when we contact family.

This is no longer our escape; it's our life. And he's ready to share it.

"Thank you for loving me *this* much," he whispers, reaching for my hand.

Our fingers interlace.

'Til death do us part, my love.

Scottie

THE WEEDS WIN. They always win.

I should surrender to the weeds. Perhaps they have a greater purpose.

"Nope. I won't surrender to you. You're no good," I mumble to myself, yanking another little bastard from the soil of my raised-bed garden while Penelope's wavy brown hair blows in the wind as Koen pushes her on the tree swing.

It doesn't last long. Miss Busybody wants out to play in the dirt.

Minutes later, rocks crunch beneath Koen's boots as he approaches me with mail in one hand and three-month-old Cedar Henry Sikes cradled in his other arm. "Promise not to cry?" he asks. "If you cry, Penn will cry.

And Henry will cry because you two are scary when you cry. So ..."

I sit back on my heels, pulling off my gardening gloves and wiping the sweat from my forehead. "Are we being audited?"

"Worse than that. We need to rename our son. It was all for nothing." He smirks, handing me the stack of mail.

"What are you talking about?" I thumb through the pile of junk, stopping on a postcard.

"No. I said no crying," Koen says.

I shake my head a half-dozen times, trying to control my emotions, but I can't.

"Here come the waterworks." Koen chuckles, squatting next to me.

I hug him, forcing him to balance with Henry in his other hand. Resting my chin on Koen's shoulder, tears covering my cheeks, I smile and stare at the postcard from Costa Rica.

"Are you done cry—" Koen starts to speak.

"Shh ... stop interrupting the universe."

The End

ACKNOWLEDGMENTS

My dear readers, thank you for "listening." 2023 was an emotionally challenging year for me. So, I took all of my emotions and put them into these characters' lives because storytelling is how I make sense of the world.

I have to give a special shoutout to my beta readers for their honesty. This is a softened version of the original story. They tried to put themselves in your shoes to imagine how you might receive the unfolding of events and the raw emotions expressed through these characters. Leslie, Jenn, Sherri, Nina, and Shauna ... thank you.

All the usual love to my editing team, Sarah, Monique, Leslie, and Sian, for making it shine.

Jenn Beach, there are never enough words to thank you for all you do. I appreciate every single official and unofficial role you play in my life and my success.

Thank you to my agent and publicist, Georgana, and her amazing Valentine PR team for getting this story into the hands of so many readers.

Thank you, Sarah, with Okay Creations, for two

perfect covers and Regina Wamba for the beautiful portrait of Price Milloy.

To everyone who read an ARC, shared in my release, wrote a review, created/liked/shared/commented on a social media post, or joined my Jonesies Facebook Group ... you are a gift. I feel unworthy of your loyalty and generosity but no less grateful. So many of you have befriended me, and all of these tiny connections have enriched my life as an author and as a person. Thank you.

Tim, Logan, Carter, Asher, and Swayze, thank you for being my real-life love story and for giving me the greatest HEA.

ALSO BY
Jewel E. Ann

———

The Fisherman Series

The Naked Fisherman

The Lost Fisherman

Jack & Jill Series

End of Day

Middle of Knight

Dawn of Forever

One (*standalone*)

Out of Love (*standalone*)

Because of Her (*standalone*)

Holding You Series

Holding You

Releasing Me

Transcend Series

Transcend

Epoch

Fortuity (*standalone*)

The Life Series

The Life That Mattered

The Life You Stole

Pieces of a Life

Memories of a Life

ABOUT THE
AUTHOR

Jewel E. Ann is a *Wall Street Journal* and *USA Today* bestselling author. She's written over thirty novels, including LOOK THE PART, a contemporary romance, the JACK & JILL TRILOGY, a romantic suspense series; and BEFORE US, an emotional women's fiction story. With 10 years of flossing lectures under her belt, she took early retirement from her dental hygiene career to write mind-bending love stories. She's living her best life in Iowa with her husband, three boys, and a Goldendoodle.

Receive a FREE book and stay informed of new releases, sales, and exclusive stories:
https://www.jeweleann.com/free-booksubscribe

Made in the USA
Monee, IL
25 May 2024

58788626R00203